Balm

Riverview

A novel by

Wes Gow

For my mother, and her endless grammatical support.
And my wife, for her fierce belief.

Acknowledgements

It seems most any creative endeavor is a team effort of some sort. I couldn't begin to name every individual who contributed to the fruition of this project: friends, family, colleagues, distant connections. The manuscript itself must have been proofed by at least thirty willing readers, some of them more than once. Simply put, this would not exist without each of you, and I am eternally grateful for your support and feedback. The story of *Balm Riverview* captures the parts we all play in each other's lives. It takes a village, as they say.

You. Me. Us.

We did it.

Contents

PART I

Homecoming

Chapter 1

LONNIE McGregor worked his way out of the tree stand with some amount of effort, favoring the stronger of his two legs. Walking was chore enough; climbing was altogether difficult. Nevertheless, he fought his way through the palmetto jungle to this post most every night during the fall and spring hunting seasons. Lonnie hunted; that's what he did. That, and turn wrenches. He wasn't very good at either, but he didn't know, so he didn't care. Lonnie wasn't what you'd recognize as mentally disabled, but he was...simple. Different, for sure. People knew him to be kind enough, with the exception of some past behavior, but he was slow in regard to academics and athletics, which was all folks seemed to reward or measure. By the time he did graduate from high school he'd already been working for his uncle's auto shop long enough to become an apprentice. He pulled long hours and hunted every chance he got. Deer were scarce this far south, but Lonnie knew just about every foxhole and squirrel's nest on the rural pastureland of Riverview.

This particular hunt passed in usual fashion: sweating on the way in, chilled by nightfall a few hours later; quiet except for the mosquitoes. He was mid-descent from the evening perch when he heard a familiar cry; long and low at first, then rising in pitch.

He'd heard it more than a few times over the years, always distant, but no less captivating. This time, however, was different for two terrifying reasons.

First, the cry was closer than Lonnie had ever experienced, as if it were almost on top of him. And second, because it was followed by another sound: a scream. The latter was unmistakably human. The first was not.

Lonnie gathered his strength and clung motionless to the ladder, still eight feet off the ground. Debris crunched and snapped off to his right, sending a shower of alarms coursing through his body. The night suddenly felt far more oppressive than comforting.

The ache in his arms from sustaining his frozen position finally drew his attention; he made up his mind to get to the truck. He slid past the last rung to land on his good leg, digging urgently through his pack for an old flashlight. His shoulders roared from the siege, but his breathing gradually slowed; he hadn't heard anything for several minutes. Lonnie clicked off the light and started down the trail he knew by heart, not wanting to draw attention to his presence. He was less than one hundred yards from the truck and just beginning to entertain the notion of having somehow imagined the entire episode, when his strong leg tripped over something large in the middle of the path.

Caught off guard and falling forward, he couldn't catch his weight on the weak leg and landed face down on the trodden, sandy soil. Lonnie rolled onto his back, holding his head. He slowly raised a hand to his cheek and felt it already warm and smarting; he'd have surface scratches and a bruise to show for it. His mind finally caught up to the moment, and he realized that whatever he'd tripped over certainly hadn't been there on his way in. Lonnie stood carefully and found his flashlight just inside the tall grass off the path. He clicked it on.

There, just beyond the reach of the dim beams, a crumpled figure lay silent and inert. Lonnie limped closer, each step throwing more light onto the object. Still several feet away, Lonnie knew something was very wrong. He was walking toward a human body, that much was evident by the apparel. The night around him seemed to be spinning as his thoughts raced to a blur. Daring to investigate further, he knelt on the backside of the figure and pulled the shoulder to roll it toward him. Lonnie screamed into the empty night and lurched backwards, once again finding himself prostrate on the ground. His light fell beside him but still illuminated the corpse. The face was bruised, battered, and bloody, the eyes swollen shut. This discovery alone would've shaken the strongest of nerves. But it was the following realization that sent Lonnie reeling: the body, despite its bludgeoned state, belonged to his cousin.

New York City, 1969
Laughlin & Lane Law Firm

BARRY Grayson took a moment amidst the fog and the traffic and the people, standing at the bottom of the stairs leading up to the imposing structure. The law firm stood like a fortress of security and opportunity. He'd imagined this moment for much of the last decade, a driving force that pushed him through college and university. Equally motivating was the juxtaposition of this very scene against the backdrop of his hometown. Despite Riverview's relative proximity to Tampa, the town may as well have existed in a dystopian parallel universe compared to his current surroundings.

Riverview was a slow, tiny plot of life embedded in the greater Hillsborough County, roughly an hour east of Tampa. A lonely, speed-trap town, little more than a blink along U.S. 301, which ran like a smuggler's route along the entire length of the eastern seaboard. The community drew its name from the Alafia River (pronounced Al-uh-fie), which bisected the town into a north and south side: the deli, library, and post office on the former, the bar and Baptist church along the latter. Alafia is translated as "River of Fire," and old prospectors told stories of the phosphorous river bottom glowing in the night. The modest collection of life gathered along its banks was a testament to human resilience, if not the fisherman and farmer's version of the American Dream. A man could live (and make his living) on the water here provided he could hack out enough jungle and keep it at bay long enough for the cement foundation to dry.

Childhood was good for most along the river in those days; between the pasture and the tides, there was plenty of opportunity and inspiration for endless summer hours of fighting imaginary Indians or pirates. Barry himself had been content enough as any boy. All that changed, however, one pivotal night in 1956, when the world of his parents' generation was undone by the vibrato baritone, impeccable hair, and sexual hips of the man who everyone would soon come to refer to only as, The King. His father, Joe, had already voiced his suspicions of Ed Sullivan (and television in general). But when he walked in one evening after a long hot day on the ranch and saw Barry sitting wide-eyed in front of musical guest Elvis Presley, he simply ripped the magic box out of the wall and heaved it into the burn pile out back. No explanation necessary, but the damage had been done. Barry's innocence about the world – and in retrospect, his own respect for his father – were fractured that night, lying in the ashes along with the family television screen.

Suddenly, the world was a lot bigger than the boundaries of his current context. Over time, Barry wondered how anyone ever got stuck in Riverview, sometimes imagining elaborate stories that were far more interesting than his own. His favorite was the tale of pirates marooned off Tampa Bay, whose descendants took on normal, undercover lives while they secretly searched for buried Spanish bullion. Tampa had a rich pirate history, and he hoped to God that some kid sitting next to him on the bus was going home to help his father dig for gold as opposed to mucking horse stalls, which was what he did most every afternoon. Like so many of his generation, the cat was out of the bag, so to speak, never to return. That fella from Memphis had ushered in a new kind of invasion, one that would be fought with guitars and mop tops instead of blitzkriegs and night raids, the spoils of which would feature a boom in American cultural revolution unlike anything before it. Families in towns like Riverview all over the country would experience the collateral damage; Barry's was no exception. Teens would neither inherit nor indulge their father's morals or his wars, pitting parents against the ever-expanding worldviews of their children.

Barry never took to music as his ticket out, but as he grew, he began to feel the once-comforting virtues of Riverview at odds with his newfound ambitions of life beyond the barbed wire fence of the family ranch. That tension, coupled with his father's increasing disapproval of his every move, had given Barry all the fuel he needed. His tunnels and gold would be through books and degrees, but he took a sort of secret oath to dig his way out and become *someone*.

Now, thirty-two, a newly minted New York City lawyer, Barry was ten minutes early for what he believed was the first day of the rest of his life. And more importantly, a life far away from his origins.

Chapter 2

Riverview, November 1978

LONNIE snatched his light and ran as fast as he could limp to his truck, wrenching the door open on the old Chevy. "No, no, no, no!" he cried with increasing volume as he fumbled for the keys. "No, no, no! Karl!" The old machine started, and Lonnie tore off for home. It was after 9:00 p.m. Uncle Richie would be close to sleep, expecting to rise again for another long day in the auto shop. Lonnie had spent most of his formative years living with Uncle Richie and his cousin Karl, moving in permanently after the episode that sent his mother to the hospital. Richie owned McGregor Motor; he was one of the kinder adults in Lonnie's life, but that wasn't saying much. Karl was an aspiring athlete like his father, with dreams of taking his imposing frame and stature north to the University of Florida in Gainesville.

16

Lonnie nearly missed the turn off lonely U.S. 301. A quarter mile later, down an oak-covered dirt road, Lonnie slammed the truck to a dusty halt outside the double-wide trailer.

"Richie! Richie! Uncle Richie! Karl's not here! Karl's not now!" He screamed almost without breath, leaving the driver's side door open and collapsing onto the stairs. A single light turned on inside the trailer, followed by a fumbling of boots and keys. Richie McGregor stomped noisily out into the November night, a loose flannel open across his t-shirt and eyes hungry for sleep.

"What the hell 'er you callin' about?" Richie found Lonnie weak on the steps below. "What's gone on? Where's Karl?"

Lonnie shook his head urgently and looked away, weeping. "No, no, no! The Tall Song took Karl. Karl's not here. Karl's not now!"

Richie knelt in front of Lonnie, grasping his shoulders and chasing his gaze. "What do you mean?" he asked, his tone fragile with fear. "What the hell are you sayin'?"

"The trail. Coming down the trail. Karl ain't now." Fighting back tears, Lonnie looked Richie in the eye for the first time and said, "The Tall Song got Karl." Richie stared, dumbfounded and disoriented. He stormed back inside the trailer and made a call to Sheriff Martin, leaving instructions with the dispatcher to have Blake meet him at the tree stand. Returning with coat and flashlight in hand, he dragged Lonnie around to the passenger side of the truck, and the two careened back down the dirt road.

New York City, November 1970
Laughlin & Lane Law Firm

THE clock on the wall read 6:25 p.m.; it may as well have been midnight. The sun was gone, again. Of course it set earlier this time of year, but amongst the tall steeples of finance and labor, that blazing beacon of hope began its descent shortly after 3:00. That is, unless you had a top-story corner office in one of these temples of worship. Barry certainly did not, but he was no less struck by the awe and wonder of such a view. He noticed a marked difference in his general mental and emotional posture whenever he had to deliver files to such a suite. Conversely, he'd begun to detect the declining slope of his spiritual state over the last few months. His first year at the firm had been difficult to say the least. Difficult and steering toward disillusioned. A rural Florida boy a long way from home, Barry wouldn't yet yield or say out loud what his gut was telling him: that this grand vision of the life of a New York City lawyer wasn't at all what he'd imagined.

"Grayson!" Barry's head snapped up off the back of his broken desk chair. The vision of a talking meatball materialized before his bleary eyes. Bob Crough stood in the entrance to his office. Had Barry's head been resting down on his desk, neither Bob nor anyone else would've known he was in there behind the disheveled mountain of paperwork. Barry made that mental note for future reference, then cleared his throat and answered, "Yes sir?"

"I need those files on the Dominion plant on my desk by 7:00 a.m. tomorrow. That gonna be a problem?"

"Not at all sir. You'll have them. Have a good evening, sir."

Bob stood and stared for several seconds. "What in the hell makes you think I'm done for the day? I got a hot date with a box of Chinese and a pack of Shermans. I'll be back in an hour." Despite the wedding band on his fat, sausage finger, Barry knew of no other indication that Bob was married, or that he had any meaningful life or relationships outside of Laughlin & Lane (not that Bob had either of those inside, for that matter). "And you can sleep on your own damn time," Bob called over his shoulder. Barry lip-synced almost the entire sentence, perfectly timing the delivery and cadence.

Bob Crough (also known to his underlings as Bob Cough or Bob Crotch), was most certainly dying. He smoked like a barge and ate like a rat. Miraculously, despite the toxins and garbage that Bob consumed, his mind was invaluably sharp when it came to corporate finance law. This made him a powerful figure within L&L, and even more so to their competition.

Not yet a named partner, everyone on Bob's staff knew this to be his single ambition, which meant that they were expected to work their asses off to see it come to fruition. The trade-off was a chance at riding his grimy coattails to their own betterment, a caustic symbiotic relationship that might result in an office somewhere far from the first floor file room, which was where Barry had been holed up for the last year of his life. A year that felt more like a decade.

But it wasn't just his supervisor that Barry could blame for his misery; the nature of the work itself had begun to eat at his conscience, a fact that he had yet to fully acknowledge. Laughlin & Lane specialized in insurance claims with a roster boasting many of the best-known brands in the industry, including Uncle Sam himself. The business of fear mongering was booming. With two world wars, a space race, stand-offs with Russia and Cuba, and chaotic conflicts in Korea and Vietnam, the American progressive war machine showed no signs of slowing down. Insurance agencies were ever eager, then, to cash in on this paranoia, collecting monthly payments in exchange for some semblance of peace of mind. However, these companies were also forward-thinking enough in their development to see the payout loopholes as their short-term key to virtually unending profits. Thus, an entire polluted ecosystem of financial law grew and festered like black mold, and firms like Laughlin & Lane were paid handsomely to see that policyholders received only a fraction (if anything at all) from their fine print contracts. For those lawyers not gentle of heart, the financial reward was remarkable. The industry, however, was beginning to take note that those with the pinnacle corner offices weren't living long enough to enjoy the fruits of their labors.

Barry saw this, if only from Bob Crough. But word was leaking that CEOs from similar firms were in a bad way, suffering and dying from various health issues or altogether suspicious circumstances. Despite this, there was still plenty of drive or naiveté left in Barry to talk himself into staying in the city for the holidays and maybe taking some time to explore upstate New York. Both were certainly better options than going home. He wasn't going home.

Chapter 3

RICHIE McGregor pushed the old Chevy well past its redline down U.S. 301 toward the pasture Lonnie hunted. *Hunted,* he thought. The kid basically just sat out there about every night. Fine by Richie. Less he had to look out for. And he'd been looking out for a lot of people for too damn long. He'd taken Lonnie in from his younger brother Tom – Lonnie's father – on the night of his tenth birthday. Richie would never forget it, and the memories were hauntingly fresh for some odd reason on this bizarre night.

Lonnie was different; everybody knew that. Quiet, thin, and awkward in conversation, he could be socially unpredictable. Only his mother, Maryl, seemed to understand his triggers, and she had devoted that first decade of his life to helping him survive in this world. But on the evening of his birthday, she'd made a grave miscalculation, and one that ended in tragedy. Something about the candles on the cake or the surprising number of people in attendance; Lonnie spiraled into a tailspin. Richie had seen it once before when Lonnie had virtually manhandled Tom at the age of eight in the church parking lot. Richie and two other congregants had to pull Lonnie off of his father, and it was all they could do to restrain him. Tom spent two days in the hospital, and had never been to church since. Maryl silently blamed Tom for instigating the event, and Tom hated all the more the fact that God had given him a simpleton for a son.

At his tenth birthday party, Lonnie erupted during another episode and shoved Maryl to the ground. She landed several yards away from where she'd been lighting the candles on the cake, and hit her head on a low shelf before collapsing into a motionless pile. Panic ensued, and sirens of all kinds arrived. Maryl was taken to Tampa General, where she was discovered to have broken her back; she'd never walk again. In the days and weeks that followed, Richie knew that Tom couldn't care for both Maryl and Lonnie, and he truly feared for the volatile relationship between father and son. So he'd taken Lonnie in. There was space in the house with only his son Karl, his own wife having succumbed to cancer before Karl was old enough to remember. Now in his late fifties and feeling the years from crawling under cars, Richie did little else but drink and fish when he could.

His son Karl, however, giddy with his coming graduation and recent university acceptance letter, had taken to playing the occasional childhood prank on Lonnie. Richie had warned him about Lonnie's surprising strength, but the truth was that Lonnie hadn't had an episode since the incident with Maryl, and Karl himself was a future collegiate linebacker. Karl had shrugged off his father's advice earlier.

The Chevy screeched to a reckless stop. Richie jumped out and was at Lonnie's door before he could open it. Trembling, he dragged his weak leg out.

"Where is he?" Richie hissed.

"Don't go, Richie. Don't go. Don't go down there, Uncle Richie!" Lonnie pleaded. Richie grabbed a fistful of Lonnie's shirt and proceeded to walk toward the path leading to his old hunting stand.

"No! The Tall Song is here! He got Karl. The Tall Song is here, and he got Karl!"

"What the hell are you talking about?" Richie shouted. "Where's Karl?" He turned on his heel and ran down the beaten footpath, leaving Lonnie limping behind him. It was after 10:00 now, and the late fall air hung in a low shroud over the flat land. Richie clicked on his flashlight and increased his pace. Rounding the big moss-covered oak, he stopped abruptly.

Lonnie moved hurriedly after his uncle, but he was well behind. Lonnie liked Richie, at least compared to his own father, and Richie seemed to care for him, as much as anyone could aside from his mother. Karl, however, while never overtly evil, was nonetheless hard on Lonnie. Teenage societies seldom favor the weak, and Karl, like most young men, possessed neither the care nor the courage to lead the reformation for his live-in cousin; the dichotomy between them was simply too great for his own ego and reputation.

Lonnie's mind was working hard to process the past and the present, until he stopped short, breathing hard, surrounded by Richie's screams.

***

KARL'S head was lying on Richie's knees, the big, vibrant athlete suddenly looked small and vulnerable, broken. Richie himself seemed shocked at the condition of Karl's body, at how badly he'd been beaten. Lonnie walked up to the scene with caution, the faint sound of gravel under tire tread in the distance. Soon Sheriff Blake Martin called out as he loped toward them. He was turning down the volume on his walkie when he rounded the corner and bumped into Lonnie.

"Jesus!" he said, out of breath. "Where's – oh my God." Blake hurried to Richie's side and knelt down over Karl. "Richie what happened?"

"I – I don't know. I don't know. He was..." Richie was talking as though he were winded, his mind racing faster than his mouth.

He held Karl tightly around his big shoulder, not letting him back to the ground. "I don't know. Something with Lonnie. Lonnie came and got me and we came back and just got here."

Blake stood, walked a few paces and placed a call through his walkie.

"Dispatch, this is Sheriff Martin. Do you copy?"

"Go ahead, Blake," said the woman's voice on the other end.

Blake instantly muffled the receiver over his chest before she could finish and jogged several paces away, disappearing into the void. He squeezed the walkie and raised it to his mouth, then paused for a moment to gather himself. He spoke carefully. "I need a code 10-87 immediately. Location is secure at 301 and Balm Riverview Road."

Code 10-87 meant that a medical emergency unit was needed on the site of a single civilian casualty. The codes were in place not only to streamline communication for such emergencies but also to avoid detailing the scene in front of family, friends, or onlookers.

"Code 10-87. 301 and Balm Riverview Road. Location secure. Copy that," said the woman.

"Have the unit reach out to me on approach for instructions." He shook his head, disappointed. Under the circumstances, that was the best he could come up with, but he wasn't sure it would be enough.

"Copy that. I'll let them know, Blake."

He waited. Nothing. Maybe he narrowly avoided making this night worse. He'd connect with the ambulance and instruct them to maneuver a quarter mile down the Grayson's property. Right now he needed tonight's dispatch operator to remain focused. He pivoted toward the scene, and readied himself for the demands of the hours ahead.

***

ON the other end of Blake's radio, Maryl McGregor wheeled her chair back from the dispatch operating board. She took a deep breath, and said a short prayer for both the family of the victim and the first responders.

New York City, September 1978
Laughlin & Lane Law Firm
BARRY stood in front of the pale bathroom sink, waiting for the water to heat up. His thin Florida blood showed no signs of acclimating to the Yankee climate despite the extra insulation he'd inadvertently added to his frame.

Looking at himself in the mirror, Barry was hardly recognizable from the naive, eager young lawyer who arrived in the capital of the world so many years ago. He was twenty pounds heavier, and slept less than he had in law school. He'd been sick and/or ailed by minor everyday injuries more often than he could remember. Worse, he was alone. Suddenly, the face staring back at him was a terrifying resemblance to the one he'd just seen in the open casket at Bob Crough's viewing.

Timing is everything. Only weeks beforehand the firm had announced that Bob would be awarded Senior Partner. After an industry lifetime of maintaining an iron fist on client payouts, Bob was earning the just deserves of his hard labor – or so he told his minions. But Bob left the office late on a Monday night and never arrived home. In fact, he never left the parking garage. Early the next morning, as Barry himself was leaving for a coffee break after another all-nighter, he saw Bob's car already in his usual spot. That wasn't uncommon, but it wasn't at all common to see his massive bulk slouched aimlessly over his steering wheel. Barry stood in the cold dawn while the medics and officers arrived and pronounced Bob dead, which they later attributed to an acute heart attack. Fifty-seven years old.

Barry washed his hands, then his face; the water in his first floor hole-in-the-wall (which could have described his office or apartment) never got this warm. He toweled off and looked in the mirror again. All of this in less than a decade. At this pace, he knew without a doubt that he'd never outlive Bob Crough. Something had to give, and it couldn't be his health any more than it already had. Barry had to get out, and he was far too gone to give a damn about pride. He unrolled his shirtsleeves, put on his jacket, and reached for the door to join his colleagues in the funeral home.

Chapter 4

SHERIFF Blake Martin knelt quietly and put his hand on Richie's shoulder. "Rich, the medical team is on their way. Can you tell me again what happened here?" Richie was still on his knees, holding Karl's upper body, rocking slightly in the blue beam of Blake's flashlight. "Rich, what do you know? Help me understand."

Richie sat still, silent. "I – I don't know. I don't know. Lonnie was out here and came home screaming about Karl. We flew straight back. I don't know."

Blake passed his light slowly along the length of Karl's frame. Twenty plus years of bar fights and gang violence had never produced a beating to this degree. Karl wasn't just beaten; he was broken, his body lying in distorted fashion as though it were being pulled to the hard earth by some incredible force of gravity. The sheriff raised his beam to find Lonnie standing close by, chewing his tongue and leaning against the old oak. He rose and strode toward him.

"It was the Tall Song, Sheriff. The Tall Song got Karl. The Tall Song took Karl!"

"Shut up with that bullshit!" Richie snapped. Before Blake closed the distance between himself and Lonnie, Richie was up on his feet and racing toward Lonnie. He blew past Blake and grabbed angry fistfuls of Lonnie's collar, lifting him completely off the ground before throwing him several feet away, landing him on his back. Richie was on him, straddling his writhing waist; Lonnie couldn't breathe from having the wind knocked out of him. "What did you do? What did you do to him?" Richie screamed into his face.

Sheriff Martin wrapped each of his strong arms underneath Richie's shoulders and heaved him off of Lonnie. "Richie! Richie, stop it!" he shouted as he now stood between the two men. He had one hand on the holstered revolver and the other extended palm out to Richie. "Now stop it! Richie McGregor, you hold your position. Lonnie, are you ok?" he called over his shoulder, never taking his eyes off Richie. Lonnie had rolled onto his side, and Blake could hear his labored breathing. "Richie what happened here?"

"I told you, I have no idea! Lonnie comes screaming home, carrying on about Karl. I called the dispatch and we came straight back here and then you walked up on us."

"The Tall Song," Lonnie whispered, coughing. "The Tall Song got Karl."

Blake turned his head to Lonnie and then back to Richie. "What's he talking about, Rich?"

"The 'Tall Song', he's sayin'. It's what he calls that damn skunk ape."

"The *what?*"

Richie threw up his arms in defeat. "What's the point, Sheriff? He's a goddamn idiot! You know those stories as well as I do!" Richie shouted as he strode toward Lonnie, who was now on his hands and knees and taking deep breaths.

"Quiet, Richie! Now that's enough." Blake put his big chest in front of Richie. "It's late, we're all confused, and right now our priority is to keep a bad situation from getting worse. We owe that to Karl, don't we Richie?" Richie stopped and slowly deflated, collapsing down onto a knee.

"If I need to I'll cuff you in the car," Blake continued. "Is there going to be a problem?" Richie shook his head, cradling it in his hands. "Good." Blake took a few seconds to make certain the answer could be trusted, then he turned to help Lonnie up. Lonnie was rubbing his jaw and leaning on his good leg, but he was standing.

Blake held onto his shoulders and asked, "Son, what happened here? Are you able to tell me?"

Lonnie nodded, drew a breath, and began to recount the events leading up to his return with Richie. "The sun was all done; I knew to come home. But then I heard…"

"What, Lonnie? Anything you tell me could help us."

Lonnie looked all around, his lower lip quivering. "I heard the Tall Song. Close. Then – then I heard the scream."

"The *Tall Song?*" Blake emphasized. Lonnie shook his head in urgent affirmation.

"I heard him close to me. Then I heard the man-scream."

"Tell me what that is, Lonnie: the Song," said Blake, trying to connect with Lonnie's eyes. "What do you mean?"

Lonnie looked away, then hung his head and leaned his full weight into the sheriff's shoulders and sobbed. Blake caught him and held on despite his evident shock.

"Lonnie," he said, quietly. "It's ok. You're ok." He slowly drew Lonnie's shoulders back and away from his own. "Listen. Can you tell me one last time? Who did this to Karl? Who is the Tall Song?"

Lonnie ran the back of his sleeves along his face, looked over at Richie, and nearly started to weep again. But he raised an arm, pointed and said, "Uncle Richie said it. Uncle Richie knows. He said it." Lonnie was on

Blake's shoulder again just as his walkie crackled. The medic team had arrived.

Riverview, October 1978

BARRY Grayson felt out of his mind, out of himself. His hands were on the wheel but his soul was very much along for the ride, engulfed in a surreal nightmare. He was going home. Dawn was breaking over the Sunshine State, and he loosened his grip on the leather steering wheel of his 1969 Jensen Interceptor. Blaze orange. The car had been a gift to himself shortly after arriving in New York. He'd never seen a vehicle like it, and anything that looked like a long way from home felt more than all right to him. The Jensen was a hatchback with a long hood, and just nearly enough room in the backseat bench for a briefcase and a lunch bag. (The tradeoff, he argued, was plenty of legroom for his frame). Regardless, the V8 engine, power steering, and four-wheel-drive combined for an irresistible offer for a country prodigal with a paycheck.

Having driven through the night, he could now clearly see all the familiar signs of his long-forgotten upbringings. Cow pastures for miles, flat as the eye could see; an orange grove, once productive, now entirely suffocated by Spanish moss, looming like an army of ghostly gray reapers. Rusted barbed wire fences lining U.S. 301 like mile markers, with small, white egrets resting along fence posts, waiting for another day of pecking insects disturbed by the cattle grazing. Maybe it was the exhaustion setting in, but there was a strange beauty here in the vast frailty, a sincerity emanating from the land itself.

And yet he knew the real mileage ahead lay deep within his soul. In fact, he realized then that he was now returning very much the way he left so many years ago: stunned. The circumstances of his departure came flooding back, memories he'd buried long ago, alongside his mother. He'd left for New York almost immediately after her funeral, and figured he'd never return. Life, however, seemed now to have successfully blunted his will, his hope, and his belief in just about anything optimistic.

Ten years and little to nothing had changed in Riverview. No surprise. But ten years in the "city that never sleeps" had changed just about everything that anyone would recognize about Barry Grayson. A former high school athlete, Barry was an all-star in three sports and a scholarship athlete on the basketball team at Florida College. Back then he had broad, strong shoulders on a slender, agile frame. Now, his scoring titles – still unbeaten – were all that remained of that shadow.

Despite his success on the hardwood, though, Barry never wavered from his pursuit to practice law in the

Big Apple. For most kids from God-knows-where, New York City probably felt like an alien orbit. For him, it was the center of the universe.

That perspective thrust Barry into channeling all of his athletic discipline into graduating with honors and studying law at the University of South Florida, outside of Tampa. The degree was a ticket out, a promise of a different future, and the waiting was more grueling than the coursework.

The tassel finally turned, and Barry told his parents that he'd be studying for the New York bar exam alongside that of his home state. That's when things went from bad to worse. His mother, of course, was crushed. Even though she'd long ago surrendered the hope of the two men in her life living happily under the same roof, Sandy Grayson was nonetheless broken by the thought of likely losing all meaningful contact with her only child. Barry's father, as usual, was at best disappointed, if not indifferent. And that had been Barry's life for as long as he could remember. He didn't believe that he and his father hated each other. But Joe was a war veteran turned Florida cracker cowboy on the back side of a once-booming industry, and Barry couldn't break through the crusted brow to get him to see that his own future lay somewhere far away from the moss and straw.

He broke the news of his plans with the intent to stay on at the ranch and help with the farming as much as he could while preparing for the exam. Barry knew this wasn't the best arrangement; he'd certainly rather divert all of his energy to the bar and get out sooner than later. The offer was gracious only for his mother's sake. Sandy, however concerned she was, embraced her son and announced with tears and fortitude that she was proud of Barry and knew that he'd make a great lawyer. He remembered eating dinner that evening in relative silence with his mother attempting to make careful conversation about possibilities in New York.

That night, as was her usual custom, Sandy had taken the canoe across the Alafia for a walk in the wildlife refuge directly opposite of the Grayson ranch. The refuge consisted of nearly two hundred acres of impenetrable Florida jungle, and it belonged to a development group of some kind that no one really knew much about. The company utilized four-wheeler pathways throughout the vast expanse to conduct research and surveys; Sandy considered these her own personal nature trails.

She had walked off the front porch after dinner and never returned. Barry could still vividly remember the color of her shirt and the apron left hanging on the porch rocker.

He gave a slight shudder. Sitting now on the side of the road overlooking his father's acreage, worn out from endless hours and miles of travel, he was too tired to keep his mind from recalling the events that unraveled that night. He'd left town shortly after her body was found and had neither spoken with his father or graced the front steps since. Until now. Despite his exhaustion, Barry was clear-headed enough to know that he was about to steer his Jensen Interceptor directly into the eye of an emotional hurricane.

Chapter 5

THE hour was nearly midnight when the medical unit drove slowly off the property en route to Tampa General. There was no need to rush. Blake Martin would make the trip into the city tomorrow, but right now he had more immediate concerns. He had to figure out what to do with Richie and Lonnie, who were basically both his only suspects and witnesses. He'd be back on this property at first light to conduct a more thorough investigation, but he had to make sure the two men standing out there in the darkness alongside him would still be alive and well by morning.

"Richie, it's been a helluva night, and we're all concerned with what happened here, certainly none more than you. I want you to take the truck home and get some sleep; I'll be in touch tomorrow afternoon after I've been back out here." Blake had mastered the art of delivering instructions like this, and his tone produced the same disarming, calming effect on Richie as it had on countless others.

"Lonnie," Blake said, turning his attention, "I'd like you to come with me to the station. We'll get you some water, a shower, and set you up in a nice room where I can take better notes on what you know. And your mother will be there." Lonnie's eyes lifted with hope and longing; Blake knew that element was key to winning him over. "Right now you're our only connection to bringing Karl's attacker to justice."

Lonnie nodded enthusiastically. "Yessir. Yes, Sheriff."

Blake turned once more to Richie and placed a firm grip on his shoulder. "Stay with me on this, Rich. For Karl's sake. We'll get to the bottom of it."

Blake and Lonnie drove to the station in relative silence. Complete silence, actually. Not because the situation was awkward; Blake had driven many miles under similar (and worse) circumstances. But tonight, Sheriff Martin's mind was racing, back to the details of a case similar to what was now unfolding. Too similar. In fact, the incident occurred very near where Karl was found. This was not Blake's first call into the woods to find a body beaten like what he'd just seen, and as they drove down the lonely midnight roads, he was replaying the images across the windshield. A woman's body, twisted and angled as to suggest no inner structure whatsoever. Dragged through the dense Florida brush. The deepest, darkest bruising. Her cheekbones crushed and caved. Blond hair discolored with black and red and gold. Oddly enough, much like tonight, two other men were standing there with him at the scene: Joe and Barry Grayson.

Riverview, June 1968

THE front porch of the Grayson farmhouse was wide enough that it should have held far more happy memories than it actually did. Sandy Grayson knew her days weren't particularly bad or unpleasant, but their lives weren't exactly light-hearted either. Then again, did she know anyone who could claim otherwise? The town of Riverview held an honesty and charm that soothed her, but life in rural Florida felt like a kind of war, not waged against fellow humanity like the world conflicts she'd grown up knowing, but against the ever-present, unknown phantasm of earth around her.

Florida could feel like an ageless, patient demon, not unlike the Lord of Lies himself: beautiful, enticing, seductive. But he was going to get you in the end. The allure of warm, emerald shores and pearl-white sand overshadowed the inland underbelly. Relentless heat and humidity, like the hot whisper of an ancient evil; violent afternoon thunderstorms that you could set your watch by. Hurricanes, hail, and tornadoes. Tangled

Spanish moss and an endless array of wild weeds that waged an unceasing campaign to engulf everything in their wake. Creatures of every size that stung and bit and killed: ants, mosquitoes, scorpions, snakes, sharks, and of course, alligators. To survive here was to live with a kind of burden that stooped your shoulders: you felt it, you carried it.

One way or another, all anyone could do was get on living in spite of it. You could never ignore it. And somehow, she thought, you came to love it. The sheer wildness of it suited her. Sandy never was a conventional girl. She came from money, but she married a quiet cowboy whose rough hands had made a fair living for them, and in those days that was nearly all a grateful woman asked of her man.

If anyone could keep the native spirits at bay, it was Joe Grayson. He'd lived through one World War, fought and almost died in another, and found the campaigns of a rancher against the natural elements practically a joy compared to the trenches and beaches of the Nazi battles. But joy seemed in low supply in Joe's life.

Sandy didn't know why, exactly, and she knew that Joe was misunderstood by most, certainly by their own son. She couldn't recall the last time the two most important men in her life had shared a laugh together. Men of her day were providers first and family men second, sometimes a distant second. The world was changing, though, and Barry's generation was afforded opportunities that war had taken from Joe's. Sandy believed that Joe understood this, but that didn't mean that he was going to take kindly to his only son trading in his boots for oxfords and a desk job. They'd come around; she hoped. Barry had just announced his plans to study for the New York bar exam, and despite her sorrow she knew he'd forge his own path and make them proud.

Right then the sun was just barely above the tree line of the wildlife refuge, heralding the beginning of what Sandy referred to as "golden hour." The swallow-tailed kites would be gliding along the thermals now, feeding on the wing. She rose off the porch, laid her stained floral pattern apron across her weather-beaten rocking chair, and headed for her routine walk down the nature trails. Barry caught a glimpse of her through the screen door as she slid the canoe into the welcoming waters of the Alafia, and watched until she landed on the opposite shore and disappeared into the warm embrace of the cypress trees and palmetto brush.

By all accounts, that was the last time anyone saw her alive.

Chapter 6

Riverview, November 1978

SHERIFF Blake Martin knew the grid of his town and the surrounding boroughs of Hillsborough County like any seasoned officer of the law should. Florida was so damn flat that an aerial view of the road system revealed miles of neat, right-angle roads, a series of clean geometrical squares and straight lines where worn asphalt bordered orange groves and strawberry fields. The irony was not lost on Blake: messy lives amongst the straight and narrow. Once again, tonight was no different. As he and Lonnie drew near the quiet station, he recalled the final scenes from the Grayson case a decade ago.

His home phone had rung just after dawn; he would forever remember the instant ominous feeling at such an early call. Barry was nervous, tense, afraid; he had last seen Sandy walking into the reserve around 6:00 p.m.

the night before. She still wasn't home now; he and Joe were heading into the woods through the back entrance off old Bloomingdale Avenue. Florida boasted more than its fair share of dangerous game: panthers, alligators, snakes, even black bears. The list of six and eight-legged predators was too long to name; an unobservant passerby could be devoured alive by a colony of fire ants if they weren't careful.

Blake was stepping out of the squad car in front of the Grayson pickup by 6:30 a.m. The two men weren't to be found. He had no experience in the wildlife refuge and wondered as he walked toward the gated entrance how he'd find Barry and Joe. But by the time he crossed the threshold into the tangled canopy, he wasn't walking in wonder; he was sprinting with clarity. Joe was screaming.

Blake followed the pitch of grief and anger for what must have been close to half a mile, the last third of which veered well off the worn path of the ATV trail. He had come upon the terrible reunion out of breath but composed himself in a moment of respect and horror.

Now, just as he and Lonnie pulled into the Riverview Police station, he reviewed the three most critical details of that fateful day. First, standing in the presence of Joe Grayson showing any emotion whatsoever was rare enough for anyone, but that experience was one that Blake would never forget. Second, the scene of Joe holding his wife was almost identical to that which he'd just responded to an hour earlier, astoundingly similar. Finally, the most poignant and electrifying detail shared by these two episodes was the fate of the victim. Sandy Grayson hadn't been beaten; she had been pummeled, practically pulverized.

Riverview, October 1978

BARRY pulled the steering wheel of his orange Interceptor clockwise to make a lazy, hesitant turn off Balm Riverview Road and onto the dusty lane that led to the Grayson ranch. He shook his head. How was this happening? He'd left New York City in a blur only a collection of hours ago after almost a decade of life in the city. *Was it that bad?* he asked himself. *Bad enough to be doing this?* He drove on at idle speed, as if some unforeseen current were pulling him toward the homestead. Nothing had changed. Nothing for the better, anyway. The ivy along the chimney that his mother always kept in check was now in full control of the vertical domain like a proud, conquering kingdom. The bay oak in the front yard that held the tire swing was engrossed in a losing battle against the smoky Spanish moss, which swayed gently as though it had all the time in the world to suffocate another helpless victim. This was a particularly dour scene given that the trees in New York were just beginning to paint their leaves all the colors of a flickering flame: gold and orange and red. While the rest of the world embraced fall, much of Florida smoldered on like a forgotten pot roast. The ground itself was green enough, at least compared to dirt. But the earth here was seemingly equal parts sand and grass, nothing like the lush, attended gardens up north.

As he slowed to a stop, he could see the four-dozen head or so of Florida Cracker Cattle grazing in the surrounding pasture, which were only momentarily interested in his arrival. Their attention, however, was quickly diverted to the far end of the barbed wire ranch, where a laboring pickup, loaded to the hilt with hay, was rocking gently down the path from the nearby barn. The herd displayed all the eager agility of an over-aged athlete, mooing and baying with anticipation as breakfast rolled closer. Dad was still at it.

Barry parked parallel to the side of the house just behind the view from the front porch. He crawled out of the hatchback and stretched his aching back. Dad's old cast net hung from a rusted nail, nearly dry rotted by now. A few fresh fish scales caught the sunlight, though, indicating the old tool's recent use.

The Alafia River was abundant with mullet, a saltwater species that took on a dark color up river, contrary to the much lighter schools that lived out in Tampa Bay and into the Gulf of Mexico. Mullet were vegetarians and therefore averse to hook and line lures; cast nets were just about the only way to harvest them. Barry wrinkled his nose. He'd grown up eating the stuff, which was a testament to how effective a layer of fried batter could be for a slime sandwich like mullet.

"Who the hell 'er you?" came a gravel voice from the front porch; it was alarmingly direct despite its soft candor. Barry whirled around to find a man not much different than he expected. Grizzled jaw, capable frame, leathered skin, and penetrating eyes buried deep under the wide brim of a stained Stetson. His father, Joe Grayson, was standing twenty feet away.

"Dad," Barry started, squinting through the midmorning sun.

"Barry?" Joe strode off the porch toward the car.

Barry closed his door and walked around to the hood, unsure of Joe's intent.

"Yeah," he sighed. "It's me."

Joe was closing with every step, and Barry could see the distrust in his eyes turn to something that shouldn't have startled him, but that was the only reaction he could process in the few seconds he had before his father was on him.

"Dad, I – "

Joe didn't give him a chance to finish. His arms shot out like huge twin rattle snakes and hooked around his son's back. Barry flinched before realizing he was embraced in the only hug from his father that he could ever remember.

Chapter 7

BLAKE Martin guided the Plymouth Fury squad car into the station. The hands on his wristwatch read 1:00 a.m. With the exception of a few pale desk lamps, the lobby was dark. Lonnie wasn't under arrest, but he didn't need to ask why they were there. Blake unlocked the door and Lonnie followed, his left boot heel scuffing the tile with every step.

"Can I get you a drink of water?"

Lonnie nodded his head.

"Sure thing. Have a seat right here, Lonnie." Blake pointed to the gray plastic chair in his office. He walked down the hall past the water jug and looked into the dispatch boardroom. Tonight's supervisor was four hours into a wild shift. Blake knocked and said, "Stop in my office when you get a second." On the way back he filled two paper cups with cold water.

"Been a long night, Lonnie," he handed him a cup, then took a sip from his own. Blake observed Lonnie's worn army surplus fatigues, presumably his hunting attire. "So, Lonnie, whatd'ya hunt out there? See many deer?"

Lonnie's eyes brightened for the first time that night. "Some deer; not too many. Lots o' rabbits and foxes, though. Lots. D'you know some o' them rabbits is bigger than the foxes?" Lonnie asked with a hesitant smile. "Or maybe as big, at least."

Blake chuckled. "No, I didn't know that," he said.

There was a soft sound of motion outside; both men looked at the doorway to Sheriff Martin's office. A pair of cracked, closed-toed leather flats appeared at the entrance, covering small feet that were slightly elevated off the ground. They were suspended in the air by a step-brace beneath them, which was attached to the wheelchair that carried Maryl McGregor around the corner into view.

"Sheriff, I would've never taken you for a – " she stopped abruptly when she saw Lonnie; Blake watched the expressions he anticipated pass quickly across her face: surprise, confusion, fear. Then her eyes filled with tears. Blake put his hand up in a motion to pause.

"It's ok, Maryl, Lonnie's all right. But there's been an unfortunate incident tonight, and Lonnie was a witness. I brought him down here because…" Maryl wasn't listening. She'd rolled her chair over to Lonnie and the two were embracing. They separated for a moment, and she wiped his eyes, then hers.

"I'm sorry, Blake."

"Don't be. I was saying that I brought Lonnie down here because I knew you were on the night shift; I thought you might be able to help him, and me, sort through a few of the important details."

"Absolutely, Sheriff. Whatever you need." She looked at Lonnie and put her hand on his arm. "What happened tonight, fella? Tell me 'bout it," she smiled reassuringly. Lonnie looked at his mother, then to Blake, then wound a loose string from his shirt cuff around his finger.

"I went to the quiet place, Momma. Like I do."

"Uncle Richie's tree stand. Sure. You like to go there. D'ya get anything this time?"

Lonnie shook his head in disappointment. "No ma'am. No things tonight. No things to hunt, anyway."

"Well, that's ok," she patted his leg. "Tell me what ya' saw and what ya' heard. Any squirrels or foxes or – " He looked up abruptly into her eyes, his hands were still. "What is it, Lonnie?" His own eyes filled with some mixture of doubt and fear and sorrow.

"Karl's not now, Momma," he trembled, "Karl's on the ground." Whatever fear had subsided in Maryl's shoulders and eyes returned in an instant. She held her son and looked at Blake.

"What's he mean, Sheriff? What's going on?"

Blake unfolded his hands and leaned his elbows across the desk. "Maryl, that dispatch I contacted you about tonight was at the Grayson ranch, where Lonnie hunts."

"Yessir, that's right." Her eyes were wide and fixed to Blake's.

"I was called to a scene along that pathway leading to the tree stand. When I arrived, Richie was there, kneeling over Karl, and Lonnie was standing nearby."

"What's happened, Blake? I don't understand."

"Maryl, Karl was dead on the scene."

She gasped and broke at the same time, tears flowing effortlessly from her eyes and rolling over the hand she'd brought to her mouth. Blake was patient and careful to keep his soft eyes on hers, like windows open on either side of a house, letting grief and sympathy flow freely.

"The reason I brought Lonnie here," he said quietly, "was to see if you can help me with one important detail that I can't seem to grasp."

She composed herself, and then the levy broke. She sobbed. She felt sick. After several moments, she managed to speak. "Sheriff, I can't. You can't ask me to do this." Blake said nothing. Maryl grew quiet again, drying her eyes with a stained, woven handkerchief.

"Ok," she managed, "Ok. What is it?" She raised Lonnie's face to engage his eyes. "Honey, what happened? Tell me. You can tell me. What happened tonight? Why was Karl on the ground?" Maryl was nauseous with the fear that she was luring Lonnie to certain doom, fully expecting her son to confess to another violent assault on a member of his own family.

Lonnie sat still, winding the string around his finger again, the last defiant thread of a once-confident team holding a button to his sleeve. He scuffed the thin, vomit-colored commercial carpet with his boot while his tongue moved quickly along the inside of his cheek. Then he inhaled deeply and looked up at the fluorescent lights.

"The Tall Song, Momma. I heard the Tall Song near to me. Then I heard Karl screaming." He shook his head and looked directly at his mother. "The Tall Song got Karl."

Blake Martin was, of course, thoroughly engaged in the conversation taking place before him. He was carefully looking for details and reactions, though exhaustion was beginning to win the day. Now, however, he sat bolt upright in his bomber brown office chair, not because of what he'd just heard, but because of what he was seeing in Maryl McGregor's face. He'd only too late put together that her emotions were likely connected to the suspicion that Blake had brought

Lonnie here to confess to beating Karl in front of her. That was a poor mistake on his part, and one that he'd berate himself for later. But whatever Maryl was afraid of hearing before was now replaced with something else altogether. The color and life had drained from her being in an instant like the bottom falling out of a bucket. She was at once completely emotionally sober and yet very distant. In the silence that elapsed, he heard three things: the soft hum of the overhead lighting, a breath escaping Maryl's lungs to the tone of "Oh my God," and the tiny tap of Lonnie's button landing on the carpet, the last of its lifelines torn asunder.

Riverview, October 1978

BARRY Grayson stood with his arms momentarily outstretched, frozen by the shock of being embraced by his father. He slowly conceded and returned the gesture.

"Dad," he smiled cautiously, "I – "

"Forget about it, son. Forget about it all." Joe's heavy hands were on either of Barry's shoulders. Barry stood there, frozen and confused. He stepped back from Joe's reach and shook his head, as though waking himself.

"No, Dad. I'm not sure I can," he looked at his father with eyes devoid of trust. "We've got a lot to catch up on. Jesus, what's this even about?" he asked with frustration in his tone. "We don't speak for almost a decade and I pull up and suddenly…" he stopped and looked away. "And who's driving that damn truck out there anyway," he pointed to the pasture in an attempt to divert Joe from seeing his own eyes welling up. But Joe didn't follow. Instead, he stood looking at his son, the faintest indication of something other than a scowl or a frown along the lines of his mouth and eyes.

"Barry, you look like hell." He was right, Barry knew. The city had long ago depleted him of the hardened muscle tone one acquires from working on a ranch. He stood his ground with his hands on his hips looking dumbfounded at his father's audacity. "Yeah, we got a lot to catch up on. But what you need is a tall stack of flapjacks and a shower. C'mon," and he turned toward the porch, leaving Barry behind. "Her name's Ellie, by the way" he called over his shoulder.

Barry, not yet having committed to Joe's offer, dropped his hands in exasperation. "Is that supposed to mean something to me?"

Without looking, Joe pointed to the pasture as he neared the screen door. "She's the one driving the damn truck." Barry looked across the sunburnt field and folded his arms against the roof of the Interceptor. "And she prefers American horsepower to sissy little imports," his father called.

"Hey, this is four-wheel-drive!" he shouted. *Whatever,* he thought. He looked back out at the pasture. A mane of brunette hair spilling out of a wide-brimmed hat was tossing hay out of the back of Joe's pickup. Maybe the miles he'd just logged were wearing on him. Maybe the Southern heat was already playing tricks on his fragile mind. Or maybe – just maybe – Barry could feel the anxiety and anger subsiding to at least a mild curiosity.

He stood there sweating through his dress shirt for a long moment, not really observing the new ranch hand as much as he was trying to figure out if he'd returned home to the right farm. His father had just hugged him, for God's sake!

"Hey! You comin'?" Joe called from the kitchen window.

Flapjacks sounded amazing. Anything did at this point. Barry succumbed to his limited options, grabbed his bag, and walked toward the home of his childhood.

Chapter 8

BLAKE Martin had been awake for much of the last twenty-four hours; he'd risen well before eight, and the hour was now closing in on 2:00 a.m. His feet and back longed to be resting in bed, preparing for another day. Instead, he was sitting in his office, elbows on the varnished desk, leaning forward with his eyes pinched in complete concentration, transfixed on Maryl and Lonnie McGregor. Maryl's expression shared a striking similarity to what his own wife wore when he caught her sleepwalking: head tilted slightly, eyes glassed, a thousand-mile stare into nothing in particular.

The linear trajectory of her own gaze now fell somewhere along a stretch of empty wall just past Lonnie's shoulder. After close to three decades of wearing a badge and countless case hours spent with persons of interest, Blake discovered long ago that silence is often the unnoticed member of any given conversation, sometimes speaking the loudest. He said nothing, only watched. Lonnie realized he'd lost his mother's attention, and he looked over at the sheriff. Blake figured they must have sat there for close to five whole minutes.

Finally, Maryl spoke, first with a silent single tear that ran down the cheek closest to Blake, then with her careful Southern accent. "Sheriff, Lonnie didn't do this." Blake said nothing. She looked at Lonnie, touched his face, and then asked him to sit outside the office. "I need to talk alone, now," she told him. Lonnie looked at them both, and then rose from his chair and closed the door behind him. Maryl waited until she heard him sit down, then looked down at her hands folded in her lap, exhaled, and silently wept. Blake opened the bottom drawer, drew out a box of tissues and carried them over to her. He sat on the front edge of his desk and waited while she dried her face and composed herself.

"Maryl," he said, "Lonnie's not here tonight under direct police investigation. Not yet." He walked over to the water cooler and poured her a small cup. She held a tissue to her mouth, still looking at her lap, and nodded. "Right now he and Richie are my only witnesses and I don't believe that either has an alibi. That doesn't immediately make them suspects, but I will need to speak with each of them further."

"I understand," said Maryl, meeting Blake's eyes.

"I brought Lonnie here for two reasons: first, I didn't want him going home with Richie under the circumstances; second, because I need your help."

"My help? How on earth could I help?" she dropped a heavy tissue onto her lap in exasperation.

"Lonnie's account of tonight's events hasn't wavered from Richie, to me, and just now to you. From all we know at the moment, which isn't much yet, he was the first person to find Karl. You know as well as I do that those two aren't exactly buddies." He paused for several seconds, looking up at nothing, before returning to meet her eyes. "Maryl, believe me when I stress how sensitive this is for me to be having this conversation with you, specifically. But given Lonnie's history, I can't be faulted for wondering how he might react if startled or cornered out there on the trail, especially in the dark."

Maryl McGregor's persona slowly but systematically strengthened like the yolk of an overdone fried egg, once soft and apt to spill, but now firm and unyielding. "Sheriff," she said with resolve, "I told you Lonnie did not do this." Even in her spirited response, she was careful to address him by his title, and Blake was thankful for that. He made no gesture to accompany his response save only to soften his tone.

"I know. And I told you that he's not under investigation at this time. But I need your help if I'm going to be able to help Lonnie."

"Help with what?" she asked, her voice rising.

"With the most specific detail of his account." Blake bent slightly forward at the waist, leaning closer as he spoke. "Who or what is 'the Tall Song'? Is that an enemy of his or Karl's? A classmate? A customer at Richie's shop? Who?"

Just as Maryl's posture rallied for a potential confrontation, she now visibly relaxed, not with relief, but with a reaction closer to awe or confusion. She held Blake's gaze for a long moment, then looked past him toward the chair behind his desk. "You said Lonnie told me what he told Richie?"

"Exactly."

"Then that means you were there with Richie to hear him tell it."

"That's right."

Maryl looked back sharply. "Then Richie already answered your question for me."

Riverview, October 1978

BARRY Grayson stepped over the threshold of the front door of the family home with all the eagerness of a dental patient going in for a root canal. Everything was at once both familiar, and then not. Nostalgia and good memories were swiftly choked by the pain of knowing that the surroundings before him were no longer blessed by his mother's presence, including the men in the room. Which reminded him of his greatest curiosity as he dropped his bag and looked over at the sound of stirring and whisking in the kitchen: what (or who) had gotten into Joe Grayson?

To be perfectly honest, he thought, there were times in New York shortly after his arrival that he figured Joe himself would fade into death without Sandy. Barry never witnessed much in the way of overt affection from him, but he knew his father held a deep – if not too often hidden – reliance on his mother. And yet there he was, whipping up pancakes, happy as a heron in a honey hole.

In the few moments that he ever extended grace to himself, Barry had come to believe that his anger and resentment were only the raw emotions of an unfulfilled longing for something more virtuous and meaningful. The truth was that he had, in fact, considered this moment many times in those first few years away, but he'd stopped tending to that haunt in his heart and it had quickly become overgrown and all but forgotten. *Like just about everything in this state*, he thought; *turn your back on a footpath and it'll be a jungle in the morning.*

"Here we go," said Joe, setting a plate of pancakes and a mason jar of maple syrup on the table, which now bore no seasonal covering like his mother always used to spread. Instead, the rough knots and scars of the lacquered pine top were showcased like badges of honor, save for a single red and white-checkered centerpiece that was now heralding breakfast. Joe sat and served himself and proceeded to fork the steaming flapjacks onto his plate into smaller bites, lathering them all in syrup.

"So how's the big city?"

Barry sat, finally. "Big enough, I guess." He dropped a few pancakes onto his blue campfire plate.

"Cooling off now, I 'magine," said Joe, pouring himself and Barry a glass of pulp-laden orange juice.

"Yeah, certainly more so than here."

"Shit, it's damn near flannel weather out there now in the mornings." Joe smiled; so did Barry. They both knew he was lying. "I wondered if I'd have ever liked it up there."

"I don't know, Dad. You should've visited."

"I did."

Barry stopped.

"Or at least I was packed and set out to. But then I realized I didn't have a clue where to find you." Barry's eyes fell. Then he looked at Joe with a question.

"What do you mean, 'wondered'?"

"Suppose the same thing you mean by 'visited'." The two men looked at each other. "What's happened, son?" Barry looked over at the front door, and noticed only one jacket hanging on the rack.

"Well, I could sure as hell ask you the same thing."

"Life's happened, Barry. I woke up one day and decided to quit dyin'. That's about it. The short story, anyway."

"What do you mean?"

Joe sighed, sat back, and wiped his mouth. "After you left, I reckon I don't know how I made it through that first winter. I believe I nearly died outta sheer loneliness and heartache, and guilt. The ranch went to shit. One night I put on my coat and walked to the barn with a torch and my gun, figuring I'd kill the cattle outta mercy and then probably myself outta pity." Joe stopped and gently stirred the puddle of syrup on his plate with his fork. "Halfway out there...let's just say I had a change of heart." A grim smile drew at one corner of his mouth. "Suddenly I cared a whole lot about living." He shrugged and leaned his elbows on the table. "Next mornin' I shaved, fed the cows, and started makin' a dent in what I'd become."

Barry sat quietly. "What about Mom?"

"I never said I wasn't still mad as a hornet's nest." Joe leaned back again. "I'm not sure if I'll ever fully square that. But she'd have been ashamed of what I'd become. I think she already was." He stabbed the final few pieces on his plate and chased the last bite with the dregs of his cup. "So I been doin' my best to move in the right direction ever since." He stood and grabbed both their plates. "Listen, once you get some rest, I got somethin' to show ya'."

Barry suddenly remembered that he was more tired than he knew, too tired and confused to protest, anyway. "Look," he rallied, "I never said I was staying."

Joe chuckled. "Never said you could." He winked. "Room's upstairs, just about how you left it. I'm gonna help Ellie with the horses and we'll talk more at dinner."

"Light on labor these days?" asked Barry.

"Not anymore," Joe smiled. "Ellie's a big reason how I'm makin' on here. She's twice as tough as most hands I've hired." Barry raised his eyebrows and nodded. Joe reached for his hat and the door.

"Barry."

"Yeah?"

"It's good to see ya'."

Chapter 9

SHERIFF Blake Martin looked directly at Maryl McGregor. He said nothing. Instead, he walked slowly back to the molded chair behind his desk and sat down. Watching a moth dance between the twin fluorescent bulbs overhead, he said, "Maryl, if you reckon what Richie told me about Lonnie's story, then you know just as well why I'm sitting here talking to you." His eyes returned to meet hers. "You also know as well as I do what Richie does with most of his free time now'days; I could smell it all over him tonight." She dropped her gaze and shook her head. "So talk slowly and help me understand what's really going on here."

Maryl looked surprised. "Sheriff, I'm telling you the truth."

"The truth about what?"

"What Lonnie's talking about."

"*What* he's talking about, not *who?*" Blake emphasized.

Maryl paused. "Yes."

"Maryl McGregor." Blake cocked his head and leaned forward with both palms flat on the desk. "Do you truthfully suggest I entertain the validity of your son's claim that his cousin was attacked and killed by some old Seminole ghost story?" He instantly wished he could take back half of what he'd just said; he usually prided himself on keeping his composure. Maryl was a faithful and valuable public servant, and she'd had a hard life between Lonnie and her husband, Tom. He knew he'd overstepped.

But Maryl was almost as gracious as she was resilient. Almost. It was now her turn to lean in. With each hand on a wheel of her chair, she whispered like an executioner, "Blake Martin. Am I to believe that you think this is the first time an attack like this has happened here?" The question hit its mark; Blake felt the sting, but at least he wasn't blindsided. He felt like he'd just rolled down his window in a car wash. *Stepped into that one*, he thought. What was worse, though, was that his own trick of conversation had now betrayed him: the silence that ensued spoke before he could.

Maryl's shoulders sagged. "Sheriff?"

"I know," said Blake. "I'm sorry for what I said, too."

"It's late," said Maryl.

"Thanks. Believe me that the last four hours have been like some sick recurring nightmare. In fact, I think I've been afraid of this ever since that incident; I was anxious the moment I got the call out there tonight."

"Then you obviously see the connection."

"Of course I see the connection *in the victims*. But that's all."

Maryl sighed quietly. "Blake, I know you want something to wrap those cold, silver cuffs around. But…"

"But what, exactly? Maryl, you can't fault my hesitation to believe this Indian nonsense."

She sat quietly. "Maybe that's the problem, Sheriff."

"What's that?"

"You can't cuff nonsense."

Riverview, October 1978

BARRY awoke just after 4:00 p.m., still wearing the slacks and undershirt he'd left New York in, his dress shirt crumpled by the headboard. He was tired and disoriented, and the shades on the windows were no match for the late afternoon sun. Lying on his back, hands behind his head, he stared up at the ceiling, in desperate need of a shower. Getting up required him to take the first fledgling steps toward figuring out his life, and he'd rather make the most of the comforts of defeat for now.

Joe was right; his room was pretty close to how he'd left it. Almost exactly, as far as he could remember. The drawers were emptied of old t-shirts and spare socks, but his Florida College basketball jersey still hung neatly in the closet, like a clean, caped costume from a forgotten hero. He watched the slats of the ceiling fan lazily chase each other around the same arc. *What in the hell?* he whispered aloud to no one. People go to New York to conquer the world, and here he lay in the bed of his youth wearing two-day old briefs and a spare tire around his waist that could've belonged on one of his dad's tractors.

All right, maybe not that bad, he said, patting his abdomen. *Some kind of success, though.* But while he was up north busting his ass, Joe was down here apparently happy as a fly on a cow patty. Maybe that, more than anything else skating through his mind, was the hardest to grasp. *Maybe I did everyone a favor by leaving,* he sighed, finally rolling out of bed. He could come home to his mother's absence and work through that. He could probably even come home to find the ranch altogether gone. But this turn of events with his dad was just about all that he could handle, not to mention this mystery maiden who was helping him out.

Barry showered and changed, and thought better about unpacking just yet. He put on the crusted square-toed boots from his closet, pleased to discover that at least his shoe size hadn't grown, and walked out to the front porch. At this hour, long shadows cast over the flat land signaled the turning of the tide: nightfall was close at hand. The rocking chairs were still there, the same ones he'd seen his mother in so many years before. Memories at every turn. Not the kind with emotions just beneath the surface, but plenty of loss and confusion, that's for sure.

"Hey there!"

Barry jolted at the voice. She laughed, hard.

"I'm so sorry," she smiled. "I'm Ellie," she said, extending a confident hand.

My God, yes you are, was the first involuntary thought that ripped through his brain.

"No, it's no problem," Barry stammered, shaking her hand and willing his heart to calm down from the surge of adrenaline. "Sorry to be so jumpy; guess I spent too many miles awake over the last few days." His fragile mind was misfiring at the sensory overload. Ellie's hand felt at once a stunning combination of power and beauty: callouses accustomed to leather gloves and pitchforks, surrounded by skin soft as warm butter. He could feel the strength and confidence in her grip, and suspected that it rose from somewhere within her being rather than a byproduct of the labor. He hoped she didn't notice that his own hands were shaped more by fountain pens and paper cuts than anything else in recent years. She seemed taller than most, but maybe it was the cowboy heels. Her thick brunette hair was no match for her eyes and smile, which fit together like emeralds in a gushing stream of snow melt. Together, they hinted at an internal energy that was as wild as any unbroken mustang.

"Yeah, that's what Joe said. All the way from New York, eh?" She took off the wide-brimmed hat and leaned against the porch rail with an ease and confidence that was inspiring.

"That's right."

"Fancy wheels ya' got over there," she smiled.

"When in Rome, I guess," he shrugged.

"Well, it's good to finally see you again; Joe's been excited all morning. As excited as Joe can be, that is."

"Yeah, I can see that," said Barry, not concealing his confusion over his dad's unexpected transformation. Suddenly his sluggish reaction time caught up with her last words. "Wait, I'm sorry," he fumbled, "have we met before?"

She looked at him with a wry smile.

"What?" he asked.

"You really don't remember me, do you?"

Barry was desperately grasping for a memory.

"Um, it's been a really long time," he smiled sheepishly.

"Barry Grayson!" she scolded, playfully. "I grew up right over there!" she was pointing down the ranch road to nothing in particular. He followed her gaze and then turned back to meet her eyes.

"Ellie?"

"Hello!"

"Holy smokes," he said slowly, as he ran his fingers through his blond, thinning hair. "Ellie! Geeze you were like...twelve when I was here last."

"I was driving, thank you very much," she said with an incredulous smile.

"Wow. I'm so sorry. Gosh it's been too long. How the hell are you? How's your family?"

"See, now it's all coming back into that big-city head of yours!"

"Ha! Yeah, big-city somethin'."

"Thanks for asking. We're doin' all right. Mom's quite a pistol even for her condition, and little brother's getting along all right."

"I'm glad to hear that, Ellie. And your dad?"

She tilted her head slightly and raised her eyebrows with a questioning look in her eyes. "Let's just say that Dad travels a lot these days, and that's kind of a good thing right now."

"Ah, I understand." He scuffed the toe of his boot along a raised nail. "Well, I wish nothing but the best for you guys."

"Thanks." They stood there for a moment before Ellie moved to one of the rockers. "So how are you, college superstar? What in the world brings you back to good ol' Riverview?"

"College superstar! Yeah I'm a spitting image of that now."

"Maybe not as far away as you think." Ellie's playful smile retreated instantly as she herself couldn't believe what she'd just said. It was Barry's turn now to cock a mischievous grin. But he exhaled deeply and looked out into the pasture.

"To be honest, I'm not sure what I'm doing back here. I guess I ran away from a lot of things; maybe I figured it's time to square it all up."

Cicadas sang like a gospel choir in the surrounding treetops. Before him lay dozens of head of cattle grazing lazily in the evening sun. Something caught his attention; something he'd missed earlier: curious pegs standing like matchsticks on top of what looked like every other fence post. "Two days ago all I knew was that it was time to leave New York. I started the car and drove, and this is where I ended up." He sounded distracted, or distant. Nodding toward the pasture he said, "What am I seeing on the fence posts out there?" He waited several seconds before he realized Ellie's silence. She had a leery look on her face as she sat staring at his observation. Then she raised her eyebrows and sighed.

"I guess it really has been that long since you've been back."

"Whad'ya mean?"

Ellie rose from the rocker, picked up her hat, and pulled gloves from her back pocket. "I'll let your dad tell you what those are. But I will tell you that they ain't *just* for panthers or coyotes." Barry looked from her back out to the pasture. Joe's pickup was moving east along the worn tire path cutting through the field and heading back to the barn. "Anyway," she said, patting Barry on the shoulder, "it's great to see ya', even if you did forget me," the playful smile returned once more. "I'm gonna head out for the day but I'm around quite a bit. I'll be sure to wear a nametag for you next time," she called over her shoulder. Even as she walked away he could see the mischief in her eyes.

He watched her climb into an old lime green '65 Ford Ranger. *Good gracious,* he thought, *no wonder Joe's still kickin'.* He figured he must have been close to eight years older than Ellie. That wasn't as much of a distance now, but it's nearly a lifetime between high school and graduate school.

He knew he'd have never guessed it was her in a hundred years, but he also knew he'd have a hard time ever forgetting her again. Not that he intended to try.

The truck disappeared over the hill and only the small dust plume was left hanging in the thick air. Barry turned back to the barn at the sound of Joe closing and latching the heavy doors, the mysterious pegs diverting his attention once again. *So, Dad, what's really going on here?*

Chapter 10

Riverview, November 1978

BLAKE Martin had called his wife after leaving the Grayson property to tell her he'd be out late. That was six hours ago. Naturally, U.S. 301 was deserted, except for the occasional overnight trucker. Tonight he felt a familiar longing to be that trucker, rolling right on through sleepy towns like Riverview, mere specks on a map. Blake had a real mess on his plate, no doubt about it. But then again, he'd been expecting to see something like this served up again. In fact, he was half surprised it had been almost ten years.

Like any lawman worthy of wearing the badge, Blake didn't like loose ends or cold cases. Unanswered questions festered into fears that hung in the psyche like a rotting cow carcass on a summer night. Maryl McGregor was a sweet lady, well respected in the town. Her damaged spine was still plenty strong enough to reign in her husband and advocate for her son. But as stern as her constitution could be, she, like so many of the generational residents of Riverview, held firmly to the stranger, spiritual aspects of the Native American presence that seemed to permeate much of the state of Florida.

These days there wasn't much overt Indian display in terms of traditions, but many of their names were still in circulation in the surrounding landmarks: bodies of water like Lake Kissimmee, the Withlacoochee and Apalachicola Rivers, and the Okefenokee Swamp connecting Florida and Georgia. Towns and cities like Tallahassee, Ocala, and even Tampa all took their names from Native American influence, and there were many more. The Miccosukee and Seminole tribes were the largest and most recognized, but there were dozens of smaller tribes that could trace their lineage throughout Florida's long and colorful history.

Like just about every other kid who grew up in or around Riverview, Blake learned about all of the wild and fanciful Indian tales that kept little boys in their beds at night and adolescents home on time. Even now as an officer of the law, these stories were too often resurrected as last ditch blame efforts, usually in crimes involving the booming agricultural industry. But one legend in particular rose above the general lore and seemed to be squarely cemented in the minds of believers, not only in his town, but evidently across the entire nation.

The 19th century began with a historic drought afflicting the Southern states, leaving many of the lakes and rivers at alarmingly low levels. The Okefenokee Swamp, then, was drier than ever before, exposing much of its almost 500,000 acres. Allegedly, a father and son took advantage of the opportunity to explore the swamp into depths yet unknown.

Early in their trek they stumbled upon a small Seminole hunting party, which urgently warned them of delving further into the swamp. When pressed for their concerns, the oldest member of the Indian group spoke reluctantly of elusive but fierce creatures that inhabited these marshy lands, in part to avoid visual detection but also to mask their natural pungent odor. The drought was inadvertently decreasing the boundary lines between the hunting grounds of the men, and those of the creatures. In fact, the father and son had not intersected a hunting party at all; according to the account, the Indians were conducting a sort of investigation into the creature's expanding range, which they were visibly alarmed by. But as they've done since the dawn of their first interactions, the white men generally disregarded the Seminole stories and forged ahead. During their two-week expedition, however, they came across tracks like that of a man's, with one considerable exception: they were abnormally large. In addition, the men claimed to have heard loud, long howls at night covering a wide range of pitch, unlike anything known to inhabit the territory. The Tall Song, the elder Seminole had called it.

Having seen and heard quite enough, father and son quickly retreated and recounted their findings, which only incited the curiosity of a large and genuine hunting party. The legend says that nine men ventured into the swamp, armed to either eradicate or disprove the lore; only four returned. The following excerpt is from a journal written by the survivor (the only known account ever recorded), who only then spoke of the horrific encounter much later in his life:

Following, for some days, the direction of their guide, they came at length upon the track first discovered, some vestiges of which were still remaining; pursuing these traces several days longer, they came to a halt on a little eminence, and determined to pitch their camp, and refresh themselves for the day. ...[T]he next minute he was full in their view, advancing upon them with a terrible look and ferocious mien. Our little band instinctively gathered close in a body and presented their rifles. The huge being, nothing daunted, bounded upon his victims, and in the same instant received the contents of seven rifles. ...[H]e did not fall alone, nor until he had glutted his wrath with the death of five of them, which he effected by wringing the head from the body. Writhing and exhausted, at length he fell, with his hapless prey beneath his grasp. ⋆

Blake Martin, along with the bravest of his elementary schoolmates, had read this very article in a poorly bound book in a hidden corner of the local library, much like many of their parents had done before them. Whispering in excited tones, the boys all shared increasingly dramatic stories of their own, personal family accounts passed down through generations of cracker cowboys, gator trappers, and fruit pickers. By then, however, the indigenous title *Tall Song* given to the creatures by the native inhabitants had been replaced with a far less poetic name: Bigfoot. Even then, in a yarn that only the most Southern state of the Union could spin, generations of Floridians prided themselves on their own unique and equally descriptive name for what felt like their own subspecies of the legend: the Skunk Ape, (taken, of course, from the awful smell often heralding the creature's presence).

The little yellow library book, with brittle pages that felt like they could break like potato chips, went on to propose that meteorological events such as droughts and hurricanes, along with dramatic increases in human growth and expansion, had forced relatively isolated populations, such as those discovered in the Okefenokee Swamp, to disband and seek out new, undeveloped territories. In addition, the book suggested that much like the effects of such growth on the habitats of alligators, panthers, and black bears, these creatures would likewise be unwittingly pitted into unprovoked human interaction, with alarming frequency and likely tragic results.

Of course, the older he got the less thought he'd given to any of these home-spun, fabricated tales. Until the summer of 1968, when his town turned upside down over the mysterious and brutal death of Sandy Grayson. In his desperate search for clues and endless hours spent combing the crime scene and surrounding wildlife reserve, the memories of these stories came lurking out from underneath years of dismissal.

Even now, after he pulled into his driveway, he stood outside in the hush of night leaning against the trunk of his squad car, staring west toward the refuge and hoping to God that the little yellow library book was everything he'd ever wished it to be, both as a young boy on overnight camping trips and now as an adult: nonsense.

* Published by Dale Cox on ExoploreSouthernHistory.com. Milledgeville, Georgia, Statesman January 1829, republished by the Connecticut Sentinel February 9, 1829

Chapter 11

MARYL McGregor squinted into the early dawn as she wheeled her chair out into the parking lot. Thankfully, the rest of her shift on the emergency dispatch board passed without incident, allowing her to focus her thoughts on the maelstrom surrounding her already fractured family. Life in a chair offered a lot of time to think. In hidden moments of weakness, she felt like a piece of driftwood, carried along by the current of life with only as much resistance as her tired forearms could muster. For years after the accident she very nearly cried herself to death, until one day she just couldn't cry any more. She would never forget that pivotal moment, sitting in front of a display of refrigerated milk in the Publix grocery store: write a note and pull a trigger, or to hell with the self-pity and start giving a goddamn. Maybe it was the refreshingly cool air emanating from the commercial machine before her, but she chose the latter.

From that moment forward, Maryl McGregor became something closer to a wrecking ball than an invalid, a force to be reckoned with rather than a doormat. She was the favorite substitute teacher, served on the town council, and picked up dispatch shifts at night. In fact, she came to realize that her chair was what actually allowed her to pursue life in a manner most women didn't dare in those days. Even now, and unbeknownst to him, she had mapped out her plan to rid herself forever from the deadbeat husband she'd mistakenly hitched her wagon to in a moment of youthful naiveté. Just about the only thing delaying the urgency of the matter was that Tom was an overnight trucker, which meant that he was out on the road for weeks at a time. Fortunately, he was on such a trip now, which is why Lonnie was pulling up in his truck. Sheriff Martin had taken Lonnie to her house to get some rest; he was returning now to pick her up.

"Hello again," she said with a smile.

"Hi, Ma'," Lonnie said with a tired grin; he was still wearing his army surplus fatigues from last night.

"Now don't get any funny ideas about droppin' me," she said as he lifted her legs and supported her torso as she pulled herself into the truck.

"Well...well, I should make *you* put the chair in the back."

"Lonnie McGregor, how dare you!" He loaded the chair and stepped awkwardly with his right leg to climb into the driver's seat.

"Between the two of us we only got one good leg to show for, eh?" Lonnie froze with one hand on the key and the other on the wheel. "I'm just kiddin' you!" Maryl said with a wink. "I'm hungry," she lied. "Let's go to the diner and get the biggest plate of blueberry pancakes you ever saw."

"Oh ok. Miss Hester makes pancakes real good."

"She sure does, buddy." Saturday morning was overcast and promised rain for much of the weekend. Perfect, she thought, for sleeping off the long night they'd both endured.

Halfway through her second cup of coffee and their third shared stack of pancakes, Maryl broke the silence. With both hands cradling her cup, she asked, "Honey, last night wasn't the first time you've heard something out there, was it?" Lonnie looked up from the huddle over his plate, searching her eyes and holding his fork like a wrench.

"No."

She nodded in approval and took another sip from the stained porcelain mug. "Have you ever told anyone?" He shook his head and swallowed a mouthful of pancakes. A waitress came and refilled their waters. "Is there anything you didn't tell the Sheriff?" Lonnie didn't look up this time and didn't respond, not directly anyway. Instead, he focused his attention on cutting his entire plate of pancakes into increasingly smaller bites, moving his tongue from one side of his cheek to the other. Maryl was patient; she read the signs. Finally, he set down his fork and scratched his head with both hands, pushing back the blaze orange hat so that it fell behind him in the booth. Reaching around to pick it up, he made vain attempts to wipe the grease stains from the cap. His mother waited.

"I saw somebody, Ma'. I heard the Tall Song, but I saw somebody, too."

"You must be a good hunter to see in the dark."

He shrugged. "I saw somebody."

"Well, can you describe them to me? Let's play that game!" she said in an excited whisper. "How tall was he?"

"It won't do that way."

"Ok," she said. "What kind of hat was he wearing?"

Lonnie shook his head again. "No, no, it won't do that way."

Maryl knew the cues; she had to ask the right question to get his memory jumpstarted in a way. He needed low-hanging fruit. Thus far, her attempts were too high for his reach. Or, something was fundamentally wrong in her request. She thought for several minutes, then raised her eyebrows in surprise at the only elements of her original questions that she could alter.

"Lonnie, can you tell me what kind of hat *she* was wearing?"

He stopped rearranging the sugar packets. "A black hat. A black hat with yellow letters."

"Does she hunt too?" Maryl asked, carefully.

Lonnie nodded in affirmation. "But not the right way."

"What's the right way, honey? What does she do wrong?"

"People should hunt deers from above. She sneaks behind the trees. And she don't wear the orange."

"Why does she do that? It's not safe to do that, is it?"

Lonnie fidgeted, eyes moving from one side to the next. "She's not hunting deers."

"Oh, well, rabbits maybe?"

Lonnie shook his head slowly. "Me. I think."

Chapter 12

BARRY stood on the porch for several long minutes after Ellie's departure. His mind was still in a fog from the travel and lack of sleep, and the unexpected changes he'd encountered over the last few hours weren't helping. Just about the only thing he did know with any certainty was his need for sustenance; he was starving. Joe would be at least a half hour in the barn prepping the next day's routine. Barry walked inside to assess the food options. As expected from anyone in the agriculture business, there's always a little bit of harvest to spare for your own table, so there was plenty of red meat in the fridge.

He went back outside and lit the charcoal grill before returning to salt and pepper a few big patties. Just as he was unfolding an old camping chair to sit alongside the grill, he remembered that his mother always made Joe keep the beer in the garage refrigerator. *Hopefully Dad hasn't gone completely reformed,* he thought as he walked around back. He opened the fridge and found two things. First, much to his delight, an entire case of Pabst Blue Ribbon was distributed throughout the far corners of the appliance. He reached for the closest, and stopped.

The reason they weren't neatly collected on a single shelf, however, lay directly in front of him: the shelves had all been removed to make room for stacks of large, white, tightly wrapped objects, like thin, stiff cuts of beef. He pulled one out, along with a beer, and set them both on the workbench. The package felt light in his hands, almost fragile. He snapped open the can of beer and took a long pull, like a wounded gunslinger before the doc sets in to remove the bullet.

As he unwrapped the package, he discovered that he was holding a crude plaster of some sort: a shallow imprint running the length of one side, and thus a slight arch along the inverse. The garage was dim in the evening light, and he fumbled through the shoe rack for the overhead bulbs. He rotated the object several times before the realization of what he was holding almost caused him to drop it. At each opposite end of the plaster, on the shallow imprint side, he could barely make out two alarming details: an indention at one end that generally resembled a heel print, and conversely, at the other end, somewhat distinguishable toe imprints. This alone was strange enough, but his next observation was far more disconcerting.

The portion of the plaster that measured from heel to toe was much larger than the length of his entire forearm, from his elbow to the tip of his middle finger. Barry was holding the cast of some kind of enormous footprint, and his father's fridge was full of them.

"You just gonna leave these out here to burn?" Joe called from the grill. Barry nearly dropped the print, and didn't bother wrapping it up before replacing it in the fridge and hustling out of the garage. Before rounding the corner, he took a quick second to compose himself.

"Just looking to see if you had some more coals. You mind burgers tonight?"

"Sounds great," said Joe, in a tone that didn't match his words. He pulled a rocking chair over to the corner of the porch near Barry's folding chair. He removed his hat, hung it on one of the chair pegs behind his head, and exhaled.

"Ellie seems like good help," Barry offered, making conversation while checking the burgers. "I'd have never guessed she was the neighbor girl across the way, though."

"Yeah she's been a real godsend. Been working here for the better part of the last three years, I suppose." They sat in silence for several minutes before Joe spoke.

"Son, that beer you got there sounds like the right idea."

"Here let me go get you...one," Barry's voice trailed off, realizing too late the dots that his father had already connected.

Joe gave him a knowing look. "Well, let me tell you one thing, it ain't a coincidence that I keep those two together in the fridge," he said with a slight grin.

"Dad, what's going on?"

"How do you mean? Other than the casts, of course."

"One of those would be enough for most folks, let alone a fridge full of 'em."

Joe said nothing.

"Not to mention whatever fire sticks you got mounted to the pasture posts out there, and never mind the fact that I come home for the first time in years, and suddenly you're the father I never knew." He poked the patties. "So I think I'm in the right by asking what the hell's going on." Joe shot up out of his chair so fast that Barry dropped the lid to the grill. He hopped off the porch and stood level with his son's chin, looking up at him with a calm intensity.

"You are home for the first time in years. Ten years, to be exact. And I'm plenty goddamn glad to see you, son." Joe bent to pick up the lid. "But I've been left to carry on in whatever way I can." He took the spatula from Barry's hand and flipped the burgers. "Let's eat, and then I'll show you everything."

He climbed back onto the porch holding the plate and grabbed his hat off the chair. "Don't forget that beer you were about to offer," he called.

They ate in relative silence with small talk about New York and the recent run of tropical storms that summer. Neither had much to say to the other's inquiries; the time for that may come after whatever explanation Joe was going to offer after dinner. Barry still couldn't wrap his mind around the dizzying events of the last forty-eight hours, and he was anxious at the thought of discovering yet another bizarre twist in this family reunion of sorts.

Joe lifted the dishes off the table and told Barry to get a jacket and bring the two rifles from his closet. Barry started to protest, but the haunting resolve in his father's eyes persuaded him otherwise. Everything had changed in the last ten years. And nothing had changed at all.

When he returned, Joe was pulling on his coat and stuffing a box of matches in the pocket. He took one of the rifles that Barry offered and checked to see that it was loaded.

"Yours, too?" he asked.

"Yeah, it's loaded."

"Good. Let's go." Joe walked off the porch and toward the truck.

"Barry, I really am glad to see you; I mean it. It's been way too long. I know I failed you in the most important ways; I reckon I'm a big reason you left in the first place. And I don't blame you." Barry stood and listened, then opened his door and set his rifle in the gun rack behind their head rests before sliding onto the cracked vinyl bench, his long legs bunched up against the dash. Joe followed suit with his own rifle, sat down beside his son, and pulled the keys out of his coat pocket.

"I hoped to have all this figured out before you turned up, for both our sakes."

"What do you mean, *figured out?*" Barry asked, frustration in his tone. Joe lifted a hand, suggesting Barry let him finish.

"Unfortunately, right now I've got more questions than answers, and what I'm about to show you and tell you – and what you've already stumbled upon – I've never spoken to another soul. I don't claim to understand it. Hell, I hardly want to believe it myself, but it's my honest-to-God recollection of what's going on here."

"Dad, you make it sound like you've uncovered some kind of drug ring or hidden cult here in our little two-bit town," Barry gave an exasperated chuckle. "What's with the paranoia?"

Joe started the truck and stared through the windshield. "I think I know what happened to your mother."

He pressed the clutch, put the truck into gear, and urged the worn engine toward the pasture.

Chapter 13

ELLIE looked in her rearview mirror, hardly able to believe what stood on that front porch behind her. Barry Grayson. *Sweet Jesus,* she whispered. She laughed out loud at the stories she and her girlfriends would spin on sleepovers or long bus rides to out of town games about *the* Barry Grayson. In their adolescent eyes he was the hometown college athlete-turned-lawyer who would one day rescue any one of them out of the confines of their surroundings, whether that be the boundaries of their homes and high school, the limits of Hillsborough County, or the state line for all they cared.

They had all dreamed of Barry as teenagers, but Ellie alone seemed the outcast in regards to any desperate yearning to leave Riverview. Most of her girlfriends had regrettably latched onto the first suitor who promised a seemingly better life than they grew up in, or at least a double-wide they could call their own. Ellie was one of the few girls from that class who went on to college, even if it was the local branch of Hillsborough Community College.

Her childhood home had plenty of its share of tension and sideways traction like so many of those from her generation: fathers working like hell to carve out a modest existence, wives navigating their own newfound opportunities from cultural changes much further upstream, and the youth of the 60s caught between their parents' values and the compelling, carnal urges ignited by the British Invasion and every homeland hero with a guitar. Even in towns as far away from the epicenter as Riverview, everyone seemed to realize that the world was changing, and those too young and naive to understand the stakes were pitted against the older generations who were desperate for the stability that the World Wars had already taken from their own lives. Ellie could feel the ground beneath the foundation of her own parents shifting, and she almost wished that the fault lines would go ahead and give way to a new future, especially for her mother's sake.

Nonetheless, Ellie embraced the times and trials of Riverview; she was at peace with the land of the fire river much the same way a person would be with a pair of weathered wranglers. Patches add character to torn denim. Still, she'd have a hell of a good laugh for the girls when she confessed to her thinking-out-loud comment to Barry back there on the porch.

She could never be faulted for being honest, at least! It's true that he wasn't all that her memory held him to be, but his own self-awareness and demeanor seemed well in tact. His blond, cigarette-model mustache certainly was. Plus, if he was gonna stick around for a while, then the ranch labor would naturally trim the excess that he'd acquired sitting behind a desk. *Listen to yourself, Ellie!* she laughed. She rolled her eyes, feeling downright silly for how light her heart felt at the sight of him after all these years. Or maybe it spoke to how much her heart ached for something to feel right, to feel unburdened.

Given her mother's wheelchair, her father's temperament, and her little brother's ongoing condition, Ellie was rarely without a heavy yoke, and unexpected moments like the sudden appearance of an old high school crush made her feel like a long-haul saddle pack had been lifted off her shoulders. Barry had hardly known her way back when, and only barely remembered her now, but that felt like enough for today.

Chapter 14

JOE let the pickup idle in neutral as he climbed out and lowered his seat forward to access the extended cab. He pulled out two long sticks that looked like some form of candle lighters, with thick wicks on their ends; one was evidently well used, the other was brand new. He lit them both and handed one to Barry. They were parked along the far east side of the pasture, along the stretch flanked by the Alafia, with the wildlife refuge sitting across the opposite bank.

"You head that way and light the sticks down to the last post. I'll go this way toward the barn and we'll meet over there at the canoe launch."

"Why the canoe launch?"

"Because that's where this will start to make some kind of sense, hopefully."

Barry sighed and set out.

"Take your rifle," Joe called.

Good God, Barry thought. By all accounts thus far it seemed that his father was a full on whack job, evidently succumbing to the mental stress over some kind of spook. He softened, though, at the thought of wondering how he himself would've handled staying here after what happened to his mother. *Who knows? Tragedy does things to folks.* Joe was certainly a kinder man. If it took a hobby like this to bring that about in him, then Barry guessed there were worse coping mechanisms.

Barry walked along the barbed wire fence for close to half a mile, dodging patches of pasture cactus and cow manure, stopping every twenty feet to extend his own torch to light another. When he finished and turned toward the canoe launch, he stopped in wonder at the scene before him. The once-lonely pasture looked eerily similar to a scene from a medieval battlefield, the line of torches standing like silent sentries against the tides of the river, or the advance of the refuge. It was an imposing and ominous picture.

Barry finally arrived at the grassy bank that sloped down to meet the muddy beach of the Alafia. He was winded from the walk, and still feeling the effects of the miles in his lower back. All that was forgotten, however, when he saw Joe loading his rifle and a high-beam flashlight into the canoe.

"Whoa, whoa, whoa, what do you think you're doing?"

"I told you I'd tell you everything."

"On a damn boat ride in the dark? No thanks."

"Relax, we're only crossing the river over to the refuge."

"Ok, so another long walk in the dark after I've already trekked nearly a mile out here. Jesus, Dad, what's any of this got to do with Mom?"

"First of all, consider me doing you a favor getting you to expend some energy. And second, this has everything to do with your mother, my wife." Joe stood up from pushing the canoe, his shoulders heaved after the exertion and he looked out at the strangely lit pasture. "Barry, I'm not proud of what I'm doing or what I'm about to tell you. Hell, like I said, I don't even want to believe it. I haven't gone looking for this as much as it's come after me."

"What? What's come after you?" Barry interrupted, losing patience.

"All of this!" Joe spread both arms out along the fencerows. "The flares, the casts, the traps," he said.

"The traps?"

Joe sighed, exasperated. "Get in the goddamn boat."

"Is there a reason we have to do this now?"

"You'll get a better understanding of who I am, of who I've become."

Barry considered slinging the rifle over his shoulder and just walking back to the house; maybe get a decent night's rest and head out to God-knows-where in the morning. Coming home had been a mistake, clearly. In truth, he had half expected to reach that conclusion, but never for reasons like this. He felt too far gone to turn back now, however, and remembered that Ellie seemed to know something of what was going on. He shook his head in a gesture of disbelief and set the rifle in the canoe. Together the two men shoved off from the haunting glow of the torches toward the infinite darkness of the forest ahead.

They crossed in silence, save for the thirsty laps of the oar and a lonely owl looking for company. Barry's boots sunk into the damp bank as he stepped off the bow and pulled the canoe ashore. Joe collected the two rifles, handed one to Barry, and grabbed the flashlight. The tree line just ahead blocked out any available celestial light, but both men could barely make out the ghostly trails from their breathing in the cool night. Joe spoke with evident hesitation, choosing his words with care.

"You asked me earlier today about how I've changed. The winter after your mother's death, I really did walk out here to the barn one night figuring I'd never walk back." He made a gesture with his rifle toward the pasture across the river.

"I was gutted, Barry. Nothin' left. I didn't have the energy to care for the cattle, much less go through the mess of trying to sell them and everything else. I'd already made up a will that left the house and property to you; figured it was the least I could do after all I robbed you of in your childhood." Even in the darkness Barry could see his father muster the resolve to look him in the eye with that word. He exhaled deeply, creating a thick vapor trail.

Father and son stood on the far banks for several moments. "I walked into the barn, thinking I'd get all the heifers out so at least the buzzards and coyotes would take care of the clean up."

"What happened?" Barry asked quietly.

"I wasn't alone," was all Joe could summon. Several more seconds of nothing but the blended voices of crickets and cicadas. "I could tell the cattle were jumpy, but I chalked it up to my being there so late."

"Who was out there?"

"I don't think it was *who*."

"How's that?"

"I've come to suspect that some *thing* was out there that night, not someone."

"Panther? You and I have fired our fair share of warning shots at those cats."

"No. Something much bigger."

"Bigger how?"

"Taller. Taller than you by a long shot."

"How do you figure that?"

"Because it was screaming at me just outside the barn." Joe sat on the bow of the canoe and removed his hat, wiping sweat from his brow.

"Screaming like a cat? Maybe it was up one of those oaks next to the barn."

"Screaming like nothing you've ever heard; nothing in your life. Barry I've been in a hand-dug hole with bullets singing past my ears, certain I was taking my last breath on this earth, but I've never known the kind of fear that tore through my spirit that night. And I've never been a devoutly religious man, probably to all of our detriment, but I felt a presence of power or evil like I've never experienced or even heard of."

"Jesus," Barry whispered.

"I was standing literally on the other side of the wall of the barn, and I thought sure as shit that it was gonna tear the whole damn thing down. The screaming and pounding." Joe's hand trembled slightly as he ran his palm over his mouth and along the back of his neck.

"I managed to gather myself and fire a few shots through the roof; I just squeezed the trigger, didn't even aim. Couldn't aim. Everything went quiet, and I heard what sounded like a loud howl in the distance, could easily have been across the river. Then the creature, or whatever it was, gave one more slam against the barn, and I heard it run off."

Barry said nothing.

"I stayed there all night, didn't dare make a run for the house. I think my body was so worked up that I must've passed out in the loft; that's where I woke up the next day, anyway. The sun was shining that morning, something I don't remember seeing or noticing for a long time before then. I tried to figure what in the hell had happened, but I couldn't get past this sense of energy to get on living, to turn it around. God, I think I was just so thankful to be alive. I missed you and your mother more than my old ticker could bear, and I wept in that loft for all that I'd lost. Wept like I've never done in my life. By all I can reckon, it seems that I came down a changed man, like there was a peace pushing against the fear I'd been drenched in the night before." Joe wiped his eyes now and put his hat back on.

"Don't take this the wrong way," Barry began.

"I know where you're going. I asked myself the same thing on my way down from the loft."

"What's that?"

"Did I imagine the whole thing? Maybe the sorrow and the despair and the beer got to me?"

"Something like that."

"Trust me, I'd be fine with that."

"But?"

"But you already found the problem with that theory."

"Where?"

"Neatly wrapped in the beer fridge."

Barry nodded knowingly. "The plaster casts."

"Yep. I walked around the side of the barn and almost vomited with the rush of fear all over again. Tracks everywhere, and mud marks higher up on the wall than even you could reach."

"From where it was beating against it."

"Yep."

They sat in silence.

"Did you get all those casts in the fridge that morning?"

"All but one."

"So it came back?"

"Not exactly. Well, maybe it did or maybe it has, but there's one other print in the fridge that I got from somewhere else."

"Where?"

Joe thumped the stock of his rifle up and down gently on the riverbank. "Right here."

Chapter 15

BLAKE Martin awoke with the familiar weight on his chest, like an invisible iron blanket bearing down on his entire spirit. He didn't always feel like this, thank God, but this morning was especially hard. Even after almost thirty years of wearing a badge, events like those from the night before, which in turn necessitated today's activities, still wore heavy on his mind. The visit to the Grayson ranch would dredge up years of pain and questions and confusion, for both parties. As he showered and dressed, he felt a moment of startling realization that he wasn't certain how much longer he could do this. He pulled the elastic band of the gold watch around his wrist, pausing to remember that he'd purchased the piece only a few days before the Sandy Grayson tragedy. Wearing his brown, pressed khakis and a white V-neck undershirt, he followed the smell of coffee and bacon to the kitchen where his wife, Kathy (Kitty to everyone else), was buttering toast.

"Good morning, honey. Late night?"

"Yeah," said Blake, his voice weary with regret and longing for sleep. Kathy Martin knew that voice; she was always hesitant to ask about it, but she always did.

"What happened?" In these intimate and delicate moments, Blake was more thankful for her than ever. She was a safe space, an attentive mind that suspended judgment or opinion, and guarded privileged information from other women in town like a Roman garrison. Throughout his career, Blake had fired a few deputies for what appeared to be technicalities, but in each case he'd learned that their wives were spilling police gossip like busted oil rigs, the effects of which were just as toxic to a small town as they were to any ecosystem. He'd rather run a ship that was short-staffed than one that was leaking sensitive information. He poured a cup of coffee and stole a wedge of toast from the pale yellow plate.

"I was out near the Grayson property last night."

Kathy rose from the fridge, forgetting what she was after and standing there with the door open.

"Karl McGregor was killed," Blake continued. "His cousin Lonnie discovered the body."

She closed the door and pulled a chair from the nearby table, never taking her eyes off her husband.

"I'm so sorry."

Blake nodded and stirred the bacon, pulling a few cuts off the burner and onto his plate.

"Yeah."

"Was it like last time?" she asked quietly.

It was Blake's turn to stand motionless, putting the pieces together of what she was implying.

"Awfully close."

Kathy brought a hand to her mouth; Blake took a sip of coffee.

"Oh my," she whispered.

Blake opened the fridge, found the strawberry jam, and scooped two small portions onto each slice of toast.

"You're headed out there this morning?"

"Yeah."

"Are you taking a hunting party?" Kathy asked with the resolve of a judge, confident in her verdict. Blake barely managed a bite of eggs before putting down his fork.

"A hunting party?" He looked at his wife with confusion, then disbelief and frustration. "Oh for God's sake, don't you start in on that too."

"Blake Martin you know exactly what I mean."

"I know what the rest of this crazy town thinks, but I hoped my own household would have more sense."

"It's not about sense, honey," she stated firmly.

"My *job* is about making sense! If my choices are common sense or some Indian swamp monster, I know which ballot I'm punching. And which one I'm arresting," he added.

Kathy sighed and walked toward the stove, turning off the burner and removing the pan. Blake sipped his coffee and tried to recover an appetite. The thought of hitching up the bass boat for a morning on the Alafia flitted across his mind, and it sounded like freedom. Turning in his badge altogether sounded like heaven.

"Blake," she said softly, "you need to consider heeding your own advice."

"And what would that be?"

"I've heard you say this many, many times: *people get hurt when they don't pay attention.*"

Blake nodded. "What's that got to do with this?"

Kathy finished drying the pan she'd just washed, hung the towel, and turned to face him.

"Most folks think that paying attention means they need to narrow their focus, notice the details."

"That's right."

"But sometimes I think it means the opposite." She stood at the sink drying her hands; Blake aimlessly stirred the cup of black coffee in circles on the tabletop.

"Kitty, I'm real tired, and I'm staring down the barrel of a rough day. You'd do best to get on with your point."

She walked to the table and sat next to him, crossing her legs under a floral-trimmed gown. "Blake, sometimes I think the best way to pay attention is to expand the view of your surroundings, increase your field of vision." Blake sighed. "Just think on this for a minute," she urged. "Think about you fishing out on the river. I've seen you do this! You're not just focused on that spot of cover on the bank; you're aware of the rest of the river, the tides and the bait, other boaters, changes in the weather."

The lines in Blake's features softened to show his interest. "Ok. So walk me through how any of that applies to this ridiculous business you and everyone else seems to believe. Hell, it's much further down the road than just *belief*. Between you and Maryl McGregor, the verdict of both this creature's existence and its involvement in these cases is a foregone conclusion!" His half-empty mug hit the table harder than he intended; coffee splashed out of both sides. "What exactly does everyone else seem to *know* that I'm apparently missing?"

Kathy leaned back in her chair for several seconds, then reached over for a napkin. She picked up his mug and wiped the coffee from outside and underneath, then gathered the circle of remaining residue from the table. "It's not what everyone else seems to know; it's what others may be willing to notice."

He held his mug in both hands and tapped his index fingers softly around the rim. "I'm sorry," he said, "thanks." They sat together in the silence and lingering darkness, the coming dawn largely overwhelmed by the low-pressure weather system camped over the county. Finally, Blake rose from the table and carried his plate to the sink.

"Honey, my job is to maintain peace and ensure justice; I can serve the people of this town best by dealing with facts, not folklore." He slid his plate into the drying rack and shook his hands into the sink before peeling off a paper towel.

"Blake, everything's got *everything* to do with belief; there's hardly a stitch of it that doesn't, not to some degree anyway. The sooner you agree to that, the better you'll be able to reckon with this world, your person, and whatever's happening to this town. Don't miss the forest for the trees, as they say."

Kathy Martin rose and retreated to the bathroom, leaving her husband standing in the dimly lit kitchen, staring out the window at the abstract outlines that were beginning to take shape and form the parameters of an existence that he was increasingly uncertain of.

Chapter 16

"YOU wanna tell me what the hell we're doing over here?" Barry asked his father over the mournful call of a whippoorwill. Joe chuckled and rose from the canoe.

"That cast is a few years old, and I've been coming over here several times a month looking for more."

"So you think it's moved on? Wait a minute, what are we even talking about? What is this thing? I mean have there been reports of something like this by anyone else?"

"Slow down there, Big Apple. I'm not sure whether it's moved on; all it takes is a tidal change and a shallow print is erased. I don't get into town much, and I'm certainly not hosting Sunday school picnics out here, so as far as I know I have no idea of any other reports."

"So what is it, then?"

"That's why we're here."

"You said this had something to do with Mom."

"It does. Let's go." Joe tossed Barry a flashlight and soon the two were walking silently along the ATV trails. Twenty minutes later, Joe suddenly stopped. "This way," he whispered, and veered off the path and into the dense foliage. Twigs snapped in protest, grapevines reached for the rifles slung across their backs. Barry was carefully sidestepping a palmetto bush when he heard Joe tell him to stop. He completed the maneuver and readjusted his gun, then he walked a few paces and stood next to his father. At first, Joe's light was illuminating nothing in particular, just more of the same mix of familiar and exotic leaves alongside fallen moss and exposed tree roots.

Then, Barry noticed several things. First, a finely lacquered wooden cross barely tucked beneath a small outcrop of ferns, standing fifteen feet away from them directly across what he now realized was a subtle clearing. Six feet to the left of the stake, Barry's light caught something out of place, a color.

A small orange boundary flag stood quietly, buried almost to the hilt. He swung his light slowly to the opposite side of the space, and found a similar flag, equally stained with mud and debris. Barry pulled his gaze to either side of himself and his father. Sure enough, two such flags were close by, creating a large square.

In the center of this little relief, halfway between them and the cross, a rope hung motionless from the canopy above, only recognizable from the grapevines by its lack of knots and angular twists. In fact, the rope was perfectly straight, because it was dangling a large rack of raw cow ribs eight feet above the ground. Finally, directly beneath the suspended offering, his light caught the pinnacles of exposed black steel, like a giant jaw lying wide open. Barry initially understood it to be a bear trap, except that the distance between the two ends made this the largest such device he'd ever seen.

Joe saw the same cold teeth and carefully walked forward to toss fistfuls of leaves onto the brutal instrument. Barry stood very still, watching him, enveloped by darkness and the orchestra of the marsh. Despite his outward posture, his mind was racing, making flailing attempts to grasp all that was before him: the chunk of cow flesh, the homemade cross, the torches, the footprints in the beer fridge, the story of his father's conversion, and the memories flooding back from beyond his control. He began to feel the metallic tinge of nausea. Without his permission, the world as he had known it only twenty-four hours ago had most likely changed forever. Last week he was a lawyer in New York City; now he was a quarter mile deep in a Florida jungle, staring at a barbaric trap designed for

God-knows-what. For a moment, he was too engulfed in self-loathing to feel any fear.

That changed immediately when the silence was shattered by the distant sound of solid wood being smacked together, one piece against another. The two men instinctively shouldered their rifles; Joe switched off his beam and whispered for Barry to do the same. The sudden absence of light magnified the effect of the darkness; they could hardly see one another. For all that Joe had recently recounted, Barry sensed that he seemed surprisingly calm and focused. Another sharp slapping sound, this time followed by a response somewhere to their two o'clock, and closer.

"Follow me," said Joe. "I want this trap between us and them."

"You wanna tell me who *them* is?"

"Later."

"Stop," Barry hissed, adrenaline coursing through his voice. "If we're about to get tossed into a shit storm then I sure as hell wanna know which way the wind is blowing. You tell me what's going on out here." Joe took a step closer to his son. The older man searched the eyes of the younger, and he smiled.

"I can explain more back at the house, but for now suffice it to say that I strongly believe that the same sonofabitch slapping those trees together is responsible for that cross in the dirt over there."

Joe's voice was filled with enough conviction that Barry made no attempt to slow his father's strategic retreat; he followed for several paces and then knelt beside him, the sound of their steps fading in time to hear the full effect of a long, lonely howl unlike any coyote he'd ever heard. Dumbfounded, Barry was filled with a sudden urge to empty his rifle into whatever was coming their way.

Riverview, November 1978

ELLIE was burning a lot of fuel pushing the little lime green Ford Ranger to speeds of personal record. The truck was far more utilitarian than high performance, even when she first bought it, but that hadn't stopped her then from experiencing the thrill of her first car with her best friends down the service road of a deserted orange grove. That late-summer celebration so many years ago had nothing on both the speed and the urgency of tonight's pursuit. She heard the familiar calls and was instantly alarmed at their proximity to the general direction of her brother's tree stand. But the second scream sent her racing through the refuge and diving headlong into the Alafia on the fastest freestyle swim she'd ever performed. By the time she located the stand she could see the glow of emergency lights; Lonnie and Richie were shouting with the sheriff. In a moment of indecision, she remained close by, but hidden, unsure of what her appearance would do. All that really mattered to her was that her little brother was safe. For now.

Ellie waited until the sheriff and medical teams walked Lonnie off the scene. Then, she summoned all of her strength to retrace her steps across the outskirts of the Grayson property, cross the river again, and exit the refuge on the far side of U.S. 301. The shoulder of the highway conveniently dipped down into an oak-covered hollow there; her pickup was practically undetectable in the night.

She couldn't be certain where the sheriff was taking Lonnie, but if there was the slightest chance that he could bring him to stay at her place, then she'd better be home. Especially at this hour. The quiet waters of the Alafia were no kind of alibi.

She turned onto her road off the main highway and had enough wherewithal to drive slowly past the dead-grass driveway before committing to it, not that she had any idea what she'd do if she saw a squad car in front of her house. Thankfully, the yard was empty. Ellie's little concrete bungalow may have only been a few miles from her parents' residence, but it was an eternity from her childhood, and that was what mattered. That, and the fact that the road ended at the Alafia made for a quiet existence. She returned and parked, closed the door quietly, and went inside, shedding her soaked outer clothing into the washer that sat in the screened-in garage. By the time she reached the bathroom, the combination of her adrenaline crash and the anxiety of her brother's plight caused her to collapse and vomit into the toilet.

An hour later, she jolted awake, lying on the bathroom floor, half-naked under a towel she didn't remember pulling over her. Nursing something worse than any hangover she could remember, she showered and dressed and ate a slice of plain toast before climbing into her truck and momentarily soaking her jeans all over again; the single bench seat was still dripping wet. She grabbed a few old towels from the laundry room, changed into dry denim, and headed out for essentially the third time in the last six hours without the sun in her eyes. It would be up soon enough, though, and she had to figure out a way to check on Lonnie without giving away her proximity to the events. He could only be in one of three locations, and she knew there was no way for her to check the police station or her uncle's trailer. Ellie was surprised, then, to see Uncle Richie's pickup peeling into her mother's driveway shortly after she had parked and checked the property.

"Where is he?" Richie shouted before the truck was even stopped. Ellie stood on the front patio, her heart racing all over again. She'd never known her uncle to be a violent man, but then again, he was her father's brother.

"Who?" she asked. "What are you doing here this early?"

"I'm lookin' for Lonnie."

"Lonnie? What makes you think he'd be here?"

"Because he ain't at my trailer or the Sheriff's office." Richie was standing just beyond the roofline, heaving and looking like some kind of angry, cornered prey that's just committed to fighting its way out.

"Uncle Richie, what's going on?"

"Wait a minute. Why are *you* here?" he countered.

"I used to live here, Richie." She hoped to have been able to steer him off the property before he connected those dots. "And I came by to pick up Mom for breakfast after her night shift."

Her uncle calmed and held his hands over his mouth before rubbing his eyes with his palms. Ellie walked down the steps. "Richie, what happened?"

"Karl's dead, Ellie."

"What?!"

"Last night. I – I can't really talk about it right now. Something happened out at the tree stand. Something or someone attacked Karl." Richie turned to her now with renewed resolve. "And I wanna make goddamn sure it wasn't Lonnie."

Chapter 17

MINUTES may as well have been hours; the human body can only sustain so much prolonged stimuli before it starts to desensitize. Barry and Joe waited in the silence, rifles ready, the hum of mosquitoes in their ears. However much time elapsed, the primitive communication had ceased. At one point they heard movement close by, but both men relaxed the tension in their triggers when an armadillo came crashing through the foliage. For their small size, the odd, armored mammals possess all the stealth of a Humvee.

Finally, Joe leaned over and whispered for Barry to follow him, and quickly. He rose and took careful, large strides over fallen trunks and washed out ditches. Soon, father and son were once again on the main ATV trail, and Barry discovered that he was in an all-out sprint to keep up with the Stetson in front of him. Before he could call out in protest, a primal scream blasted through the low fog shelf that had settled below the tree line, followed by an equally powerful smashing through the forest that may as well have been a Vietcong landmine.

His heart nearly fell out of his chest; whatever he'd gotten himself into, or however familiar Joe was with these bizarre circumstances, Barry was way out of his depth. In New York, one had to quickly develop a habit of looking for reflections to check your back: storefronts, windshields, subway windows. But in the sulfur swamps of Florida, you apparently ran for your life from unknown goblins.

Whatever started giving chase behind them was gaining ground, despite never seeking the path of least resistance that the Grayson men were racing down. Joe almost slipped on the line of damp leaves and scallop shells left by the low tide, but recovered quickly enough to leap effortlessly into the canoe. Barry followed and heaved the vessel into the river up to his knees before jumping in; Joe was already pulling hard with a paddle, practically dragging Barry behind him. Together, they traversed the natural barrier in seconds. They were standing back inside the pasture fence line when they heard the now-familiar sounds of sticks smashing against each other, inside one hundred yards of the banks of the refuge, sounding very much like a vigorous warning.

Barry stood on the passenger side of the truck, catching his breath and staring across the river that now felt like either a lover caught in a lie or an old friend finally telling secrets. He looked at the rifle in his hands. Not only was his personal life firmly upside down, but whatever innocence was left of his youth either fell out of that canoe or lay trounced underfoot somewhere in the vast expanse before him. Even now, the image of the wooden cross almost made him vomit, and the mountain of emotional baggage that stood before him felt more overwhelming than any challenge he'd ever faced, like a dormant disease once held at bay now coursing through his bloodstream.

Joe was sitting in the truck; he leaned across the bench and knocked on the inside of the passenger window. Barry didn't notice, or didn't care.

"Hey!" Joe's muffled voice came from inside. Finally, he climbed out; the truck was still running. "C'mon, let's go." Barry shifted his eyes from the refuge to his father, and climbed in, pulling his long legs into the small cabin. The two bounced along in silence all the way to the ranch house. Joe parked and shut off the engine; neither made any motion to exit.

"Son, I know this is – "

"What in God's name are you doing out here?" Barry quietly interrupted, still looking through the windshield at nothing in particular.

"Excuse me?"

He turned now to look at his father and repeated the question, slowly.

"What do you mean, '*What am I doing out here?*' I'm trying to survive! Ain't that clear enough from tonight?"

"No, you're not."

"And how the hell do you figure that?"

"The hired help, the dramatic torches, half a freaking cow donated to some kind of prop trap. Christ, Dad, you've got Mom's grave marker out there! You're not *surviving*; you're running some kind of sick scare scam. I wouldn't be surprised to learn that you've got Halloween hayrides out there now."

Joe sat behind the wheel looking at his own flesh and blood as if he'd just discovered that his only son was an alien from another galaxy; and in some ways maybe he was. He stared at him for several seconds, incredulous. "Have you lost your goddamn mind?"

"Took the words right outta my mouth," Barry said.

"Don't you ever again accuse me of something like profiting off what happened to her, what happened to us. Are we clear? Because, boy, I will defend her honor to my own death."

"That's not what I meant."

"Then what the hell do you mean? How do you explain what we just heard out there?"

"I have no idea, Dad! Why don't you offer an explanation?" Barry burst out of the truck and walked several paces into the night. "You got guys out there banging shit around? Is that why you were so adamant about going over there tonight? What am I supposed to think?"

Joe closed his door and walked toward Barry, his hands resting on the silver and turquoise belt buckle he'd had for as long as Barry could recall. "Why don't you *want* it to be what it is?"

"Probably because I don't know what *it* is! How do I know you didn't drink that whole barn story up?"

Joe sized up his son for a long moment. "I forgot," he said, "you've been a big city lawyer for too long."

Barry's arms collapsed to his sides. "If that means I'm predisposed to the facts, then guilty as charged."

"Come in here." Joe turned and walked toward the garage, flipping on the light as he entered.

"Those plasters are hardly convincing," Barry called over the sound of Joe rummaging through the contents of the refrigerator. "Anyone could have easily – " Joe flung a tightly rolled grocery bag at his chest; it bounced off and Barry caught it around his waist.

"What's this?"

"Let's call it hard evidence," Joe said with a sneer. Barry held it, looking suspiciously at his father.

"Where'd you get this?"

Joe chuckled, "You'll see."

"My God, I don't want to have to testify – "

"Just open it."

Barry slowly unwrapped the brown sac; he could feel that the contents were long and firm, like popsicles or frozen hotdogs, only larger. He looked inside, then back at his father, before carefully extracting a white, freezer-wrapped package, taped together in a manner that suggested a fear of the contents escaping on their own.

"Go ahead, open it up," Joe said as he tossed his pocketknife.

Barry opened the blade and ran it along the overlapping edges, neatly cutting through the tape. He set the knife and package on the workbench, and gently opened the thick paper. The task was not yet finished. Just as he'd prepared countless steaks for freezer storage, the first layer was always a generous portion of thin plastic wrap, followed by the thick, stiff paper he'd just cut through. The general outline before him was anything but a steak. Whatever lay hidden in that inner lining was as long as a hammer, and felt nearly as heavy, if the tool's weight were evenly distributed.

Barry found the edge of the wrap. Out of habit, he held it firmly in one hand and, raising it in the air over his receiving hand, he carefully jerked the package up and down, using the content's own weight to unwrap itself. For the duration of his childhood and adolescent years, Barry had performed this very maneuver thousands of times in an efficient effort to get whatever red meat was on the menu that night onto the grill. Typically, though, he'd be doing this long after the back strap or flank steak had been left out to thaw, so that what fell into his hand would be soft yet still somewhat firm.

That was one major difference from tonight; Joe had just removed the package, thus the object would still be very hard, as he expected. The second, most distinct difference was what sent him barreling out of the garage and finally giving way to the nausea he'd been suppressing. What fell into Barry's own hand had once belonged to someone else's: fingers.

Chapter 18

AS if Barry's world weren't already spinning, the rules and parameters of his reality were now utterly shattered. He wiped his mouth with the back of his hand before reaching for the garden hose, rinsing his mouth of the acidic residue and scooping water over his face, hair, and onto the back of his neck. He spat several times and drew his hand over his mustache in a long, slow gesture of recalibration.

Joe walked out, carrying the unwrapped bag, and set a Pepsi-Cola on the sidewalk next to him. "Here, take a few sips."

Barry cracked open the can and savored the sugary syrup. He sat in the glow of the garage, arms locked around his knees, staring ahead at the rusted out basketball goal at the end of the driveway. It stood like a faded monument of forgotten days. He'd raised the money and set it all up himself; the net looked like the next thunderstorm would be its last. The memory lingered only a few seconds, but he was thankful for the momentary transport.

Barry took another sip, wishing it were something much harder from a small glass; then, he summoned all of his remaining resolution and returned his focus to the package that Joe had set down beside him. Even now, knowing what he was going to behold, he could hardly believe what was lying next to him. Two severed fingers, that much was clear; neither of them a thumb. If he wanted to look any closer maybe he could determine the right or left hand. It seemed impossible, however, to determine which two fingers they were due to their sheer size and scale. One was close to twelve inches long, if not longer; the other was smaller, but not by much.

The scene was something of a terrible, mind-bending paradox in that the fingers were more human in their nature than any other resemblance on the planet: three segments, nails, hair. All immediately recognizable as human-oriented. And yet they were unlike any human being Barry had ever heard of. Aside from their inexplicable size, there were other features that stood out. First, Barry noticed their color in regards to human races. They clearly didn't belong to any white, Indian, African, or Asian man. Second, they possessed a musculature and girth that suggested alarming power.

Beyond these observations, one final element was clearly more un-human (or more animal-like) than any other. The ends of each finger boasted thick, sharp protrusions that, given their anatomic location and the shared characteristics of his own species, might be considered nails. But no one would call the business end of a grizzly's paw a "fingernail." In similar fashion, then, something much closer to the claw of a dangerous predator extended menacingly from each of the fingers that sat there sharing the sidewalk with him.

Riverview, November 1978

ELLIE collapsed into a threadbare folding chair after Richie's taillights disappeared in a cloud of dust. Her head was spinning from the night before. The sun was now piercing through the tangle of fern-laden oaks; a small hawk was crying loudly from her perch with an enthusiasm meant to be taken seriously. A lizard ran along the edge of the sidewalk and snatched an ant, while a barely visible scorpion lay tucked beneath a discarded sneaker. A new day of survival was dawning. *Where was Lonnie?* She'd never seen her uncle like this, and she felt doubly compelled to find her brother before he did. It would have been a relief, she considered, to learn that he was in a holding cell, at least safe from Richie's vengeance, and she shuddered at the thought of her father coming home from his trucker route. God knows what he'd do.

Tom – she quit calling him *Dad* a long time ago – behaved as though he held some kind of long-standing feud with his only son. She suspected that he probably blamed Lonnie for everything gone wrong in his life. Not that much had gone wrong for him, necessarily, not for a working man in a rural town back then, anyway. Probably he was jealous of his brother getting the football player and him getting stuck with Lonnie. *You bastard*, she thought.

She was momentarily lost in the memories of the last decade, awestruck that she'd turned out halfway decent, when her head snapped to attention at the sound of an approaching vehicle. Tom's truck came sauntering over the slight ridge. Ellie's heart fell for a moment, until she saw the silhouette behind the wheel. Her father only ever drove with his right arm draped over the bench with his body slouched against the corner of his door in a give-a-damn posture. The person now driving his truck toward her was leaning forward, both hands on the wheel, and nodding his head ever so slightly. Lonnie.

For as long as she could remember, and many years before he was driving, he would methodically count the small lane reflectors in the middle of the road, checking them off silently by nodding his head. Now, any time he got in a vehicle, regardless of whether the road had reflectors or not, his head bobbed slightly out of habit. She loved him all the more for it.

Lonnie pulled up on the grass and parked, with Maryl's door facing the house. He climbed out and gave Ellie a curious look. Before he could ask what she was doing, her arms were around his neck; she was sobbing.

"Well, I'm all wet now, all wet," he managed to say underneath the weight of her hug. His sister laughed and pulled herself away before walking around to open the passenger door.

"Good morning, honey," said her mother as Ellie reached around and underneath to haul her into the wheelchair that Lonnie pulled out from the pickup.

"Morning, Mom."

"Looks like we've all had a long night."

"Yeah," Ellie said, wiping her eyes.

"You had breakfast?"

"No, I thought I'd come over and ask you the same thing."

"Oh, I wish we'd a' known! Lonnie and I just came from Hester's Diner."

"Mmm, I could go for some of her pancakes."

"Ma' tried to eat all of mine," chimed Lonnie.

"Your mother hardly ate a thing," Maryl protested. "Not after last night." She looked up at Ellie and said, "But I reckon you know all about that."

Ellie's eyes hit the ground.

"What on earth were you doing out there, Ellie?"

Ellie looked up at Lonnie, who was licking the bill of his hat and vigorously trying to remove a stain. "I was worried; I've been worried."

"About what?" Maryl asked.

"About all this talk of the Grayson property, all the fire sticks and what happened all those years ago. I'm worried about Lonnie out there at night."

"Fire sticks?"

Ellie sighed. "Joe lights 'em on his fence posts. I know he thinks it'll keep something out, something he won't talk about."

Maryl searched her daughter's eyes. Lonnie slapped his hat back on, leaving the bill resting high above his forehead, and gripped the handles of his mother's wheelchair.

"Anyway, we've got bigger problems," Ellie managed. "Uncle Richie was just here and told me about Karl."

Lonnie took his hands off the wheelchair and stepped back. Maryl's suspicious gaze retreated to shock, "Richie came here? How long ago?"

"Not ten minutes before you pulled in."

"Ok, c'mon let's all get inside," she called over her shoulder. She looked back at Ellie, "Then I want to know exactly how you're wrapped up in all this."

What was true as a kid is all the same today, Ellie thought. *Nothing gets past Mom.*

Chapter 19

"JESUS," Barry said, hanging his head between his legs. "What have you done?"

"What have I done?" asked Joe. "What's it look like?"

"I don't know, Dad! I'm looking at a pair of fingers that look a lot more like my own than some gorilla's. So you tell me. *What have you done?*"

Joe sneered at his son. "Barry, if after all this you still can't grasp what's across that river, then there's not much else I can do other than drag the whole carcass back. Make no mistake, I fully intend to do just that, but even then I'm not sure it'd be enough for you."

"Enough for what? Enough to make me believe you weren't guilty of murder or manslaughter?"

"What the hell are you getting at?"

"Look at what's sitting between us, Dad. How are you so convinced that these belong to a species other than our own? How do I know there's not some genetic freak show out there finding it just a little more difficult to hold his own can of Pepsi tonight?"

Joe gave a slight chuckle, then reached into his breast pocket for a Camel cigarette. "Trust me," he said, offering one to Barry, "he'll hold nothing but maggots soon enough."

"Good God." Barry stood and wiped his face again and dusted off the seat of his pants. He lit the cigarette and took a long pull. "This was a mistake," he said to no one in particular.

"What I did was a mistake?"

"No. Coming home."

Now Joe stood, still holding his rifle. "Why are you here, Barry? Why'd you show up unannounced after all this time and blow smoke all over what I've just confided in you?"

"I don't know."

"Bullshit."

"And if I did what would it matter to you?"

"It matters to me because you're my son, and I think you do know."

Barry sighed and threw the empty can into the garbage. "The city was killing me, or at least I knew that it would."

"How'd you figure?"

"A few weeks ago my boss died in his car of a heart attack. He was younger than you," Barry said as he looked at Joe. "He wasn't the first, and he won't be the last."

Joe set his rifle against the house. "I'm sorry."

"Yeah. One mistake after the next."

"Listen, you getting outta here in the first place was hardly a mistake."

"Years of work chasing a dream only to find it killing your soul? Sounds like a waste of time to me. Now I'm back at the beginning with nothing to show."

"New York wasn't your dream."

"Come again?"

"That place wasn't your dream, Barry. That's not why you busted your ass in college and law school."

"Please. Enlighten me."

"You wanted a father, a home, and the chance to love and help people. That's more than just a place or a job."

Barry felt a slight fracture on the grip of his emotional state. He didn't want to try speaking right then for fear that his lower lip would tremble and the hot, salty upwelling in his eyes would overflow onto his unshaven cheeks.

"I failed you, son. And your mother. I know that. Very seldom does a day pass without at least a fleeting regret. You're here now, and I'd hate to see you go. I don't have all the answers to this madness wrapped in a neat box like I do them fingers. We've seen and heard the same things tonight, but it looks like we're either coming to different conclusions or you've got a disposition that I don't. But I aim to see this through and figure it out, whatever it takes."

The two men were quiet. An ensemble of tree frogs filled the empty space, and the occasional bat darted against the moonlight overhead.

"Dad," Barry asked, "what happened? Really. What's really lying there on the ground?"

"You know as well as I do," said Joe, "but something in you won't accept it."

Barry sighed.

"Long after you left," Joe continued, "I kept revisiting the site of your mother's death, looking for anything. One night – well, let's just say I discovered that I wasn't alone. What we experienced tonight didn't scratch the surface. Luckily I got my machete up before being pummeled myself. The creature hollered so loud I figured folks in Ocala would'a heard it. That was enough to give me time to get out before reinforcements arrived."

"So there's more of them?"

"Evidently."

"How many?"

"I don't know. But I suspect their numbers are few."

"Why?"

"Look at it, Barry. You said it yourself: those fingers look similar enough to yours and mine, at least compared to anything else."

"And that doesn't bother you?"

"You think it bothered me in the war?"

Barry paused, unsure of how to respond. "Anyway," Joe continued, "they're sure as hell more like us than they are rabbits, which means life is slower and longer and probably harder."

"And you think this is what killed Mom?"

"I do."

"Why?"

Joe reached into his pocket, pulled out a Ziploc bag and handed it to Barry.

"God I'm tired of bags tonight."

Joe laughed and motioned for him to step back into the light of the garage. Barry followed and examined the bag. It was full of what looked like hair or fur.

"What is it?"

"I found about half of what's in there a few days after your mother's funeral, all over the palmettos where she was killed."

Riverview, November 1978

MARYL McGregor wheeled herself into the kitchen and put on a pot of coffee. "You look like you could use some," she said to her daughter.

"Thanks."

"I'm sure you haven't eaten. I can whip up some eggs."

"No, no, that's ok."

Maryl gave her a disbelieving look. Lonnie sauntered over to the kitchen table in his oversized hunting boots and jacket, feeling very much like a third wheel.

"Ellie," Maryl began, "tell me what you know. How are both my children caught up in this business?"

"This *business?*" Ellie folded her arms. "We're adults, mother, and we're not laundering money here."

"Well, somethin's going on!" Maryl's voice began to crack. "Right now your brother is under suspicion of manslaughter, your cousin is dead, and I can hardly bear the thought of losing you two." She held her emotions, but not before two hot tears made their escape and left trails down her cheeks.

Ellie's eyes welled and she swept across the kitchen to hug her mother, grabbing a fistful of her brother's jacket and pulling him into the sob session against his will.

"We're not going anywhere, Ma'," she whispered.

Maryl pulled away, "And how do I know that? How do you know that?"

Ellie poured a cup of coffee and sat at the table next to Lonnie. "I was there last night."

"Doing what on earth?"

Ellie sighed, her eyes fell. "Ever since Lonnie started hunting out there, I've been looking out for him on occasion. I was at Ritchie's a few days ago, and I overheard Karl tellin' a friend that he was gonna scare the Jesus outta Lonnie one last time."

"Oh, Ellie," Maryl mourned.

"I came across through the refuge," Ellie gazed into her mug, "by the time I got there, Karl was already – "

The front door crashed open before she could finish, and Uncle Richie came stalking in like a crazed grizzly.

"Just what I figured," he sneered.

"Rich, they just got here, I swear."

"Shut up!"

"Now that's enough!" Maryl shouted, propelling herself forward across the kitchen. "Richie McGregor, you can march your ass right outta my house faster than you barged in."

"Your house, huh?"

"Oh save it. State your business this instant before I call the Sheriff."

"You know exactly why I'm here. And you know why my boy's dead on a gurney at Tampa General!" Richie shouted with increasing volume.

Ellie's heart was racing like a suffocating songbird. Lonnie sat with increasing agitation, working furiously to shove a toothpick through a crack in the kitchen table, feeling the tiny muscles in his wrist and fingers burn as shavings were forced from the main beam and onto the tabletop.

"Your boy killed mine!"

"You don't know that, Richie!"

"I know it as well as I see you rotting in that chair."

Maryl reached for the butcher's knife and swung it hard at Richie's thigh. He jumped back, grabbed a phone book off the counter, and hurled it at her. The heavy volume caught Maryl square in the mouth, snapping her head back with ferocious force, spraying blood into the air and spilling her over backwards out of her chair.

Lonnie was out of his seat before she hit the floor, leaving the toothpick barely hanging underneath the table. He launched himself at Richie, grabbing the breast pockets of his coat and charging full bore as hard and as fast as he could through the living room before the two crashed over the recliner and against the wall. Richie's head cracked like a bullwhip and left a cannon ball crater in the wood paneling. His nephew fell on top of him, still holding his jacket up around his throat. Lonnie squirmed with the energy of a squirrel fighting for his life, kicking the toppled chair away as he worked his knees up onto his uncle's chest. Then he swung, and swung, and swung, rhythmically alternating between left and right, left and right, repeatedly connecting with Richie's face. He noticed that it only took two rounds with each hand before his knuckles were covered in his uncle's blood. Maybe he would've stopped from eventual exhaustion. Maybe. But he wasn't anywhere near finished when his sister's strong arms disrupted his rhythm and pulled him off.

She was screaming and weeping. Lonnie's chest was heaving. Richie wasn't moving.

"My God," Maryl murmured through a bloody towel held over her mouth. "Is he breathing?"

Chapter 20

ONE hundred miles north of Riverview, a man swung his Ford Pinto into a Gulf gas station, driving like a split-second decision, or maybe a last ditch effort. Probably some combination of both, seeing as how he wasn't there for fuel. He came to a halt right in front of the glass doors, shut off the car, and flicked his last cigarette butt to the pavement before walking inside to reload. He was a smaller man, with stout forearms, receding hair, and busy eyes that were baked into a perpetual wince. His name was Tom McGregor. He grabbed a case of beer, three packs of Pall Malls, and the latest issue of a centerfold. He dumped the purchases into the trunk, but not before lighting a fresh stick. Then he fished around the dash and emerged with a fist of small change and a worn handheld notebook that he flipped through urgently on his way to the payphone.

He pulled the turn-wheel dial to the correct digits and took a long pull from the cigarette while he waited. "Good afternoon, is this Miss Kate?" he asked, with the perfect cocktail of endearing confidence and humility mastered by any seasoned preacher, salesman, con man, or politician. Truth be told, Tom considered all of those professions to be one and the same.

"Yes it is," the lady said sweetly, "and am I speaking with Reverend McGregor?" The question was basically rhetorical; she'd been expecting his call and was excited to tell her family that night that she'd personally spoken with the travelling evangelist.

"Yes ma'am, guilty as charged," Tom chuckled into the receiver. "I just wanted to let you kind folks know that I'm makin' good time and I'm thrilled to share what the Good Lord has in store for us all this weekend."

"Goodness, that's wonderful. Thank you Reverend. We are *so* excited to see you again! Will you be stayin' in the parsonage?"

"Oh no ma'am. I wouldn't want to trouble ya'll."

"It's no trouble at all, Reverend!"

"No no, I insist now. Plus I've got a dear grandmother just outside of town who'd have my head on a platter if I didn't visit."

"Well, I can certainly understand that."

"Mmm, yes, the refining age of wisdom carries with it the right to make certain demands, am I right?"

Kate laughed effortlessly.

"I'll be along by five o'clock tomorrow, ok?"

"Yes sir. The service starts at six, so that'll be just fine."

"Wonderful. You have a blessed day, Katie, and ya'll join me in prayer for this weekend, Amen?"

"Amen, Reverend! You drive safe, now."

Tom hung up and took another drag, smoke billowing from his mouth and nostrils as he strode back to the Pinto. He cracked open a beer and sat down on the splintered top of a worn picnic table. The forests of Ocala were less than two hours from Riverview, but they may as well have been another state. There were hills here, changes in elevation. Great horse country. Tom had considered resettling here after he retired from "trucking." He smiled. *Goddamn fools,* he thought. Fools everywhere. Back home and up ahead. And none of 'em had a clue what ol' Reverend McGregor was up to.

He had a lot of miles to log before pulling into Tallahassee, but he had plenty of time to gather his thoughts before the weekend revival tomorrow night. He would take this moment to reflect on the season of harvest from his hard labor. For the last several years he'd traversed the state in his old pickup and trailer, hauling an expansive tent into just about every sleepy Baptist town in Florida. The Sunshine State, he learned, held a dark secret, and one that he aimed to cash in on.

While the massive peninsula featured endless miles of postcard beaches, the reality was that this limited collection of resort towns was hardly the only picture of Florida, maybe not even the most accurate. Less than ten miles inland from any mixture of sand and ocean and you'd be standing in a starkly different world. Twenty miles further, and you'd never know you were that close to paradise.

This was where Tom McGregor worked and played, all at the same time, and his years of tilling the soil were finally paying off in a big way. He could hardly believe that a lifetime ago he was once himself a Baptist pastor. *What a show,* he thought, swirling the last quarter of beer around in the can. He'd seen loads of other pastors come and go, mostly for some kind of general moral or financial failure. He chuckled. Years ago he discovered that his home state was basically comprised of a thousand Riverviews, each one featuring an urgent religious stronghold of congregants drunk on conservative politics, medieval morality, and hellfire antics. Why, then, would he limit his reach to only one? He resigned from his pulpit, bought a tent, and was none too happy to leave his disabled wife and estranged son for the open roads and limitless riches of honorarium offerings.

The plan was simple, and easier than he'd ever imagined. He'd roll into an unknown speck on a map on

Monday, post fliers for the open tent revival, and by the end of the weekend he'd have a wad of untraceable cash and yet another "flock" to add to the touring circuit. He carefully nurtured this following for years before ditching the circus tent act and upgrading to the local climate-controlled sanctuaries. Now, he could collect in a long weekend what he used to hustle for in a blazing week of summer. Business was good, beer was cheap, and no one outside of Riverview was wiser to the life and times of *Reverend* Tom McGregor.

Riverview, November 1978

BLAKE Martin was too early, and he was halfway to the Grayson ranch before he realized that. His tense conversation with Kathy that morning must have temporarily thrown off his sense of time and routine. He made a rule of never conducting domestic investigations before 8:00 a.m., preferably even 9:00. He wasn't hungry, but he knew he needed something in his stomach to appease the nauseating feeling of acid swirling around inside. A plate of Miss Hester's pancakes sounded perfectly suited for the job, and at this hour he'd have the place mostly to himself to collect his thoughts.

The sun was rising over the oaks and orange groves; Blake could barely make out a few deer in the farthest pasture. A roost of turkey vultures had just taken flight out of a dead pine tree, the victim of lightning or ivy, or maybe both. Blue herons stalked the ditches alongside each shoulder, meticulously searching for crickets or tadpoles. Life was slow around these parts, but it was there, at least, for those who paid attention. Blake found beauty in the struggle, and a sense of clarity when it came to priorities. There wasn't much time for fuss when life itself was hard-won.

The squad car eased into a parking spot and the sheriff removed his western-style patrol hat upon entering the diner. As was his habit, he sat at the booth furthest from the door. Given the hour and the nearly empty room, his table was the last before entering the double doors into the kitchen. A young gal he didn't recognize came to take his drink order, and he promptly added a stack of pancakes with his coffee.

"All righty, then," she smiled, "I'll get your coffee right out." She walked a few paces back to the kitchen and pushed open the easy saloon-style door. Blake looked behind him and was about to ask if she'd put the butter on the side when he caught a glimpse of a face that stole the thought out of his mind. He stared at the doors long after they closed, then leaned back slowly in his chair, his physical posture a manifestation of the sudden collision of both intrigue and shame. He should have remembered earlier, but he was glad to be reminded now.

Raymond Muskee was the kitchen manager at Hester's Diner and had been for most of Blake's career. The Riverview regulars boasted that he made the best grits this side of the Chattahoochee. But Blake wasn't interested in grits this morning. Not now. Raymond Muskee was the living local authority on Cherokee history in these parts, as well respected as he was knowledgeable. Blake felt deflated. Not only had he forgotten what light Raymond could shed on these most recent events, but he'd also suddenly recalled the visceral terror he'd felt all those years ago when Mr. Muskee told the story of a ten-foot swamp devil to a wide-eyed troop of Boy Scouts in the glow of a campfire.

The spirited blonde set his coffee down on the table with a small handful of creamer packets.

"Oh, it's ok, just black, thank you." Blake returned the creamers. "Hey, could you do me an odd favor?"

"Sure!" she chirped.

"I saw a face back there I've known for a long time."

"Mr. Muskee?"

"That's right," he smiled. "Would you ask him to join me for a cup when he gets a minute?"

"Yessir I'll ask right now; we're slow this mornin' anyway."

Chapter 21

ELLIE was going to need a second cup of coffee, because at that very moment she was cleaning her first off the floor of her mother's kitchen, and her uncle's blood off the living room wall and carpet. Maryl leaned against the counter, still holding a damp rag to her nose. Lonnie stood like a guard dog, never diverting his attention from Richie's motionless form, almost daring him to wake up.

"Lonnie," Ellie called. "Lonnie!"

His eyes snapped up to meet hers.

"I asked you to dump this bowl and fill it with hot water." Ellie was kneeling beside Uncle Richie, gently soaking the blood off his swollen face. Lonnie took the bowl into the kitchen; Maryl touched his forearm as he passed.

"Honey," she whispered.

"I won't let him, Ma'."

"Won't what?"

"I won't let him. He won't do like that to you." He poured the pale red water down the sink and filled it again.

Maryl turned her chair around to face him. "Oh, honey, look at your hands." Her eyes welled as she reached for them. They hurt like hell, he realized, and looked like they'd been run over by an aerator. She reached over the sink, wet a fresh towel, and began dabbing his knuckles. Lonnie winced and bit his tongue.

"Ma,' I don't care about them. Don't worry about them. Ok? It's ok, it's ok."

"Son, you must clean your hands; they'll get infected."

A low, incoherent groan emanated from the living room. "Hey. He's moving. Bring me that damn bowl!" Ellie called.

Lonnie carried the bowl carefully to Ellie's hands, pleased with himself for minimizing spills in his haste. The two of them watched as Uncle Richie made a failed attempt to roll onto his side. He collapsed onto his back, eyes still shut, and no indication that they were going to open any time soon.

"Jesus, Lonnie. You could've killed him."

"Yeah."

His sister looked up to find him standing over her looking intently at their own kin. "Did you hear what I said?"

"Yup."

"Well you need to be careful. You could end up – "

"Can I see the rag?"

"What?"

"Can I have that rag? That rag you're holding."

"It's covered in blood." He reached out and took it, and stepped in behind his sister, wedging himself into the space between the wall and his uncle.

"Lonnie, don't go and make this – "

"Ellie," Maryl called from the kitchen.

They were silent together, as Lonnie carefully dabbed Richie's swollen face.

***

RAYMOND Muskee seemed to glide through life with the ease of an athlete: quiet, composed, efficient. Blake imagined the every-day tasks that produced angst and friction for most others came without effort for Raymond; the lug nuts of life seemed well-oiled when the wrench was in his hands. If there were ever moments of struggle, they were sufficiently hidden from view. Until this morning. In fact, Blake wasn't sure which he was more struck by: the information Ray shared or the evident signs of mental and emotional toll it took to deliver it.

"Good morning, Ray."

"How are you today, Sheriff?"

"I've been better, to be honest with you."

"I'm sorry to hear that."

"Oddly enough, I was hoping you could help."

Raymond's eyebrows rose in surprise. "I'm happy to offer what I can."

Blake laced his fingers around the mug and stared at the contents.

"Would you like a refill?" Ray asked, halfway out of his chair.

"No, no, I'm fine, thanks," Blake waved him off. "Sorry; I'm just not sure how to begin," he chuckled nervously.

"Let's start with how I can help you."

Blake took a sip of coffee like it was hard whiskey, wishing that it was. "I need to know the difference," he began slowly.

Raymond leaned in slightly. "Between what, exactly?"

"Between the past and the truth."

"I'm not sure I follow you, Sheriff."

Blake held his eager eyes, and spoke quietly. "How much truth is in those stories you used to tell the Boy Scouts?"

Mr. Muskee relaxed into the back of his chair and nodded, looking out the window at the sun squinting through the shades of the diner. An osprey patrolled the retention pond across the street, and an angry mob of songbirds of various species united their efforts against a trespassing hawk.

"May I ask what brings you to these questions?"

Blake sighed patiently through pursed lips, sounding like a kickball with a slow leak. "There's been another…incident," he said.

Raymond allowed the sheriff's statement to settle into their presence before speaking. "Similar to the last?" he asked.

"Practically the same, with the exception of a possible suspect."

Raymond's eyes returned to Blake's.

"A human suspect, Ray," he clarified.

"Then why do you seek information from me?"

"Because I want to know if they're my *only* suspects."

The two sat in silence for several seconds. "The past," Raymond began, "is only a point of reference; it always lives on."

"What's that supposed to mean?"

"We all carry our past in however we abide in the present. An experience in your life many years ago, good or bad, still plays a part in shaping how you live today."

Blake shifted on the bench. "I understand that, Ray, but how does that inform the case I'm working on?"

"Are you really looking for another suspect? Or just hoping to clear one?"

Blake shook his head. "I shouldn't have done this. I'm sorry, Raymond."

"For what?"

"For wasting my time and yours. I began this conversation against my better judgment, against my gut. But I figured I should be more open-minded, pursue all possible leads, real or imagined."

Silence.

"I will do all I can to assist you. I apologize for my distance; you can imagine that such inquiries into the stories of my people are met with hesitation."

"A young man's been killed, Ray. Last night. Just like last time. I was different then; I want justice now. Is there something in the outskirts of this town that I oughta know about?"

It was Raymond's turn to take a deep breath. "I have suspected as much."

"And just so we're clear, we're talking about the stories I mentioned earlier."

"Just so we're clear, I'm talking about those driven from this land and harassed into the margins by countless generations."

"The same that may be responsible for the deaths of two innocent victims?"

"Sheriff," he said, rising from his chair, "motive is always the most humane element of any action."

"So what am I supposed to do?"

Raymond thought for a few seconds. "Be very careful," he said, "then find me on the peninsula. Tonight. We'll speak more openly then."

The high-school waitress burst through the kitchen doors with a big smile and a plate of hot pancakes. She stopped short momentarily when she saw the expression on the two men's faces, but delivered the tray with a half-embarrassed smile.

"Thank you," said Blake, as she hurried away.

"May I ask you something?" asked Raymond.

"Sure."

"A moment ago you said you were different now, and that you wanted justice this time. What, then, did you seek so many years ago?"

Blake picked up the syrup and poured it generously across the stack. He placed it carefully next to the assorted jellies and said, "To be right."

Chapter 22

BARRY awoke an hour earlier than usual, though he wasn't at all sure what "usual" was anymore. He lay flat on his back and stared at the ceiling fan. Every thread he chased in his mind segued into another, spinning him around in a maddening cycle of disbelief and, eventually, depression. He'd been distracting himself during the daylight hours by punishing his neglected body with the work necessary to keep a cattle ranch operational, and he could tell that he was beginning to return to the form of his athletic days long ago. That at least helped to ease the mental weight of knowing his world had changed forever. New York was long gone, a colossal waste of time as far as he was concerned. His father was holed up on the outskirts of sanity waging war with schoolyard legends. There were frozen fingers downstairs for Christ's sake!

Mercifully, there'd been no further incidents since that discovery and their alleged encounter across the river, which felt like a short lifetime ago now. He'd give absolutely anything to wake up from what he could only hope was the worst nightmare of anyone's life. What was he gonna do? Sticking around on this clown farm any longer simply wasn't an option. He could head south. Miami was booming and any firm down there would love to add New York City experience to their pedigree. Barry hated the heat but at least he'd have the ocean, not to mention far more manageable winters. Miami in February sounded about right.

But just as he was beginning to imagine himself with a Bahama shirt and a tiki drink, a surprising thought pulled the whole production down: *Ellie.* What about her? She was a pistol, that's for sure, and certainly helped to ease the manual labor of the past weeks. But where was this emotion coming from? *Probably from those wranglers around her hips,* he smiled. Not to mention the way her eyes and smile seemed to affect the whole of creation around her, like a triumphant dawn after a midnight storm. Still, she couldn't possibly tip the scales on keeping him here, but he had to admit a fondness for her that had gone previously undetected. Waking up to the thought of spending the day in her vicinity was a good reason for slow rolling the process of making his inevitable exit. He laughed. *Jesus.* What had he gotten himself into? He rolled his eyes and pulled the covers over his head. *Doesn't matter,* he thought, *because Ellie will be here for coffee in an hour.*

The doorbell rang down on the first floor. In the weeks he'd been home, Ellie always arrived at the same time; this was too early. He dressed and went downstairs. He swung open the door, prepared to chide her for not bringing donuts.

"You know you really oughta – "

The two men stood looking at each other.

"Oh, I'm sorry," he fumbled. "Can I help you?" He watched the color drain from the sheriff's face, eyes sinking as though he were aging right there in front of him.

"Barry?"

"That's right."

"I – I'm sorry. I didn't know you were home."

"That's ok. Came on a whim, I guess."

Blake was holding his hat by the brim, turning it in his hands. Barry scratched at the doorframe.

"It's good to see you," Blake said. "Mind if I come in?"

"No, of course not. I'm sorry. I was just about to make some coffee."

"Thank you." Blake stepped into the living room, realizing too late that he had not prepared himself for the gravity of revisiting this very room after so many years. Stomach acid churned up to his taste buds, and he asked kindly for a glass of water.

"So you're sticking around for a while?"

"Yeah, for a spell anyway."

"I'm sure your father's glad for the help and company."

"Oh, I'm not so sure about that," Barry said with a sarcastic smile as Joe strode down the steps.

"What help?" Joe chuckled as he shook Blake's hand. "Good morning, Sheriff. What can we do ya' for?"

Just as he expected, Joe wasted no time.

Blake had long ago accepted a life of uncertainty when it came to the Graysons, given his inability to bring about resolution or closure to that fateful case. Perhaps Joe's willingness to get straight to the point was born from a desire to get him out the door as soon as possible; perhaps that in and of itself was kindness.

"Gentlemen," he began, "I don't know how to say this so I'll get right to it. I'm here to make you aware of an incident that occurred on the outskirts of your property last night."

Barry looked up from pouring the coffee; Joe slowly fastened the last button on his flannel.

"What happened?" Barry asked.

"I'm very sorry to tell you this, but Karl McGregor was killed."

The three men said nothing for several seconds.

"Do I need to ask how?" Joe said flatly.

Blake looked him in the eye. "The circumstances are very similar, Joe." There wasn't much else to say.

"What in the world was he doing out there?" Barry asked.

"Seems he was paying a visit to his cousin, Lonnie, though I'm not certain of his intent. I'm sure you two are aware that Lonnie has a tree stand out in that corner of the property?"

"Yeah," Joe nodded. "He asked me about that years ago. To be honest, I'd forgotten until now. How's Richie?"

Blake sighed slowly and chose his words carefully, "Pretty much the same as you two would expect." The Grayson men knew what the sheriff meant; they'd both been there before.

Joe stared into his coffee mug in silence, then his gaze shot back up to meet Blake's, his eyes now betraying a keen interest. In most any other instance Blake would've asked about Joe's sudden reaction just then, but he'd been waiting for this question.

"Did the kid see anything?" Joe asked

"No." Joe was unapologetically searching Blake's eyes, looking for a tell. Blake didn't blink. "But what he heard is of interest."

"Howling."

"Excuse me?"

"That's what he heard, isn't it?"

Blake drummed his fingers on the contents of his standard issue utility belt: Smith & Wesson on the right, radio on the left, cuffs in the back. He looked at the floor and then back at both men. "Yes," he said, "that's what he described. Just before the sound of his cousin being beaten to death."

"Jesus," Barry whispered.

The static of Blake's radio interrupted the solemn atmosphere. "Attention all units. Attention all units. 10-91 domestic at 489 Clearfield Drive. One male unconscious. Medical unit en route. Repeat: 10-91 Clearfield Drive, medical unit en route."

Blake grabbed the dial and turned it down, but not before the dispatcher gave the address. Barry froze, expecting the same reaction from the sheriff.

"Sorry about that," Blake said, returning his attention back to the conversation at hand. "What?" he asked, looking at Barry.

"The McGregors live on Clearfield."

"Shit." Blake grabbed the radio off his belt and mumbled orders into the receiver. "Joe, Barry, I'm sorry," he said, with evident honesty in his eyes. "Given the circumstances, I need to respond to this, but I'll look in on both of you again as soon as I can to answer any questions. In the meantime, I'd ask you to keep to yourselves and of course avoid that area around

Lonnie's stand until we can properly investigate." Barry nodded, and Blake bolted out the door.

A moment later, Joe looked at Barry, grabbed his coat, and followed suit.

Barry didn't need to ask where either of them was going.

PART II

Merge

Chapter 23

BLAKE Martin veered onto the shoulder of Clearfield Drive in time to see an EMT unit carefully threading a stretcher through the narrow doorway. The usual crowd of onlookers had gathered on their parched lawns and front porches. He could see Ellie and Lonnie standing on the threshold. Ellie looked shaken; Lonnie looked like usual: nonplused. That was a surprise. Not the expression, but the fact that Lonnie wasn't on the stretcher himself. Even without knowing the details of what he was walking into, he figured Richie must be involved. Blake grabbed his hat and strode toward the scene. He intercepted the medical team and inquired about the patient.

"He's alive. Beat to hell, but alive." The sheriff stood there as they continued on to the transport ambulance, shaking his head. *Beat to hell,* he thought. Exactly. He looked toward the house and saw the two McGregor siblings staring at him; Ellie seemed to put the pieces together and drew Lonnie back inside. Blake knew he had no choice, now.

"Mornin', Sheriff."

Blake turned and saw his deputy walking toward him with a thick clipboard. He sighed and reviewed the paperwork, "What are the details?"

"Neighbors called in the dispute. Two witnesses saw Richie McGregor speed onto the lot, twice."

"Twice?" Blake asked.

"Apparently members of the family weren't home the first time. The same folks said they heard shouting soon after arrival before the fight broke out inside."

"Have you been inside?"

"Yes sir, but only for a moment before the medics arrived."

"Ok. Hang out here for a second." Blake turned toward the trailer. "And tell all these folks to get to work," he called over his shoulder.

Blake gave the courtesy of knocking and found Maryl at the door. Her spine sat upright, but her face betrayed the shame. "Come in, Sheriff. I'm very sorry you have to be here."

Blake didn't move at first. He looked hard at her and asked, "Did he hit you, Maryl?"

She tilted her head as if analyzing his words. "Not exactly."

"Well, I do need you to tell me *exactly* what happened."

"Yeah. Come in. I'll pour you a cup of coffee."

Blake walked inside, removing his hat. "Ellie, Lonnie," he nodded.

"Good morning, Sheriff," Ellie smiled bravely.

He was about to engage her with a question and then stopped short, having spotted the deep dent in the wood paneling. Blake stared at it and sighed, the badge on his chest reflecting a spot of sunlight on the wall next to it. "Why don't we all have a seat in the kitchen."

Maryl handed Blake a warm mug as her two grown children pulled chairs around the table. In the pale light her face was even more swollen. Despite her appearance and condition, she spoke with the same Southern dignity as always.

Blake listened carefully as his dispatcher recounted the details of that morning, following her gaze across the trailer to the head-height crater at the finish. A long, tense silence permeated the room.

"Thank you, Maryl," Blake said, hands folded around his mug. "I'm very sorry for what happened here, what's happened to all of you in the last several hours. Lonnie, you did a brave thing, defending your mother."

Ellie lowered her gaze and looked down at the table. "But?"

"I've got to think and act very carefully here, with everyone's interests in mind," Blake nodded out the window. "I can't ignore the fact that Lonnie's been at the scene of two violent attacks in less than twelve hours."

Ellie shifted in her chair to protest.

"Honey…" Maryl said quietly, putting a hand on her daughter's arm.

"Ellie, this isn't easy for anyone," Blake said. "To some degree, regardless of what I think or believe in the moment, I've got a responsibility to uphold."

"Sheriff, if you cuff Lonnie, you damn well know that he's as good as guilty," Ellie blurted.

Blake shifted his focus from Ellie to her brother. "Lonnie, you are guilty, in this assault. Intervening on behalf of your family is one thing. Beating a man – your uncle no less – within an inch of his life is another." He returned his attention to mother and daughter. "Now, are these two events connected? At this point I can't speak to that. But given Lonnie's connection to last night, I simply can't ignore this." Blake's eyes were steady, but not without sympathy. He reached behind his back for the handcuffs.

"Sheriff, you can't do that! You know we can't – "

"Ellie!" Maryl raised her voice. The room fell silent. "He's right," she said slowly.

Lonnie found the splintered toothpick he'd wedged under the table earlier. He reached for it and examined the remains closely, carefully pulling thin wooden threads off the mainmast to reveal a resolute structure. "Ma'," he said, looking at both of the women in his life, "it won't do like that. I'll be all right."

***

JOE Grayson pulled slowly off the dirt access road well before he reached the area that Sheriff Martin described as the crime scene. Much like a proper medical examiner would appreciate, he knew how important a clean slate was for plastering evidence. He grabbed his tools from the bed and began walking slowly toward Lonnie's tree stand. Several species of songbirds set aside their differences to sound the alarm of a kestrel circling intently overhead. An osprey with a fresh catch called to its mate from the branches of a pine tree. Either side of the service road was lined with a wall of Florida grasses and brush, which harbored all manner of insect and reptile somewhere within its growth. Joe walked along carefully until he found what he was looking for: a break in the brush line. This was the trail Lonnie McGregor took to get to his stand.

Joe could clearly make out the fervent activity from the previous night in the soft, sandy soil. His seasoned eye could identify at least three different prints in the disturbance. He paused a moment before entering, crouching close to the ground. Joe suspected the emotions to arrive, and he was ready for them. What he was about to walk into felt frighteningly similar to another scene he'd scoured so many years ago, and one that continued to haunt his mind.

He had carried her in his arms out to meet the medical units; he'd never forget the strange thought of how stark their emergency lights glowed even in the daylight. Neither would he forget the sensation of how rigid she hung in his care, or the sensation of surrendering her to the stretcher. All of it came back, there and then, and soon after the shock of loss came the surge of purpose. Joe Grayson aimed to finish what was started, to fill his whole freezer if he had to with everything that those two fingers were attached to. This wasn't about discovery; it wasn't about science. This was about justice, or vengeance, or some concoction of both.

He swallowed hard and pushed aside the branches of a large palmetto bush, like a cowboy entering the swinging doors of a saloon. Joe stuck to the outer edge of the beaten footpath, walking in a tight, single file line. Hunting an encounter area for signs took just as much discipline and focus as following the blood trail of a wounded animal, maybe more. One had to constantly reign in the desire to look ahead in order to focus intently on what was directly beneath their gaze. Eventually, Joe came upon an area of paradox: significant soil disturbance alongside what could be mistaken for animal bedding in the form of worn, bent grasses. This was where Karl had been beaten, and where Lonnie found him lying.

Joe's focus sharpened onto the scene, first from a standing position at several angles, then kneeling and even lowering to all fours at several points. There were so many prints from everyone involved last night that he was losing hope of finding anything of interest or value. He rose slowly and lit a cigarette, waving wisps of smoke out of his eyes. He spit and hung his hands on his pockets, teetering on the brink of calling the whole thing a bust, when he spied something he'd missed. Not a print, but a small offshoot branching from the main trail. A varmint trail, probably used by opossums and armadillos. He stepped carefully over the site and leaned his worn canvas jacket into the vines that covered the smaller path. The terrain sloped just slightly but quickly downward before leveling off again, resulting in a sort of basin that held more moisture than the main path.

Typically this common topographical feature wouldn't have held anyone's interest, but Joe was frozen to the spot, wearing an expression of shock that slowly morphed into some combination of confusion and disbelief.

Chapter 24

BARRY stood alone, leaning against the kitchen counter, holding a cup of coffee. He was barely awake from another fitful night's sleep. Sheriff Martin and his father had just run out of the house. He knew the one with the badge was going to diffuse trouble; the one without was probably going to do nothing more than stir up more of it. He took a sip, thankful at least for the solitude. Was this real life? Was this really happening? Could this get any more absurd? He'd come home. That's it. He'd achieved his goal of practicing law in the most important city in the world, and he'd left it all to come home. Most would applaud him. Everyone with a conscience would affirm his decision. And yet everything had gone sideways almost from the moment he'd crossed the threshold of the homestead. Now he couldn't even get through the morning brew without some new development. If he had any less empathy he'd pack his meager belongings and drive away now. Forever. It sounded like paradise.

Still, there it was, that something that drew him, called him, kept him. He sighed and reluctantly reached for the flannel he'd tossed on the counter. He dumped his coffee down the drain, and thought about its connection to his own life, and then grabbed his keys and headed for the Jensen. *Might as well join the parade,* he thought.

***

TEN minutes later, Barry was turning onto Clearfield Drive. Thankfully, it looked like the scene had already dissipated. *What am I even doing here?* In the weeks they'd worked alongside one another, he sensed a friendship develop between them. But was that enough to warrant this kind of house call? He felt out of his depth. So much so, in fact, that he drove right past the McGregor residence. This kind of domestic nonsense was exactly why he'd left in the first place. And now here he was, back amongst the jungles of parcel swamps and trailer parks. Sure, Ellie was different from the usual cast of Riverview characters, but how much? He didn't have time to answer that. Before he knew it he'd turned around and parked next to her truck. She was standing in the doorway of a gray-sky doublewide. The worn pine wheelchair ramp measured their distance like something between a warning and an invitation.

"Hey," he fumbled, climbing out, "I'm sorry. I just wanted to see if you guys were ok."

"No that's all right. Thanks."

He stood near the hood holding his keys; she leaned against the pillar that supported the overhang.

"So...maybe I should give you some space."

"No," she said.

"No?"

"No, we're not ok." She was weeping before she finished, and sliding down the pillar.

Barry was holding her before she hit the ground.

Chapter 25

THE pale pink telephone in the motel rang like an alarm clock next to the King James Bible. Tom McGregor stared at it and smiled at the irony before picking up.

"This is Reverend McGregor speaking, how are you?"

"Tom."

"Hello?"

"It's me."

A long silence.

"Rich?" the Southern salesman charm was gone.

"Yeah."

"What are you doing? Why are you talkin' like that?"

"I'm in the hospital."

Tom sat up in bed, the gas station magazine landed softly on the shag carpet.

"What in the hell for?"

Silence.

"Karl's dead," Richie's voice started to break up.

"Who? What're you talkin' about, Richie?" He could hear his brother sobbing on the other end.

"It's gone too far."

"Goddammit what's happened?"

Silence.

"Richie?"

"He's dead, Tom. Karl's dead."

Tom was pacing the room now in his V-neck undershirt and tall black socks, tangled in the phone cord.

"Jesus Christ. How?"

Silence.

"He'd gone out to the tree stand to scare Lonnie or something," Richie managed.

"You better be shitting me!"

"I ain't shitting you!" Richie hollered.

Silence.

"My God," Tom whispered. He could hear a nurse trying to calm his brother. Richie asked her to leave.

"Richie?"

"Yeah."

"What's happened to you?"

"The kid flipped on me. Nearly beat me to death."

"Both of you?"

"Well, that's what I ain't certain of just yet," Richie's tone had snapped to an ominous resolve. "But you can be damn sure I'm gonna find out. You better call off your spook, or I'm gonna find him too and kill him myself. I'm through with this madness."

Silence.

"You're a goddamn genius, brother."

Richie coughed. "Did you hear me? Karl's dead, Tom; my boy's dead!"

"Calm down Richie, I understand – "

"You don't understand shit! My boy's dead, and he ain't the first. And if this doesn't end now, then one way or another he ain't gonna be the last. I'm gettin' out of this."

"Oh no you're not, brother."

Silence.

Tom stood still, feet shoulder width apart, facing the vanity mirror. "You're out of your depth," he said quietly, "you're way past the oyster bars in this shit storm. You said it yourself: Karl ain't the first. There's not any more blood on my hands than yours, and don't you ever forget that." Tom let that hang in a few seconds of silence. "Now you listen to me. Whether you realized it or not, I'm about to throw my own flesh and blood into the fiery furnace for the sake of the greater good."

"What do you mean?"

"I mean you're gonna press charges."

"On who?"

"Who do you think, for Christ's sake? Lonnie!"

Silence.

"That boy lost it again in a fit of rage and assaulted his own uncle and cousin. Hell, for all we know right now that may even be the truth. It ain't gonna take much to convince a jury of that."

Silence.

"This has gone too far, Tom. I don't want no part of this."

"Oh yes you do. You'll want every part of your share, which'll be more than enough for you to put hundreds of miles between you and the sacrifices you've made."

"I didn't sacrifice my own son for this!"

Silence.

"No, brother. You didn't. Lonnie McGregor murdered your son, and my precious nephew."

"How the hell you think that's gonna hold up?"

"Because the whole town knows he put his own mother in a wheelchair."

Silence.

"You stay the course, brother. I've gotta go share the news of the Good Lord with the sheep of his pasture. I'll be back in town soon after, and you can be damn sure I'll check all the threads on my end. That spook's screwed up once already, and if he's to blame here again then I'm more than happy to cut him out of the plan, literally. I'll set this right, don't you worry. But either way, Lonnie takes the fall and we carry on."

Tom hung up the phone and looked intently at it in his hands, as if noticing the shade of pink for the first time. He slammed it down onto the bed and ran both of his hands through his fishing-line hair. He looked at the gold wristwatch and breathed deeply. It was almost time to perform. He set his shoulders back and rolled his neck side to side. Then he reached into the closet for his dress shirt and tie.

Chapter 26

BLAKE Martin shot a glance into his rear view mirror. Lonnie McGregor was looking down at something. This struck him as odd; most everyone else he'd ever seen from this angle always looked out the window, as though the last vestiges of their freedom were fading before their eyes. Lonnie was looking down.

"Lonnie?"

"Yessir?"

"You ok?"

"I'm ok."

Blake knew he was walking a fine line engaging anyone in the backseat in conversation.

"Your mother's going to be all right."

"Yessir."

"Lonnie?"

He was still looking down.

"You almost killed your uncle, son."

Lonnie looked up, right at Blake through the mirror.

"He knew never to touch my mom." Something in Lonnie's delivery immediately caught Blake off guard. After a few seconds of consideration, he realized that it was the curious combination of both the utter lack of negative emotion coupled with the tone of positive urgency. Lonnie may as well have told Blake that Richie knew he had ordered chocolate ice cream, not strawberry.

Lonnie was looking down again.

Probably a good thing, Blake thought; he was just now turning into the station.

***

BARRY slowly pulled out onto U.S. 301. The midday sun was peaking and any semblance of fall temperatures was quickly retreating. He'd just spent the last hour in the presence of a very pretty gal, and he'd promised to do anything he could to help. Typically that would be reason to at least smile. After all, Ellie looked amazing in what could very well have been clothes she'd slept in. In contrast, his face wore hard lines. Barry was deep in the throes of mental and emotional conflict. Selfishly, he hated that all this had hit the fan in the narrow stretch of time that he'd returned home. He could still hardly believe he'd even come home in the first place. And to find all this! He felt guilty for such feelings, if only barely, and couldn't help admitting that there were certainly far worse scenarios than being a shoulder for Ellie McGregor to cry on.

In addition to this surprising development, an entirely new wave of emotions was churning, like a tropical depression somewhere in the Caribbean that a local weatherman was tracking. To the best of his knowledge, he'd come home to regroup, to escape the confines and noise of a crowded city in an effort to chart a new course. Instead, he had been immediately confronted with memories that kept him from this flat, swampy jungle in the first place: his mother's murder. Even now, at noon on a November weekday, Barry had just consoled a woman whose cousin had recently been killed under alarmingly similar circumstances.

Which brought about the mental strain showing up on Barry's face and forehead. Two violent homicides, a decade apart, under a shroud of mystery. Both within a square mile of each other, and both occurring on or near his family's property.

Part of the burden, he realized, was that he either didn't know what or how to feel at this moment, or that he was falling well short of what seemed like emotional expectations of how one ought to feel under such conditions. As he drove down the scorched highway toward nowhere in particular, he sensed a new emotion: anger. All he'd ever wanted to do was get away from this boat-ramp-blip on a map and secure a better future for himself. Now here he was, beckoned back here by an unforeseen force, only to find himself wrapped up in some implausible, Hardy Boys' adventure that had his mother's murder scripted into the plot. If there was, in fact, a transcendent deity in the universe, then it was some kind of insensitive; that, or it possessed a sick sense of humor when it came to writing chapters in Barry's life.

He was heading to the ranch, or at least in that direction. However, Barry had no desire to discover what his father had been up to. The meager offerings of the town of Riverview lay ahead of him, and suddenly the first good idea he'd had in a long time entered his mind.

Dan's Three Corners Bar sat just across the Alafia Bridge, at the intersection of "middle of nowhere" and "a long way from anywhere." A map identified it as the point where Balm Riverview Road dead-ends into U.S. 301. A poetic and absolutely true location. Nonetheless, a few cold cans and a side of something fried sounded more like good therapy than a decent lunch. Barry pulled in, and suddenly felt more at home than he had at any point in the previous weeks.

Chapter 27

FIVE miles west of Riverview, near the mouth of Tampa Bay, U.S. 41 bisects another small, quiet town. This one, however, boasts a curious history. A tourist attraction at best, but nowhere near enough novelty to pay the bills. The days of glory are passed, and fading evermore. Businesses are closing, selling their stock and leaving only the locks on the doors. Vacancy creates opportunity, but not always of the contributing kind.

A block off the highway, the orange logo of a once-proud Gulf gas station fights bravely against the decay, to no avail. Inside, the stench of stale, stiff air hangs like invisible banners suspended from the stained ceiling. Every surface seems slick to the touch with humidity and dampness. Despite the stillness, the quarter's disarray and abysmal state conjure an ominous hesitation. One can hardly imagine anyone living there, at least anyone healthy, or anything human.

Suddenly, a grunt disrupts the moment from somewhere down the hallway, followed by the jarring blast of a telephone ring.

More grunting, then stirring, then the fumbling and clanging of hard plastic.

The ringing stops.

From clear outside the room, a voice can be heard on the other end. Screaming. Furious. Threatening. Giving orders.

A grunt of agreement, like a sad resolution.

The receiver is carefully returned, with patient control.

Quiet.

Around the corner of the room at the end of the hall, the sole occupant lies in a pile of rabble: cans and wrappers and cartons of all brands.

He is unmistakably human. But undeniably different.

Chapter 28

DAN'S Three Corners Bar was named after the triangle used to rack billiard balls on a pool table, or at least that's what Barry believed. It was an odd name for an establishment, but then again, it felt just about right for a town like Riverview. The rotting, white-washed walls had stood at that very intersection for as long as Barry could remember, outlasting the fury of countless hurricanes and disgruntled housewives. There were no windows, but the front door was always open, facing U.S. 301. As a kid, Barry would often crane his neck from the back seat to try to catch a glimpse of what went on inside that den of sin. *Were people fighting? Passed out over tables? Making love on the floors?* All he ever saw from that angle were the outskirts of a pool table, flickering beer brands, and the occasional passing patron. Buying your first beer from Dan's was something of a secret rite of passage, and when he had come of age, Barry would never forget the experience of discovering the awful truth of the place.

Farther north outside of town, 301 intersected Highway 60. If you turned left, you'd be heading into the underbelly of old Tampa, and straight down what was quite possibly the longest stretch of strip joints and boobie bars along the Eastern seaboard. In fact, the Port of Tampa ensured consistent cash flow through these establishments. Huge, well-lit, unashamed temples of lust, all within a mile or two of each other, clearly competing for customers, like adjoining car lots, or even churches, for that matter. Dancers and dollars ruled the nights along "skin row."

That was sin city, that was Highway 60, and that was what Barry had expected to find inside the splintered siding of Dan's Three Corners Bar.

The scene was anything but. To his great shock and surprise so many years ago, he discovered it to be decidedly normal. No fights. No brazen waitresses. No live bands. Hardly any house music at all, in fact. Just men looking to enjoy solitude or camaraderie and essentially escape their realities, if only for a spell.

Which was exactly why he was pulling in today; the thought of liquid inebriation felt like a godsend. His tires crunched on the unpaved mixture of sand and shell, and in a few moments he crossed the threshold from blinding light and stale heat into the dungeon of darkness and suspended table fans. Nothing had changed, not in the slightest. Barry slid onto a stool and pulled a few dollars from his pocket. "Because The Night" by Patti Smith crooned from a wounded jukebox.

"What'll it be, soldier?" asked a spritely old fox.

"Whatever's cold and deep fried."

"Now you're talkin," he pulled a towel from his shoulder and wiped his brow. "Got catfish or chicken sandwiches, pick yer poison."

Barry had adopted a rule in such scenarios: always go with the air-breather. God only knows where the *ratfish* (as he called them) came from. He ordered the chicken, no onions, and a side of fries, then took his first long drink from the golden pint glass. Cold and old. Nothing had changed. He wiped the foam from his mustache and noticed the facial growth that had been gaining traction since his return, stubble that hadn't graced his face in all his years in New York. He was just then realizing the opportunity now afforded to him to grow a beard in the winter. Might as well.

Suddenly, the solitude and isolation he'd sought was soundly disrupted.

"Good God Almighty. Barry Malorie Grayson!"

The man's voice came from directly behind him, clear and loud and disbelieving. Barry didn't move.

***

RAYMOND Muskee reflected on his recent choice. The '64 Chevy pickup ambled on away from the diner. He'd done the unthinkable: Raymond was taking a lunch break. In all his years he could not recall a similar experience, but circumstances dictated such actions. Sheriff Martin's inquiries that morning weren't altogether unexpected; maybe late, but not unexpected. Raymond was the closest thing that Riverview had to offer as a genuine Native American tribal chief. He wasn't a chief, not by federal government papers, but his seniority and heritage alone were enough to pull rank even off the reservation.

Raymond turned left past the deli and into the parking lot of the Riverview Library, a small, unassuming structure with tall windows and a single wooden door. The inside was quiet, as usual, but particularly empty on this weekday lunch hour. Precisely why he'd come.

Mrs. Harrison was carefully reorganizing a row of children's books from what must have been a rowdy bunch. Raymond knew that what looked like a simple and mind-numbing part of the job brought this saint sincere joy. The woman loved books nearly as much as she evidently loved margarine, and she possessed an insufferable patience with children.

"Oh!" she gave a start. "Goodness, Raymond!" she laughed. "I never heard you come in."

"My apologies, young lady," he smiled and bowed slightly.

"Oh now you stop that," she chided. "What on earth brings you down here, and without a pair of guava turnovers for me?" She peered out over the rim of her glasses, and her tone had turned from jovial to mockingly serious. Freida Harrison had a sweet tooth that brooked no trespassers.

"Aha, but you think too little of me, Ma'am." Raymond produced a small white paper bag from behind his back and presented it like a coveted trophy.

"Ray Muskee, you are a good friend." She beamed and closed her eyes, receiving the offering with both hands and relishing in the temporary transportation. "You're too kind," she inhaled deeply through her nose and her shoulders sagged with deep contentment as she exhaled. "Now," she paused, "what brings you in here bearing such peace offerings?"

Raymond laughed. "A very simple request, I'm afraid. I need to make a call. An urgent, private call."

Freida nodded. "Well, you've come to the right place at the right time. You know where it is, and I'll be out here with my treats."

"Thank you, Mrs. Harrison."

Raymond walked back behind the counter and into a pale yellow office. Freida's attention to detail wasn't only for show; her personal space was equally pristine.

Stapler, tape, and hole puncher neatly aligned in one corner of the desk; a canister of pens (all the same) and highlighters (all yellow) in the other. A large calendar in the middle, upon which rested a perfectly squared stack of books, no doubt to be returned to their shelves. He glanced back out at the floor as he closed the door; Mrs. Harrison wasn't in sight. Raymond knew this was the only phone in the building, and he knew that he could trust his old friend. Still, the nature of this call was sensitive enough that he hesitated to follow through, even in the silence.

Nonetheless, he reached for the phone and dialed the number by heart.

"It's a beautiful day at Ocala Wildlife Sanctuary," said a soothing, patient voice. "This is Thomas speaking. How may I help you?"

Raymond smiled. Thomas Night Song was a good young man. "Hello, Thomas," he said.

"Standing Oak!" Thomas broke stride from his work tone and spoke now with genuine enthusiasm. "It's great to hear from you."

"It's good to be heard, my friend. How are you?"

"Well, thanks. The sanctuary is busy with fall guests. And you? How goes the swamp?"

Raymond laughed. Ocala was just shy of two hours north of Riverview, but it boasted a more robust forest and even slight topographical features, at least compared to the flatland marshes of his hometown. "The kite eats well in the swamp today," he said, referring to a small bird of prey found along the banks of the Alafia.

"That's good."

"I suppose you're calling for Dancing Brook."

"Yes, is she nearby?"

"She was out on a scout this morning after heavy rainfall last night, but I think I just heard the ATV. Hold on a second."

"Thank you, Thomas. Good to hear you."

"You as well!"

The line fell silent for several seconds; Raymond listened patiently to the general sound of long-range murmur and scuttle. The sanctuary was a beautiful place, and he envied the view of the forest now as he glanced out at the rows of books in the little library.

"Hello, brother!" came a joyful and jumpy voice.

"Dancing Brook. How are you, baby sister?"

"Wonderful. The forest is beautiful this morning. And you?"

"I am...well," he said slowly.

"What moves you so down in the swamp?"

Raymond hesitated. "It's more about what else may be moving down in our swamps."

"Oh," she replied, glancing sharply over at Thomas to make sure her sudden change in tone hadn't alerted his suspicion.

Silence.

"The song of the dead will be sung again."

Silence.

"I see. You know what? Give me just a second and I'll check for you. I think it's in my office. Hang on I'm going to transfer the call."

Raymond knew that Thomas must be in the room. Dancing Brook picked up again from her office.

"I've got it, thanks. Thomas could you do me a favor? The ATV was grinding this morning and needs an oil change. Excellent, thank you."

She closed the door.

"I'm here. What happened?"

"I'm not sure exactly; it's too soon. Sheriff approached me this morning with news of a young man beaten to death."

"You haven't been able to examine the body?"

"No. He was found only last night."

Silence.

"Sarah?" he asked.

"Yes?"

"He was found very near the same location, only this time across the river, on the refuge."

Silence.

"Jesha," she whispered.

"Have you reason to suspect any unrest up there?" he asked.

She sighed. "Not directly, not that I would have been burdened by had we not spoken. Not yet, anyway."

"Tell me," Raymond said.

"Their patterns are spoken of by the forest, and they are consistent."

"But?"

"But there have been no lights in the night skies for many days."

"A troubled darkness," he said.

"Some would say," she offered. "But it may be too early to judge."

Silence.

Finally, Raymond spoke. "Let's speak again soon, ok? I'll learn all that I can."

"Ok," she said. "Ray?"

"Yes?"

"Use a serpent's caution."

"I will. And you do the same."

He lowered the phone into the cradle. The relentless sun poured through the single office window. If today were like most, it would soon yield to the passing afternoon thunderstorm. *Then,* he thought, *the view outside would match the stirring within.*

Chapter 29

BEN Ford was a lot of things. He was stocky and thick, just north of overweight, with forearms like the average man's calf muscle. He boasted a beard that should have been a registered voter, although it certainly didn't give Ben the appearance of anyone who cared much about politics. He was also, ironically, an Eagle Scout, which to his great pleasure, always garnered a sort of disbelief and recalibration. Ben was a lot of things all wrapped up in a confusing paradox. But one thing no one could ever accuse him of was being ambitious. No sir. Which made Ben the perfect wingman. He and Barry had lived some high times in the lowlands of Hillsborough County, and he was the only person in the whole world who called the tall prodigal by that fictional middle name: *Malorie.*

Barry didn't turn around. He took another long drink from his pint glass, and smiled.

"Hey Bare!" Ben called again. Barry could hear him walking closer.

"Man, what the – "

Before Ben could finish, Barry spun counter clockwise off his stool with a swiftness that could only be attributed to the toning effect that the ranch work had produced upon his faded athletic days. He could feel his core taught and agile, and he'd timed his move perfectly. Ben was mid stride and utterly defenseless to the velocity of Barry's haymaker. The blow would've dropped most men like a soaked towel: heavy, clumsy, and void of any consciousness.

But Barry didn't smash his old buddy, partly out of choice, and partly because his follow through would've missed anyway. Ben wasn't there. He wasn't like most men. Adding to the paradox of his perception, Ben Ford was surprisingly nimble for a heavy-set, bearded fella. In this case, his reaction time was quick enough to avoid the first strike, but nothing else. He was lying on the uneven hardwood floor, whimpering in a fetal position.

"Oh Jesus no!" he screamed.

Barry laughed like he couldn't remember.

"Malorie my ass, you sucker," he smiled as he helped his friend up off the floor.

"Is that the thanks I get for helping you get Mandy Adams?"

"*Thanks?* Jeez, you got me tangled in a real hornet's nest that time."

"Maybe. But a hornet's nest with huge jahoobies, am I right?"

They both laughed.

"I'm assuming that's your little orange acorn parked out there?" Ben asked, hopping onto a stool and holding a finger up to the barkeep.

"That thing's got a V8 and four-wheel-drive," Barry countered.

"Yeah sure. Nothing says 'MAN!' like a two-door orange import."

"Like that stupid orange sweatshirt?" Barry asked.

"Hey, man, it's the home team, the Buccaneers!"

Barry grunted. "I'll take my *import* over that sorry excuse for a football squad."

"Whatever. Anyway, what the hell are you doing here?"

"Wouldn't I like to know," Barry said.

"I haven't seen you in years. Too damn long," Ben said, wiping foam from his mustache and sizing up his old friend. "Still got that right hook, though."

Barry took another drink. "Feels like that's about all I got these days."

Ben reached into his pocket and produced a pack of Lucky Strike cigarettes. "What's going on?" he asked, lighting one and offering another to Barry. "I thought you were livin' the dream, gettin' your toes licked by beautiful women?"

"Hardly. Mostly getting my ass handed to me by dying old men."

"Oh man, Joe ok?"

"Huh? Oh yeah. No, not Dad. Joe's healthy as a horse. Physically, anyway," his voice trailed off as he lifted his glass again. "No, I'm talking about New York. Watching your boss literally work himself to death, and then being the first one to find him dead, kinda changes your perspective."

"Shit, man."

"Yeah."

"So you came back here to regroup?"

"Something like that, I guess," Barry sighed.

"Well, this is a good place for that," Ben said confidently.

Barry set down his glass and motioned for a refill. "You talking about the bar or the town?"

Ben considered the question, "Both, I reckon."

"I'm not so sure about that."

"Ah c'mon, man. The pace is slow, and the people are honest. That's as much as anyone can ask for, and what a guy like you needs right now."

The two sat in silence, save for the background noise of clanging utensils.

"Guess I hadn't thought about it that way," Barry said.

"I wouldn't sweat it if I were you. You're not gonna end up a has-been sideshow like the rest of us anyway."

Barry gave him a confused look. Maybe it was the beer doing its job, or maybe he'd been away for too long. "Has-been sideshow?" he asked.

"You know, like all those Gibtown freaks."

Barry nodded slowly, grasping memories, but thankful at least for even a fleeting moment of lightheartedness.

"So what's going on, then?"

"Ben, I'm gonna need a lot more of these to answer that question," he said, directing his eyes to his half empty glass. "Suffice it to say that for now that I'm a bit rudderless. I'm not really sure what brought me back here. I had no intention of sticking around this long, and I gotta get out before I get sucked in too deep."

"Sucked into what?"

Barry finished his glass and lifted a finger to the barkeep.

"Lemme grab that sandwich for ya'," he called. Barry watched as he disappeared into the kitchen. Nothing had changed. Dan was still a careful old hawk about making sure guys didn't leave his property too loaded. *Good on him,* Barry thought.

"Ben, I can't talk about this yet, but shit's gone down again."

"Like what? Like you and Mandy Megaboobs?" Ben laughed. Barry didn't. The former lowered his glass slowly while the latter lifted his refill and thanked Dan for the plate.

"Oh man, you mean like last time?" Ben whispered, the corners of his eyes wincing as he spoke. "With your mom?"

Barry nodded without looking at him. He set the cigarette into the ashtray and bit into the fried chicken sandwich.

"Jesus, Barry. I'm sorry."

Silence.

"When did this happen? Or can you say anything?"

Barry wiped his mouth. "Last night, if you can believe it."

"Shit." Ben stared into his glass. "I mean, is your family ok?"

"Yeah, well, it's just me and Dad. It wasn't either one of us. But it happened on our property. Again."

"Anyone I know?"

Barry's mouth was full, and he gave him a look like he ought to know better.

"Ah, I'm sorry."

Barry swallowed. "No, it's not that. I mean, no, I'm not going to say anything right now, but you should know that there's no one in this town that you don't know."

Ben chuckled. "Yeah. Guess that's one thing that sticking around will do for ya'. For better or worse, anyway. So what are you going to do?"

"Do?" Barry asked, surprised.

"Yeah, man, you're the fixer."

Barry rolled his eyes.

"C'mon man!"

"C'mon what? Fix what?"

Ben lowered his glass with mock authority and turned on his stool to face his friend directly.

"Barry Malorie Grayson. I know you've got a birthmark on your ass and a crush on Elvis Presley, God bless him." Barry glowered, trying not to smile. "But I know you've got a big heart beneath all those brains and brawn."

Barry made an attempt to interject.

"No, no, no. Lemme finish," Ben insisted.

Barry yielded.

"My sister's got this batshit crazy little boy. Wild as hell. I've watched that dumb kid go on hunger strikes and take countless ass-beatings for not eating his greens."

"What the hell's that got to do – "

"And he reminds me of you," Ben interrupted.

"What?"

"The kid's stubborn. He knows what he wants, and he's not letting up. Ever. It's annoying as hell right now, but the truth is he's gonna need that in this life. You've got that. I've seen it. Not just with your fancy-pants degree, but in other ways."

Barry wasn't returning Ben's stare.

"You won't let go of something that bothers you. You're like a coon in a paw-trap. You're not letting go."

"And where's that gotten me, Ben?" Barry could feel his usual inhibitions folding under the drink. "I've got one parent on his last marble and the other under a makeshift cross in a goddamn swamp. That's some lineage!"

Dan looked down at them from the other end of the bar. Ben sat quietly before speaking.

"My grandad was a trapper," he said softly. "He used to tell me that in all his years, there were only a few times he ever came across a coon that got out before the dogs came."

"How's that?" Barry asked, feeling the need to amuse his friend after his outburst.

"Blood."

"What?"

"The bastards pulled so hard against the trap that the blood from their paw would finally allow them to slip it through and make off with the prize."

"Ok," Barry said, urging Ben to get on with his point.

"He said that whenever he came upon a trap like that, one with no bait and fur and blood all over it, he'd always smile and be glad for the fella."

Barry took his last bite.

"You get what I'm sayin'?"

"I'm in too deep, buddy," Barry gently flicked his empty glass. "Talk slower."

"Getting what you want never comes without cost."

Just then the dark, quiet bar flooded with daylight as the front door slammed against the wall. The two men looked over and saw Joe Grayson framed in the doorway, letting his eyes adjust to the sudden darkness, his face wrought with urgency.

"Speaking of cost," Barry whispered.

Chapter 30

THE elder Grayson walked into Dan's Three Corners Bar like a fish on four legs. He certainly looked enough like everyone else inside, but there was something altogether different about this one. Faded Wranglers, ageless boots, and a thin-striped flannel shirt. Evidently nowhere necessarily important to be. But the gait, straight back, and the tucked in shirt all very quickly singled out a man who had intention and purpose. The tarnished eagle belt buckle probably helped, as well.

Joe made a beeline to his son, and Barry braced for the worst. What on earth could his father possibly want in here other than to drag him into some deeper level of delusion? Through the haze of the beer coursing through his mind and body, Barry amused himself by wondering if Joe would order the chicken fingers. Whatever he imagined, he couldn't have prepared himself for what happened next.

"Hey there, Ben," Joe smiled, extending a hand.

"Afternoon, Mr. Grayson," Ben returned, enthusiastically.

"The usual today, Joe?" Dan interrupted from out of the kitchen.

"You bet, Dan. Thanks."

In the five seconds it took for all of this to unfold, Barry was already playing catch up. Maybe it was the drink, but at the very least it was a combination that included several punches that he never saw coming. He'd watched his father traverse the space of floor like a slow motion train wreck. Not that he cared what anyone in the bar thought, but he'd figured that in a matter of seconds he'd probably have the very last nail in the coffin of his reasons to get out of Riverview fast. His jaw had been clenched, waiting to absorb the proverbial blow. Now, however, not only was it relaxed, it was practically dragging on the floor.

The first misstep came at his father's amiable greeting to Ben. Barry remembered Joe not caring much for Ben, and the reasons were still apparent today. The older man's shaved cheeks, defined jaw, and cinched flannel didn't have much in common with the younger bearded, disheveled, hang-about. To Barry's amazement, however, the two greeted each other like buddies on a bowling team.

The second and third points of confusion came from Dan, the owner and barkeep. In all his years of sitting at that bar, Barry had never heard the silver fox call anyone anything other than "soldier" or "sister," and the two were not always relegated to gender. In fact, President Carter himself could've walked in on the campaign trail and no doubt would have been greeted as "sister," if greeted at all. But Dan addressed his father with an unmistakable air of shared respect. Unbelievable. That alone, however, paled in comparison to the discovery that Joe had a "usual." Dan never seemed to care what you or anyone else ordered, and there was hardly enough variety for anyone to have an order unique to them. A small selection of beers that all tasted like the river, and everything on the menu was fried beyond the point of recognition anyway. But Joe had a "usual." Once again, Barry was left wondering who this old salt was and what he'd done with his real father. Actually, he wasn't even sure he cared.

"How's the ranch, Mr. Grayson?" Ben asked.

"Hundred head a' cattle will keep you movin'!" Joe smiled as he snapped open a can of Pabst and pulled a stool out away from the bar to see both of the younger men.

"Is that what's got this old jock lookin' like his All American days?" Ben asked, pointing to his pal.

Barry shrugged, but Ben was right. Weeks on the ranch had certainly been kinder than years behind a desk. Had Ellie noticed? That thought, perhaps more than anything else, was a clear indication to cut off his tab. He felt like a fool for wondering.

Joe slapped his son on the shoulder and said how thankful he'd been for the help. "You're welcome to join any time, Ben," he winked.

"Mr. Grayson, I have a severe allergy to that kind of work."

"Truest thing you've said all afternoon," Barry said, pulling bills out of his wallet and placing them under his glass. He took one last draw from the Lucky Strike and crushed it in the tray.

Dan gathered the pile of glasses and currency after bringing Joe a plate of chicken bites and okra, both fried into submission.

"Thanks, Dan. Say, I'm here to catch these guys, and if they're leavin' then I'll take mine to go if that's all right."

"Just bring the plate back," was all they heard as the Riverview icon disappeared behind the swinging kitchen doors. The three men made no objection. Dan didn't really care where or how you ate your food. Just don't steal the kitchenware.

"We'll stick around," Ben offered.

"We will?" Barry asked.

"What the hell've you got to do anyway?" Ben joked.

Joe took a long pull from his can.

Barry watched his father for a few bites. "What'dya need me for?"

"Gotta show you something." Joe didn't look up from his plate.

Barry rolled his eyes. Here we go. "You get the rest of the hand to round out the collection?"

Joe's eyes shot up from the bar, and they sat in the silence created by his sudden lack of chewing.

Ben, standing next to Joe and two seats from Barry, found a sudden interest in the creaking ceiling fan overhead.

"Well, come on," Barry continued, "it's just Ben. You guys seem like pals anyway."

Ben fidgeted with his wristwatch, something old with a silver metal band. "Good to see you, Mr. Grayson. Barry I'll see ya' around. I think I'm   gonna – "

"Whoa, whoa, whoa. You're not going anywhere. You're gonna want to hear this. C'mon! It's the latest from the funny farm."

"Don't do this, Barry" Joe said, quietly.

"What? Isn't this what you want? An audience? Isn't that why you came?"

"And why'd you come, Barry?" Joe countered.

"Oh, believe me I came here thinking it was the last place I'd find anyone."

"No, I mean home. Why'd you come home in the first place?"

Ben stood watching the scene unfold, torn between a desperate desire to disappear and a selfish fascination to eavesdrop.

"No idea, Dad."

"Really? Nothing you can think of?"

Barry lifted his palms to the ceiling in a show of surrender.

"Well I've got one," Joe offered.

"Do tell."

"Right here in front of your friend?"

"Apparently you two are bar buddies anyway, so what's it matter?" Barry asked.

"Ok." Joe drained his Pabst, crushed it to the depth of a small pancake, and placed it neatly on the empty plate, alongside his silverware and a single bill that more than covered his order. "I think you came back to figure it out."

There was a long silence.

Barry shook his head and hated himself for indulging. "Dad I've had my life figured out long before I left."

"That's not what I'm talking about."

"Then what?"

Joe stood and pushed his stool in. Even then he wasn't taller than his son.

"I think you came back to figure out who or what's responsible. For her murder."

The two men were looking directly at each other's eyes, fully alert despite the beverages.

"Don't bring her into this," Barry said slowly.

"I didn't. You did. The moment you pulled onto the homestead."

Barry looked away, straight ahead at the rows of glasses stacked upside down; they seemed as though they were waiting for quitting time. He thought about knocking his father's lights out, and miraculously thought better of it. Joe stood his ground next to him, patiently.

"I'm going out to the truck. I came here hoping to find you; there's something you might want to see." And with that he turned and walked out. Sunlight poured in for a brief moment, then the darkness engulfed them once again.

"Guys, I feel like I intruded," Ben began, "I really should be – "

"C'mon," Barry said shortly. He stormed off his perch and grabbed a fistful of Ben's Buccaneers sweatshirt and dragged him along toward the door. Ben was protesting urgently, but Barry ignored it. If he was going one step further down this God-forsaken rabbit hole, he wasn't going alone. Barry opened the door and turned to face his friend.

"Sorry, buddy, but you're neck deep now, and frankly I need you. I feel like I'm losing my goddamn mind here. All I wanna do is get outta here forever, but I can't shake this sense of responsibility that something's happening or going to happen. And I oughta be here when it does. You were right. I can't leave it alone. Never could. Maybe that's why I'm standing here. But if I'm gonna be any good to anyone, then I need someone I can trust."

Ben stood there, looking more shocked than a few beers ought to allow for. He looked Barry up and down, then stammered, "Oh – ok. Ok. Yeah. I'm in. Whatever you need." Then his posture straightened and his shoulders resolved. "Let's get it done," he said.

Barry smiled, not altogether sincerely. Ben recognized it instantly. "But if I wind up naked in a cow pasture I'm gonna – "

"Believe me, before long you're gonna wish that was the worst you could be getting into."

The two crossed the threshold and shielded their eyes as they adjusted to the afternoon sun. Joe was parked in the far corner of the shale lot and just sliding onto the single bench of the pickup. Barry grasped the driver side door as Joe started to back out.

"One condition, Dad. For now."

Joe grunted, both hands on the steering wheel.

"Ben gets eyes on whatever it is you've got to show me."

His father peered over his shoulder at Ben.

"And why's that?"

"Because you and I are so far down, and so emotionally invested, that we need a fresh perspective."

"And that's Ben?"

"No one else in this town I'd insist on."

Joe looked ahead through the windshield. Seagulls were waging a gang war across the street against a murder of crows over an old pile of fast food. He put the truck in park and left the engine running.

"What are you doing?" Barry asked.

"I'm showing you. Both of you."

"Right here?"

Joe climbed out and motioned the two men over to the bed of the truck. It looked empty, until Joe reached to the corner tucked behind the driver. He gently pulled a long, wrapped towel out into view, but not out of the bed. With one hand he slowly unwrapped it until the very last fold, then he paused.

Three men lined up along the side panel, all leaning against the bed of a pickup and staring down into it.

Joe looked down the line, focusing on Ben.

"Hey, don't worry about me," Ben said, realizing the intent of Joe's stare. "Between my sister's baby and my old man's health, I've seen just about everything." To Barry's surprise, even Joe gave a subtle snort of laughter.

"I don't know how much Barry's told you," Joe said, "but last night Karl McGregor was killed. His cousin Lonnie was hunting out on our property, and he found him. No idea yet if there's any connection. At least between those two."

Ben nodded, his face showing concern for the family. "What other connection would there be?" he asked.

"The condition of Karl's body apparently looked a lot like my mother's," said Barry.

"Oh my God."

The three men stood in silence. Nearby, the crows were celebrating their hard-earned victory.

"Ben, there's a lot more to this that we can't get into now, and maybe that's for the better," Joe said, gravely. "I went to that crime scene this morning and found something. To be truthful, I was looking for it. Or something like it, anyway. I've found others, but nothing like this."

Jesus, thought Barry, *here we go again.*

Joe reached in and pulled the last flap of cover off the object. There, in the bed of the old Ford pickup, on a clear November day like any other, three grown men stood very still, two of them trying to process the information for the first time. They were all looking at a long, white, shallow object. Easily over two feet long, close to three, and about a foot wide in its entirety. The ridges were deep, and the tread was unmistakable.

It was the largest shoe print any of them had ever seen.

Chapter 31

BARRY rested his elbows on the side panel of his father's pickup and laid his forehead on his overlapping fingers. His head was spinning. Every new thought was intercepted by either an unsatisfying conclusion or an altogether new thread. Does this affect the contents of Joe's beer fridge? Was something like this missed at his mother's crime scene? If so, that meant human flesh and blood was to blame, and that meant someone he'd been longing to find for a long time was out there somewhere, at large. What could they have possibly wanted with his mother in the first place? And how does someone with a boot print the size of his thigh go unnoticed?

"I've gone round and round myself," Joe said quietly.

Barry raised his head to look at nothing in particular. The pickup idled with subtle effort, like the way an old man shifts in his seat, waiting for his wife in a department store.

The two Grayson men suddenly noticed their new comrade wandering slightly away toward the tailgate, eyes on the nearby trees following an agitated squirrel.

"Ben?" Barry asked.

He didn't respond.

Barry called again.

Ben spoke without facing them. "Do you guys know those things are actually pretty damn tasty? Gamey flavor, different from chicken, but good. Hardly worth the effort to skin, but lots of meat on the hind legs at least."

Barry looked at this father, then back at Ben. "What are you not telling us?" he asked.

Ben kept his attention on the treetops, like a faithful hound. "Tree rats," he said. "That's what my old man calls 'em."

For a moment, Barry was strongly reconsidering his decision to bring Ben into this. Maybe he'd grossly underestimated the toll that this town could take on a mind over time. Maybe his wingman wasn't avoiding the question; maybe he wasn't withholding anything. Maybe he was witnessing the effects of dirty river water and a deep fried diet, driving a man to get distracted by a squirrel and process that information as a viable, coveted, food source instead of a worthless rodent or pest.

Ben took a step closer to the tailgate and looked directly at the cast, sharply focused, jaw clenched.

"I think I know that boot," he said softly.

"What?" Barry and Joe both tensed.

"I think so. Can't be certain."

"What makes you think you know the owner of a boot print that size?"

"Don't know 'em directly, but I may know where to find him. Or at least where to start looking."

"And where's that?" Joe asked, carefully covering the cast and tucking it into the corner of the bed.

Ben looked at Barry. "C'mon, guys, you both know this place. Where all the freaks hide out."

The two Grayson men gave each other questioning looks.

"Your own house excluded, I'm at a loss," Barry said.

Ben casually flicked off his friend.

"Gibtown," said Joe.

Ben nodded. "Yup."

"Gibtown?" Barry asked.

"Yeah," said Ben, "Gibtown, Gibsonton. And I've heard of this thing, too."

"*Thing?*" Barry asked with emphasis.

"C'mon, Malorie, keep up. The Gibtown Giant. You don't remember this?"

"Mercifully not. Must'a been bird-doggin' chicks that day."

"Anyway," Ben continued, unamused, "our Scout leaders used to scare the shit out of us with this stuff!"

"One of us, apparently," Barry smirked.

"Oh, don't gimme that garbage."

"All right, all right, enough of that," Joe waved. "What else do you know about this?"

Ben collected himself. "Only that he's got a mangled hand. Not that he wouldn't be recognizable enough as it is."

Joe looked at Barry. "Mangled how?"

"I dunno. Never saw him myself. Just heard he was missing some fingers or something."

Chapter 32

GIBSONTON pretty well epitomizes any and every town in Florida that isn't next to a world-class beach, an international airport, or a mouse-eared theme park: most everyone there is running or hiding from something. If vacationers were passing through on their way to the coast, they'd probably find themselves staring out the window in a kind of wary awe. If they were younger, they'd probably ask, "What does anyone do for fun here?" If the travellers were into their family years and beyond, then they'd probably ask something like, "How does anyone wind up here?" The answers to the former don't matter, and one can pretty well guess anyway. But the stories behind the latter are wide and varied, and none more colorful than those belonging to the mysterious residents of Gibsonton (affectionately coined, "Gibtown").

Every ten years the Federal Government takes a population census. Folks from all walks of life are temporarily employed to search down every dirt road in the country and discover who lives where. You can imagine the characters they encounter. Such a day spent with an ID badge and a clipboard in the town of Gibsonton, however, would be like something between a real life horror picture and a backstage pass to the traveling freak show. Because that's exactly what Gibtown was.

Every slick production has a darker underbelly, and The Ringling Brothers Circus was no exception. A circus is unlike any other travelling entertainment in that it "employs" both man and beast, and many of those four-legged top ticket sellers don't hail from anywhere near a northern environment. Thus, the most Southern state in the Union provided a natural wintering headquarters. To their credit, the early town council of Gibsonton saw an interesting opportunity. They created odd, circus-friendly zoning ordinances that essentially allowed residents to keep just about anything they wanted on their property: large transport trailers, supplies, tenting, even elephants grazing in fenced pastures. So one can imagine that if the animals felt welcomed, then so did many of the sideshow human performers and other "carnies." Inadvertently, then, Gibsonton became home to the marginalized, to those who found solace and community in the carnival business. Marquee tickets like Monkey Girl and Lobster Boy were known by their real names at the gas pumps and grocery stores of the tiny town.

It was interesting at first, and most residents were glad to find a reason to be proud of their hometown, but the trickle soon led to a flood. Word spread fast throughout the industry and the sideshow community. Before long, Gibsonton boasted the largest Showmen's Association in the United States, along with a museum, annual tradeshow, and an assortment of carnival artifacts that became legendary landmarks.

One such landmark sat prominently displayed right alongside U.S. 41, which ran straight through Gibsonton. There, in front of a dilapidated inn and sea food restaurant, stood an enormous boot, fastened to a large concrete platform for all to see. It was said to be a size twenty-seven.

The makeshift monument had weathered not only the elements, but also the battles with angry snowbirds who failed to appreciate the novelty. Barry had forgotten all about it. But Tom McGregor hadn't. In fact, his Ford Pinto was speeding down Interstate 75 from Tallahassee at that very moment, eager to conduct and settle business in the sleepy sideshow town.

Chapter 33

BLAKE Martin needed coffee, never mind lunch. The details of the last few days were spinning in his head, coursing through his veins. The McGregor domestic racket had thrown a wrench into everything, and he imagined it would only get worse when Richie fully regained consciousness. The crime scene at the Grayson property proved disturbing, partly because it appeared to have been tampered with. He was careful to conserve his energy and pick his battles, but he had a good hunch that Joe had paid it a visit before his deputies could. They'd found what looked like the remnants of a plaster composite. It would have appeared out of place in the context, but given that it may have been used on a very large print only furthered Blake's suspicions. Still, he couldn't be certain, either about Joe or about what might be a print. The latter detail was particularly puzzling because it was nearly impossible to imagine a print that size belonging to anything that wasn't prehistoric.

But that's why he'd left work early this evening and was now pulling into a secluded clearing that jutted out onto a point in the Alafia River near the mouth of Tampa Bay. The Peninsula, as it was known to locals.

Raymond Muskee stood next to his pickup, looking out in the direction of the great estuary. As he parked and shut off his lights, Blake wondered if Raymond was remembering his ancestor's relationship with the river and bay, and the teeming harvest of fish they supplied.

The surrounding wood was alive with crickets and cicadas; a whippoorwill sang her soothing lullaby nearby. "Beautiful night," Blake offered.

"Yes, indeed," Raymond returned, still looking away. Blake now stood next to him and shared his focus.

"Thanks for meeting me, Ray."

"You're welcome, Sheriff."

The two men stood together; they were both lifelong residents in their town. Neither had known each other particularly well, but both shared a mutual respect for the other.

"Sheriff, I've known this river and these tides for many years. The red fish and the snook, the dolphin and the shark, the alligator and the sea cow."

The twilight hid much of their features, but Blake could easily hear the concern in Raymond's memories.

"I've felt the pains of the generations of my people, the loss of their range and their dignity." Blake lowered his head and removed his hat, examining the inside of the rim. "So it is with great hesitation that I speak with you on the matter of your interest," Raymond turned now to look directly at Blake, "for fear of what that information in the hands of a white man may do to me and my people."

Blake returned his gaze confidently, and Raymond could see empathy and honesty in his eyes. "Raymond, I know what I represent to you, what my own people have been responsible for. It weighs on me every time I put on this uniform." Blake looked out into the darkness. "I know the stories of my own grandfather, the days of the reservation round-ups. And I hate 'em. A man's life oughta transcend his skin or his heritage. In some respects, this town isn't different from any other this side of the Mississippi. But the way I see it, there are two very important differences, and they're standing right here."

Raymond looked at Blake, and nodded. "You have my trust, Sheriff. And my warning."

"What's that?"

"First, what you are about to learn is not easy to grasp, much less for me to adequately articulate; there are some things that do not so easily fit within the lines of the white man's world, or any man's understanding of the world for that matter."

"And second?"

Raymond sighed slightly. "That there may indeed be danger in our swamps. Though it is too early to speak for certain."

Blake nodded. "Go ahead, Ray. What you say here tonight is shared only between the two of us and the critters."

Raymond took a few steps forward through the tall grass in no particular direction, collecting his thoughts. He turned to face the sheriff, and a smile crossed his face. "Sheriff, you've read the little yellow book in the library, I presume."

"I have, like most of us when we were kids."

"How difficult is it for you to question the authenticity of that account?"

"I guess it depends on the day." The two men could see the other smile. "But I'd be lying if I said I wished it weren't true."

"The good news is that it isn't. At least not all of it."

"Ok," Blake said hesitantly.

"The bad news, for you, is that the inerrancy involves the final description given by the surviving members of the hunting party."

"And what's that?"

"The allegation that any of them survived at all."

A whippoorwill spoke on behalf of Blake: distant, haunted.

"What are you implying?" Blake asked.

"None of them returned, Sheriff. Not alive, at least."

"So how was the account recorded?" Blake countered.

"As they say, Sheriff, 'History is written by the victors.' It won't surprise you, then, that a white man's account will never reveal complete failure. Especially not one involving the Indians at that time."

"Failure in what regard?"

"The events are true, so far as I know, but all nine men were later discovered to have met their fate in the swamp."

"I see. How were they found?"

Raymond paused. "They were pieced together, in a fashion, like puzzles."

"I don't understand."

"They weren't found whole, Sheriff. But enough of the important parts was discovered to account for all members of the party."

"They were torn apart?"

"Yes."

Blake looked up at the tree line, eyes wincing not from the sun, but in an effort to process. "You know as well as I do that there's not a puddle in this land that isn't claimed by an alligator. And gators kill in that fashion."

"True, but with one distinction."

"What's that?"

"The alligator does not climb trees."

Blake shrugged slightly. "I don't follow you."

"Sheriff, everything that was found from what remained of those men was first pulled down from the tree tops."

"Jesus," Blake whispered, and returned his attention to the inside rim of his hat, taking a few steps to lean against the hood of the squad car. He shook his head. "I feel like I have to make some assumptions here, Ray. The first being, of course, that these creatures exist at all."

"That's correct, but first you must know that my people hold to a belief very different from yours."

"I'm not sure what I believe in," Blake said, "but different in what way?"

"Several years ago a video surfaced of a terrible hoax."

"The California tape. The Bigfoot."

"That's right. A blasphemy as far as I am concerned. But this hulking, upright cow has become the face of the legend my people have long known about."

"So how is it different?"

"I'm glad you're willing to ask. A creature depicted in that costume does not exist in that environment, nor any on this land. Far too large to be a forager, and much too slow to be a predator."

"What about bears? Black bears. They get plenty big, and we got 'em not far from these parts."

"Sheriff, picture the largest man you've ever heard of."

"I guess maybe one of those wrestlers on the TV."

"Now what if that man were turned loose, naked in the woods, and forced to survive with only the resources at his disposal."

"S'pose they're practically naked on the TV anyway," Blake chuckled.

"After a few months, in what condition would you expect to find that man? Specifically, would you expect him to have maintained his wrestling weight?"

"I see what you mean."

"But why?"

"Because he couldn't sustain that mass on seeds and weeds."

"Correct. And have you ever tried to play the predator in the forest, Sheriff, with no weapon to use? Have you ever tried to sneak up on so much as a squirrel?"

"Ok then," Blake said, "are we just talking about a size discrepancy?"

"I'm saying that what the white man calls Bigfoot is no more a creature than the hat you're holding in your hands."

Blake stood up. "Wait a minute, then how have your people ever seen them?"

"We have never seen the white man's figment of his imagination."

"So you're saying the Bigfoot – or whatever you want to call it – doesn't exist?"

"I did not say that."

"For Christ's sake, Ray, what am I doing – "

"Wait," Raymond held up a hand. "You asked me about the Tall Song."

"What's the difference?" Blake asked, his patience passing with the outgoing tide.

"The Tall Song" Raymond emphasized, "is believed to be as much spirit as it is flesh. Not entirely either. And in that sense, it is far closer to our own species than the white man's ape."

"So it can be seen?"

"It can, but rarely without great effect."

"Why's that?"

"The Tall Song is a servant of the earth, a ruthless protector of the land and guardian against those who would bring it harm in some way. Their origin is older than our history, and they walk the land where and when they are needed. They are willing to do the work that the gods of many cultures are not."

"Like murder."

"According to our laws, yes."

"According to anyone's laws, Ray."

"Does a bear stand trial?"

Blake rolled his eyes. "In the diner you made mention of a species that's been hunted and harassed. Is that why this thing is here?"

"I was referring to my own people, then."

"So then this spirit creature is the protector of your people?"

"Not exclusively, no."

Blake put his hat on slowly and inhaled deeply. "Forgive me for asking, Ray, but how is it you know all of this? Even the information about that hunting party."

"My great grandfather."

"He told you?"

Raymond looked back out toward the bay. "He was among those in the search party who found the bodies."

Chapter 34

THE last defiant rays of sunlight were reaching above the far western tree line of the ranch. As it did every night, the sun dipped beneath the emerald waters of the Gulf of Mexico, disappearing for a time before rising again over the Atlantic.

Barry was in the barn, mucking the last stall and rationing out the evening's oats. Manual labor, at least, kept his mind from hyper focusing on his present reality. Given the developments of recent days, he wasn't sure how to extract himself from this narrative. However, what proved far more worrisome was a growth of some kind in his head (or worse, his heart) that he'd only recently discovered: he was no longer completely certain he wanted to leave. Barry could hardly admit it to himself, and he knew he couldn't exactly pinpoint the reasons. Maybe that's what hours of inhaling horse manure will do to a person.

He was just beginning to cart the last load out of the barn before washing out the wheelbarrow and turning in for the night, when he rounded the corner and ran straight into Ellie McGregor. Miraculously, the contents of the haul remained intact, but they both laughed and admitted that neither was certain the same could be said about their own bladders.

"You very nearly scared the shit outta me, or at least *onto* me," Barry smiled. "What's up? I thought you were taking some time off?"

"I was," she began, "or I am, I should say. But…"

"But what?"

"But I needed to see you. I mean I need to ask you something."

Barry nodded and gave a wry smile. "It's the perfume, isn't it?"

"Excuse me?"

"The horse shit. You smell it on me and you can hardly resist."

"You jerk!" Ellie laughed and hit Barry hard on the shoulder. "Plus, what does that make me? Some kinda giant fly?" She hit him again. She was lithe and powerful, and he knew he'd feel that bruise tomorrow morning.

"Ok! Ok! I didn't think that one through." Barry lowered his hands, wary of a final barrage. "So what's going on? How's Lonnie?"

"He's ok. Um, that's actually what I need to talk to you about." The flirting was gone from Ellie's eyes, their natural beauty overwhelmed now with deep-felt concern. She walked inside the barn and sat down on a bail of hay; Barry followed and leaned against a stall, thankful to rest his lower back. "Barry, I don't know how to say this, so I'm just gonna come out with it."

"Ok," Barry said.

"Richie is pressing charges against Lonnie."

Barry stood opposite of Ellie with his arms crossed. His lawyer mind butted in line ahead of empathy. "That's pointless on his part," he began. "You and your mom were right there and..." he stopped short. "I'm sorry, Ellie," he said, "I shouldn't be trying to fix it. I really am sorry to hear that; I'm sorry all of this has happened to your family."

"No, that's ok. Thanks. I know you are. And actually, fixing it is kinda what I was hoping you'd mention."

Barry gave a confused look. "Sure," he said slowly, "I'll give you any information I can."

Ellie looked down at the toes of her boots. "That's not all, I'm afraid."

"I don't understand. I can give you more than information?"

"No, well..." she smiled faintly in an effort to keep it together, "we may need more than that. But besides, what I meant was that's not all Richie is pressing charges for."

"What else could he possibly – "

"Murder," she interrupted, and the tears flowed over the levy of her will. "He's pressing charges against Lonnie for Karl's murder. Lonnie's in jail." She lowered her head and wept.

Barry was off the stall in a moment and moving toward her, but she was faster. He'd already held her sobbing frame once, and as much as she loved it, Ellie wasn't going to play the damsel in distress again. She rose and was pacing through the barn. "We can't really afford a proper lawyer; but I can't imagine a court-ordered public servant will give a rat's ass about my brother," she was wiping her cheeks with her back to Barry. She turned suddenly to face him, with resolve and longing in her eyes. "Barry, would you – "

He was already there, and he felt ashamed at the reaction in his head. *Would he represent her brother as his trial lawyer?* She finished the question and was about to begin an apology.

"Ellie, there's really not much I can do. I'm not a defense attorney."

"But you're a lawyer," she pleaded.

"And in all my years up north I was in a courtroom about as many times as you've been in one."

"This is Riverview, Barry. You and I both know it's a long way from New York."

Once again, pragmatism was winning out over the human connection. His mind was racing about all the details of figuring out how to pull this off, how to revisit all he'd learned over a decade ago in a vain attempt to adequately defend someone against prosecution.

"It's ok, I shouldn't have asked. I thought…"

"Ellie, wait." His shoulders slumped slightly. "I wasn't – I'm not even sure how long I'm going to be here."

She straightened to her full height. "Well. By all means, Yankee, don't let us give you a reason to stay." She'd barely completed the sentence when the tears returned, and she was out and around the corner before he could respond.

Shit. He shoveled it, smelled like it, had apparently stepped in it, literally and figuratively, and it had all just hit the fan. He shook his head and glowered at the conflict going on inside. He'd wanted nothing more than to get out before getting trapped. He'd felt the noose tightening. *Then why didn't you go, Barry? You're the one still standing here, hanging around. You knew this would happen but you're the one who stayed.* He picked up the shovel and swung it hard against a stall beam. It splintered in half like a toothpick, the business end crashing into the far corner. He wound up and swung again, splitting what was left and leaving a nice dent in the aged beam.

His shoulders were heaving from the sudden rush of anger and adrenaline.

But right then and there, Barry did what he'd been avoiding for too long.

He made up his mind.

Chapter 35

RICKY Branch wasn't much of an eight-year-old boy when it came to kickball and foot races. What he lacked in athletic coordination, however, he more than made up for in detail and observation. If you'd known Ricky, then, you wouldn't have been surprised to learn that he spotted the two strange men walking quickly off the shoulder of Bloomingdale Avenue and disappearing into the wildlife refuge connected to the Alafia. He'd later describe their height and hair color and the assortment of accessories they were carrying: a lantern, large sailor bags, and general "excavation tools," as Ricky put it. His mother humored him with interest at the dinner table that night, but Ricky knew she was grasping at straws to get his father to notice him. For a long time after that night he imagined a deputy arriving at their doorstep and inviting Ricky to come down to the station and identify the men the way he saw it done on the TV. That would certainly impress Jennifer Shaw, and maybe even get him a kiss.

The two men Ricky saw that evening would never set foot in the Riverview Police Station, though they'd no doubt gladly have chosen that fate over what befell them. Florida is flat enough that a person can see a long way from even a moderate height. For example, given the right atmospheric conditions, you could see the Confederate flag waving proudly on Beer Can Island at the mouth of Tampa Bay all the way from the Alafia Bridge.

The duo did, in fact, venture into the refuge that night, along with the supplies that Ricky carefully noted. They had planned for a long job ahead. But before the dawn rose, both men were nowhere near achieving their goal. They were in the treetops, actually.

Fall and winter mornings were the clearest of the year, absent of heavy humidity. You could've seen the flag on Beer Can Island on a morning like that. Neither of the two men did, because both were completely dismembered, with limbs and entrails dangling amongst the moss of a cypress tree like barbaric, medieval Christmas ornaments.

Raymond Muskee woke up in a cold sweat that night, and never made it back to sleep. At first light, he was stepping carefully through the refuge, hardly breathing.

Chapter 36

ELLIE pulled into her driveway in such a state that she almost clipped the driver side mirror on the mailbox. She slammed the door, went inside, and sat on her bed. She wasn't crying anymore; that was done with. In fact, she was hardly emotional at all, at least not visibly. Inside, however, she was something between the two extremes of seething with anger and numb with indifference. Not because she didn't care, but because maybe this was the final straw that would wear her down forever.

Nothing in her life was how she'd hoped, but she'd stopped that nonsense a long time ago. Hope was too hard. Her family, immediate and extended, was extravagantly dysfunctional, and she felt enormous guilt for even admitting that. In fact, that's most of what she felt in her life: guilt. Guilt for being "normal." Guilt for resenting the fact that the rest of her family wasn't. Guilt for being pretty. Guilt for sticking around and guilt for wanting to get out. And now she felt even more of it for trying to get Barry to help and then for her anger at his response. The anger had subsided, though. She couldn't blame him for getting out; maybe she oughta do the same. Just leave. Leave and never return. Start over. Be thankful for the life you do have, and quit wasting it here. Write a note for Mom, say a prayer for Lonnie, give Dad the bird, and just leave. She could do it.

Maybe she would have right there and then had she not seen headlights peering through her house, followed by footsteps scuffing the cracked concrete outside her front door. Ellie froze, knowing she should move. But she waited. The lights stayed on well past any late delivery, and whoever was outside was either a complete fool or unsure of their next move. She heard a heavy boot land on the porch; they must have tripped on the small single step. She'd done it for a week after moving in.

Still no knock or call. Finally, in a moment of adrenaline shock, she leapt from her bed, fumbled through her tiny closet, and emerged with a Remington 12-gauge shotgun. It wasn't loaded, and she had neither the time nor the fortitude to change that, but the sound of the pump action alone would deliver a strong message.

She crept out of her room and practically jumped through the ceiling when a powerful knock from the front door resounded through her living room. Ellie could see a tall figure in the half moon window at the top of her front door. Whoever it was, they were plenty big enough to block out the headlights.

Another knock, followed by something she desperately wanted to hear but couldn't imagine from whom: a voice she recognized. "Ellie? It's me."

She must have had a hundred conflicting thoughts racing through her mind, because it took another call from the unexpected guest to jolt her into action.

"Hello? Ellie? You there?"

She ran the gun back into the closet, pulled her hair back, and slowed only seconds to calm herself before opening the front door.

Barry turned around to face her.

"Ok," he said. "I'll do it."

PART III

Engaged

Chapter 37

YARD time. Lonnie hated it, for this was the time of day when inmates were without structure. The only thing he loathed and feared more than a lack of predictability was when other people were thrown into the mix. He liked the confines and anonymity of the auto shop: few people in general, and no one without a tool and a task. One afternoon in the second grade Lonnie made the grave mistake of being noticed on the playground. Suddenly surrounded by a pack of snarling boys, he did what most any cornered creature would do: he fought to survive. Once the others saw blood most of them ran. "Lookers," he called them. There were far more lookers than actual fighters. The boys who didn't run away that day got it worse than the first out of sheer effort. That was the end of Lonnie's social interactions that year, partly because he was quarantined by the teachers during recess, but also because everyone knew then to stay the hell away.

The incident in seventh grade study hall was hardly different. Everyone picks on the weakest of their pack, until the weakest kicks their ass. Lonnie never considered his actions in any heroic manner; for him, fighting to survive was as normal as needing to eat throughout the day. So when the bombardment of spitballs and rubber bands reached their zenith that day, Lonnie spun out of his chair like a maniac, his right hook moving like the outer bands of a ferocious hurricane. Bryce Granger lost three teeth in one blow, and Lonnie nearly lost the use of his hand. From that day forward he was happily sentenced to closely monitored janitorial duties every day during study period.

Prison felt no different from life in general for Lonnie, with one very important distinction: the population ratio of lookers to fighters was inverted in here compared to the outside world. And so it was with a particularly rapid tapping of his index finger against his temple that Number 476 limped out into The Yard, fueled by awareness, anxiety, and fear.

The Yard was a square of maintained lawn, fifty yards on all sides, with two cracked but often pressure-washed squares of concrete equal distance from each other and the nearest perimeter, like two very large stone steps through an apartment garden. The first patio had a basketball rim at either end, not quite a full court, but it could be used as such if those interested wanted to play a single game instead of dividing the block into two. The second patio held all the familiar trappings of a long-forgotten bodybuilding facility: benches, bars, dumbbells, and plates, all thoroughly rusted and torn but neatly racked or stacked.

Lonnie was interested in neither option. Balls in any sporting context only made him nervous, and the concept of hard work through repetitive motion felt mind numbing, even for him. Loitering wasn't allowed, which left only one viable option for anyone not looking to lose his Yard time. And as much as he hated this segment of the day, he couldn't bear the thought of never stepping out into the sun.

The usual sounds began to fill the air: basketballs snapping and banging against concrete, iron weights chiming together, and all of it filled with the grunts and howls and hollers of adult, athletic males. Lonnie moved warily around the far side of the basketball court toward one of the guards. As he drew within speaking distance, the guard kept one hand on his lowered shot gun and used the other in a stiff-arm fashion to direct Lonnie where to stand, making sure to maintain a triangle between himself, the inquiring inmate, and the basketball game in front of him.

"Yessir, Number 476?"

"Sir I'd like a pack o' them seeds. A pack of seeds, please."

"Excuse me?"

"For the garden over there. Seeds for the garden."

The guard didn't follow Lonnie's direction, both because of his training, and because he didn't need to. A small plot of raised earth lay in a rotted box on the far side of the Yard, weeds spilling defiantly out of the baked, forgotten clay. Once upon a time a group of granola-crunching fruit loops tried to introduce a gardening program to inmates of a few different security detention facilities like this one. Officer Jim Fooshee had been on the job less than a year at the time, and that was plenty long enough to know that such an endeavor would only create far more problems than the bleeding hearts were looking to solve. It did. One inmate was killed for taking a liking to it, and the effort was scrapped inside of a few months.

Now, there was no storehouse of seeds and certainly no plastic rakes or spades, but the Warden at Jim's jail decided to leave the remains of the garden to spite those who created it in the first place. Prisoners needed very little, he believed, and creativity was certainly not one of them.

Lonnie knew none of this, only that a different guard assured him earlier that day that Officer Fooshee oversaw the gardening program, and that he'd be more than happy to show him the storehouse during Yard time.

Jim looked out now over his aviators before pushing them back up the bridge of his nose. As he did so, he caught a glimpse of Officer Marren smiling on the other side of the weightlifting court. Jim chuckled, then spat a plug of tobacco onto the ground.

"Ohhh, you - want - the - seeeeeds," he emphasized in a slow, broken sentence, as if he were talking to a deaf person. Jim pulled the whistle off his barrel chest and blew it loud and long. Lonnie stumbled back and covered his ears. All activity in the Yard stopped abruptly, and everyone's attention focused on the exchange taking place between Officer Fooshee and Number 476.

"Officer Marren!" Jim shouted into the stillness. "Do we have any seeds left so Number 476 can play in the sandbox?" Both courts erupted in a mix of laughter and derision.

Jim turned back to Lonnie, pleased at the opportunity Marren had presented to him. "I'm sorry, Number 476, looks like we're all out. Would you like a ball instead?"

The inmate closest to the pair had been in the process of trying to dribble out of a jam when Officer Fooshee interrupted their game. He took two steps now toward Lonnie, "C'mon, dummy, come play ball!" He heaved a chest pass that struck Lonnie's head with such velocity that his ears rang till the next morning. The ball slammed against the broadside of his face, lifting him off the ground and leaving an imprint of the seams across his cheek. Jim Fooshee laughed his ass off, and for the span of a few short seconds he didn't completely hate his job or his life.

Chapter 38

BARRY Grayson pulled into the Hillsborough County Jail; the fresh white lines of parking spaces were gleaming on the new blacktop. Tax dollars at work. In the week or so since his commitment to the case, Barry had seen very little of anything (or anyone) except his old law school journals. The courtroom was what everyone envisioned when they thought about practicing law, and yet in actuality it was where the vast majority of lawyers spent the least amount of their professional careers. He had helped prepare dozens of cases in New York, but he'd never been required to defend or represent any of them himself in front of a judge and jury. Barry knew just enough about the rhythm, cadence, and language of the drama to hold his own in a conversation, but the thought of taking center stage himself made his palms slick with perspiration. Fortunately, he didn't have any time to dwell on the matter as the formal hearing was scheduled for three days from then. This afternoon he would meet with his client officially for the first time.

He was escorted to a small, sparse room with a wooden, rectangular table and four commercial grade metal chairs. The walls were white only in that they were absent of any other color; mostly they were a pale shade of disregard. Barry seated himself and pulled a legal pad out of a small brown briefcase he'd bought second hand just the day before.

Several minutes later, the door opened and an armed guard followed Lonnie McGregor into the room, all the way to his seat across from Barry. Lonnie shuddered as he slowly lowered himself onto the unforgiving chair, using his cuffed hands to pull his left leg around in front of him. Finally situated, he raised his head to meet Barry's surprise. Lonnie's right eye was swollen shut and a shade of purple that was closer to black than anything else, the way a particularly mean thunderstorm looks on the horizon. One side of his lip looked like it was full of dip, and he was breathing with effort through his nose. Barry gathered himself and glanced up at the guard.

"Same shitty service despite the shiny new parking lot, eh?"

The guard's gut vibrated with laughter. "Careful, buddy."

"Will the DA be so careful if I insist he pay a visit?" The guard glowered. "What are the employment options for a recently terminated corrections officer? Probably about as bleak as what drove you in here in the first place."

"You just lost five minutes, hotshot. Keep talkin' and we'll call it a day right now."

Barry pulled out a pen and returned his attention to Lonnie. "That'll be all, officer. For today." The guard grunted and stepped outside, pleased with his self-proclaimed victory.

"Lonnie, you may not remember me, but my name is – "

"I remember," he said, nonplused. "Basketball. Basketball and red shoes." Barry had worn red suede Nike high-tops during his days on the court.

He smiled gently at happier times. "That's right. The red shoes."

"I don't like red, though. Not red."

"Why?"

"Pain. Red is always pain. Always." He inhaled deeply through his broken nose, and looked at the table. "I was red."

They sat in silence. "Lonnie," Barry began, "you saw red on Karl. How did that get there?"

Lonnie looked at Barry through his good eye for a long moment. "I didn't hurt Karl."

"I know you didn't. I believe you. But someone else thinks you did, and I'm going to make sure they believe you too. Will you help me do that, Lonnie?"

He nodded gently, rocking forward and hunched over as though he were cold.

"What happened? How did Karl get red?"

"The Tall Song hurt Karl. I heard the Tall Song, and it hurt Karl."

Barry was prepared for this, but not for the confidence in his client's tone. The door of hope was closed before it ever opened. Barry chose his words carefully. "Have you heard this before?"

"Yeah. I hear it sometimes across the river."

"Only *across* the river?"

Lonnie stopped rocking, Barry stopped writing. "Lonnie?"

"I've heard it on the pasture. But…"

"But what?"

"Different."

Barry leaned forward. "What's different about the pasture, Lonnie?"

"The song."

"The song is different?"

"Yeah. I – I don't know how. It's just different."

In that moment, Barry felt a pang of guilt. Guilt because suddenly insurance law in New York felt like heaven. Guilt because he wanted to pull the brown striped tie off his neck and walk away. Guilt because he wanted to slam his head on the table. He was staring at his sparse legal pad when Lonnie broke the silence.

"One sounds like a lie," he said.

Barry looked up. "A lie?"

"The one in the pasture sounds like a lie."

"How?"

Barry could see that Lonnie was clearly frustrated that his lawyer wasn't keeping up. Maybe now he understood the black eye.

"The song in the pasture isn't the same. It's a lie."

"Lonnie, the noise you hear in the pasture sounds like maybe someone is pretending to make the same sound across the river?"

"Yeah."

Barry considered this, then braced for the moment of no return. "Lonnie, which sound did you hear the night Karl was killed?"

"The Tall Song. The truth."

Just for clarity, good measure, and maybe a bit of added sting, he asked, "Lonnie, what exactly is the Tall Song?"

"You don't know?" Lonnie asked, with all the sincerity of a four-year-old who fears you've never heard of Santa Claus. "I thought lawyers always read books. You should read the book. In the library."

***

BARRY slung his briefcase through the open window of his Jensen Interceptor, sending it crashing into the passenger door. *Thank you, law school,* he thought. *Thank you, effort, persistence, and work ethic. Ladies and gentlemen of the jury,* he imagined saying, *my aim is to prove my client's innocence by exposing the goddamn Sasquatch as the real criminal responsible for the brutal death of Karl McGregor.* He turned the key and screeched out of the lot. *Good-bye, career.*

Chapter 39

THE Alafia River is an underdog, a dark horse, an afterthought in a land barely above sea level, surrounded by water, and plastered with lakes, rivers, bays, and ponds of all sizes. If you were to fly into Tampa International Airport, you'd see so much water that you might begin to wonder if the land itself didn't somehow manage to take root and simply grow up around it, trapping puddles of the stuff to form the landscape below. In fact, just north of Tampa is an area aptly named "Land O' Lakes." The Hillsborough, Palm, Manatee, and Little Manatee rivers are all longer than the Alafia, and they all boast either much larger, or in some cases, more protected estuaries. Unlike those, however, the Alafia runs almost directly west-to-east, as though it aimed to traverse the state. But nearly six miles from the mouth of Tampa Bay, the river takes a sharp left turn, due north. At this juncture, the river begins to narrow significantly, becoming more intimate with the land on either side. There's a small island at this northernmost tip, just before the Alafia begins to veer south again and even out its original course.

The island itself is insignificant, certainly less than one hundred feet long and no more than thirty feet wide at the most. It's a young boy's playground and a smuggler's landmark, torn straight from the pages of Mark Twain's inspiration. What is significant, however, is the curious shade of color in the water near this point.

The starboard side of the island, like the rest of the river, is characterized by dark, murky water and a slick, muddy bottom. The left side, though, features shallow, crystal clear water, flowing over nearly white sand. If you were to follow this trail of liquid sapphire in search of its source, you would discover something resembling the mouth of a cave looming just ahead. A freshwater creek pours out from underneath a canopy of guardian oaks, intersecting the black water of the river. It's a beautiful, serene location. Schools of mullet glide over the small shoal; kingfishers and herons patrol the banks. The creek continues northeast for miles, ambling silently through a marsh jungle that would otherwise be impassable. The land is curiously uninhabited to this day, forgotten even amidst a surrounding and rapidly developing sprawl.

Chapter 40

BARRY drove past the turn, but not because he missed it. The left onto Balm Riverview Road off of U.S. 301 would've taken him to the ranch. Instead, he blew through the yellow light with increasing speed, as if he'd been given a head start on a road race. Commercial desolation lay before him, with little more than gypsy trailer parks dotting the landscape as if they were hewn out of the undergrowth itself. His tie was yanked to the left and his shirt collar was opened but still restricted, like a victor lying pinned underneath a vanquished foe. Windows down, one hand on the wheel. "Roxeanne" by The Police, chiming over the radio station.

Barry was heading south. He needed time to think, and a change of scenery. If his career were going down the can, then he'd rather go down off the grid as opposed to being flushed down because he played by the books. He was in a tight spot, no doubt about that.

Lonnie wasn't mentally handicapped, and Barry knew he could make that case if necessary. In fact that was just about his only hope. But Lonnie also had nothing to lose, from his perspective, and he wasn't backing down from his original story, however far-fetched it seemed. Something was missing.

Twenty minutes later, Barry came to a stoplight that he hoped would lead him to some answers. He flipped on his blinker and slowly pulled right onto Gibsonton Drive.

A small sign made of scrap lumber was dressed in fading paint and read, "Welcome to Gibsonton." Traffic was light for midday, comparatively, and Barry's sports car stood out like a peacock in a chicken coop. He'd forgotten to account for that. He pulled into a yellow brick general hardware store, which resembled a converted Post Office. From here he planned to walk the few blocks through the heart of the town, an exercise that he figured couldn't take more than a half hour. A sandwich shop sat across the street, laboring under the sun and daring another summer thunderstorm to take its best shot. He was hungry, and this looked as good a place as any. Instinctively, Barry looked in the direction of oncoming traffic before crossing the two-lane road.

He stopped, one foot on the asphalt, caught in mid-stride. The road was clear, but something caught his eye, just off the road sitting high and out of place. Maybe a hundred feet away, a pile of whitewashed concrete beamed like the torch of a lighthouse. The platform was crudely shaped, but functional; probably four feet tall.

Barry had seen displays like this in historical settings like St. Augustine or Key West; they usually held a plaque of some sort that shared a piece of significant information pertinent to the location. He was walking toward it now, and maybe he'd find such an engraving upon closer inspection. But even from that distance it was evident that this altar wasn't intended to feature data alone, for the flat plateau of its crest exalted a very different kind of history lesson: an enormous, black, knee-high riding boot.

Chapter 41

BLAKE Martin rarely skipped lunch, not because he was overweight or lazy, but because he was orderly. Structure and familiarity hung like a warm bathrobe around his shoulders. Kathy religiously packed him a modest pail with a thermos of coffee every day. Come to think of it now, he realized, that was a big reason he didn't skip lunch: the coffee. He drank so much of it throughout the day that his sandwich and fruit were basically consumed to take the edge off the acid, not that he needed any more of that these days. Ever since that call to the Grayson property weeks ago he'd been feeling the faint but discernable signs of anxiety that he'd come to recognize in his adult years: neck stiffness, gassy stomach pains, a metallic aftertaste that he couldn't brush or rinse out, even an odd, dull pain in his groin at times.

Blake had long ago accepted the baggage that came with the badge, but cases like this (which were mercifully rare in his town), made him consider the life of a schoolteacher or phosphate miner. Punch in, punch out. Recently, he'd been taking far too many gut punches.

His conversation with Raymond Muskee had done little to shed any kind of light on this case. In fact, he was sleeping less and coming up completely empty from the dredges of his analytical exercises. From a higher altitude, he knew there were pieces missing from this puzzle, and that it would be impossible to identify the full mosaic without them. He was beginning to wonder, however, whether he actually wanted to find them. Ignorance truly is bliss; that much was true from his own marriage. Kathy's life was much lighter than his own simply because he kept her from all the underbelly happenings, all the domestic disputes and robberies, the drunks and homosexuals. She may find out in time from her own gossips, but her friends were always amazed that she was often the last to learn about the juicy news despite her proximity to the person who was usually the first to know.

Raymond certainly wasn't his only concern. The crime scene on the Grayson property had evidently been tampered with. Blake and his deputy found tracks and prints that were noticeably more fresh than the others, despite what appeared to be an attempt at covering them. What was more alarming, however, was the white, chalky residue they'd found several yards from the focus of their attention, seemingly outlining a depressed area just off the beaten path. At a first glance from some distance, the outline resembled the general shape of a foot.

Closer inspection revealed that to be impossible; it looked nearly large enough for Blake to place his entire lower leg inside. He knew the intruder must have been Joe, and he could guess that the chalk was plaster, but he certainly wasn't sure what the elder Grayson had found or discovered from the casting, or what he was on to. More importantly, once again, Blake felt the sensation of standing pressed against the outer wall of one corner and weighing the decision of whether to look around it. He felt ashamed, in fact, for even thinking there was a choice in the matter.

He could go easy on himself, however, seeing as how he was once again turning off onto the dirt road leading to the Grayson ranch. Like it or not, so long as he wore the badge, he was going to press forward. Joe knew things that he didn't, and he aimed to close that gap today.

***

BY the time Barry arrived at the makeshift monument he could already see that what was left of the boot couldn't possibly last much longer. The toe was completely torn off, exposing a threadbare sole. The shaft rose tall and imposing, leaning forward as if it were daring the next afternoon thunderstorm to do its worst. Even still, it was cracked and dry-rotted throughout. A single piece of rudely bent, rusted rebar served as the primary anchor and security device. It was buried into the concrete on either side of the boot, and it punched through the shaft halfway up the leg. The effort had a visceral, barbaric feel to it, like a permanent crucifixion. Barry felt the change in his temperament, a shift from curiosity to concern.

"It ain't gonna bite ya', stranger!"

Barry's oxford loafers spun so fast on the soft soil that he instinctively grasped the monument for support. The voice that boomed so clear and strong in his ear was howling now in a raspy cackle. A quick, scaly hand shot out from a grey suit jacket and caught his shoulder.

"My apologies, Mister…" The stranger was peering up at him, one eye closed and the other nearly squinted shut, as if Barry's face was the beam of a halogen bulb. "What's your name, son?"

"Barry," he said reflexively, wishing he hadn't.

"Pleased to meet you, Barry," the stranger said with a salesman's smile. Barry didn't recall accepting a handshake, but now he wondered how long the two had been at it.

"Come to see our museum, have ya'? We gotta charge admission, ya' know." Another bout of asthmatic laughter, the kind that usually precedes some kind of a well-rehearsed pitch.

Barry gathered himself. "Yeah, I suppose so. Are visiting hours still open?"

"Always, ma' boy. Always." The stranger was still evidently sizing him up. "What can I do ya' for?"

"Just passing through; figured I'd find out what was sitting over here."

"Oh yeah, Big Al. Still stoppin' traffic is he?"

"Who's Al?"

"Who indeed?" the stranger smiled. "The King Kong of big top entertainment, he was."

"How's that?"

"Well, Mister, eight feet tall makes you the king of just about everything, don't it?" he wheezed through another fit of laughter. "Ol' Al practically invented the sideshow acts of Barnum Bailey; just about built this whole town, too."

"Wow," said Barry, in genuine surprise. "Is he still around?"

"Nah, nah. Al passed nearly fifteen years ago now, maybe longer. But as you can see, he's still drawing crowds, ain't he?" The man's smile faded quickly as he looked once more at Barry. "Say, have we met before? What did you say your last name was?"

"I didn't," Barry said, "but it's Grayson. Barry Grayson."

The stranger's face went slack despite the glare of the sun. He recovered quickly, but not in time for Barry to pick up on some element of shock or fear or disdain.

"Watch yourself out here, Mr. Grayson," the Southern salesmanship was gone now from his tone, "folks here are wary of strangers, like the way a stray dog's been beaten and abandoned. Ya' can't really blame it for biting." And with that, he seemed to slither away from whichever direction he had appeared.

"I didn't catch your name," Barry called.

"Didn't give it, Mister!" The stranger walked on.

Chapter 42

BLAKE Martin pulled up to the Grayson homestead alongside Joe's truck. He closed the door slowly and paused a moment to appreciate the scenery, but more likely to delay the nature of this visit. He was sad to consider the fact that the only times he'd been out to this secluded property in the last ten years was to deal with troubling news. Despite that, he'd always been fond of the location itself: open pasture gently flanking the river, with the quiet refuge growing wild beyond it. He could see why Joe hadn't left, even now after all he'd experienced.

A sudden movement in the distance caught his attention. The hour was relatively young, but the night ruled this time of year, and the evening began its campaign heralding the moon earlier every day. A light began to glow out near the barn, a flickering, kinetic dance. Then another. He strode to the porch with urgency and could see now that the lights were following another object, a white cowboy hat. Every time it paused, another flame appeared. Joe was walking his fence line, lighting torches atop the posts.

"For God's sake," Blake sighed. He wanted nothing more than to sneak back to the squad car and speed out undetected. But that was too late; Joe was staring right at him. He covered the remaining distance, patiently lighting the wickets before finally blowing out his torch and walking through the gate toward his uninvited guest.

"What can I do for ya', Sheriff?" he asked upon approach, without lifting his eyes beneath the brim of his hat.

"Evenin', Joe," Blake chuckled. Joe stomped his boots on the porch deck, took off his hat, and sat carefully into one of the two rockers. He didn't motion for Blake to join him. Crickets sang softly, unaware of – or maybe looking to ease – the evident tension. Blake slid over to lean against one of the posts supporting the roof over the porch, his back to the pasture but his person facing Joe.

"Joe," he began, "I don't like the purpose of this visit any more than you do, but I've got a job to do, and frankly I need your help. Given that we both want the same thing I figured – "

"That ain't true, Martin," Joe interrupted, staring out at the flickering torches.

"What's that?"

"We don't want the same thing," Joe said, turning now to look at Blake.

Blake sighed. He knew this wouldn't-be easy.

"I'm sorry you had to come out and see all this," Joe nodded toward the pasture.

"You wanna tell me about it?"

"Not particularly, but I imagine I'll have to."

The two men occupied the silence of the descending darkness.

"Joe, I think you were out at the crime scene before my deputies arrived. I noticed a few traces of white plaster residue. I'm not here to demand anything from you, but you gotta trust that the angles we're both coming from are at least well-intentioned. I'm here for help, Joe. I got a funny feeling that there are pieces to this puzzle that I'm missing, and I think you may know the general shapes."

Joe chuckled. "Careful what you ask for, Sheriff."

"I don't get that privilege in this job," he said.

To that, Joe glanced up sharply and held Blake's gaze. "Ok," he said with resolve as he stood and walked off the porch.

"Where are you going?"

"To grab a few beers. I think you should come with me."

***

RAYMOND Muskee nearly dropped the receiver as he lifted it off the wall; a single lamp illuminated the darkness of his home. He had to dial the number twice, his breathing forced under control as he listened to the ringing.

"Hello?" came a woman's voice on the other end.

Breathing.

"Hello?" Dancing Brook was nervous now, having been awakened in the middle of the night.

"There is no light in the sky now."

"Raymond," she exhaled. She took a moment to gather herself, leaning up on her pillow. "I've noticed the same here. Do you suspect anything? Or anyone?"

"Not yet," he lied. "But there is a stir on the river refuge."

"How can you tell?" she asked.

Silence.

Raymond began to move the phone toward the receiver, pausing to whisper, "Because I've been walking amongst it."

Dancing Brook sat bolt upright in bed, before realizing her brother had hung up.

Chapter 43

BARRY crushed the can of another Pabst Blue Ribbon in his large hands and sat staring out into the darkness; the Alafia flowing silently before him, the bridge watching quietly overhead. He and Ben used to fish down here for hours as kids, catching little more than catfish and mosquito bites, daydreaming of stealing a first kiss under the overpass. In the haze of the last few days and the buzz from his beers, Barry almost mustered an admiration for life's ability to carve new, unexpected paths into the fabric of a dream. Not long ago he'd been practicing law in New York City. Now, he was nearly a beer away from being drunk along the banks of his childhood haunts, tossing rocks into a murky river like the final scraps of his career. In less than two days he'd be standing in front of a judge and jury for a preliminary hearing, during which he had to produce the grounds of defense for his client.

He stood slowly now, dusting the sand from his khakis and reaching up to straighten his tie before realizing he'd ripped it off long ago after leaving the jail. He stood at moderate attention, cleared his throat, and strode a few paces forward, parallel with the river. A mullet jumped and splashed nearby.

"Your Honor," he said in pompous mockery, "my client has been wrongfully accused and I wish to present the jury with grounds for considerable doubt regarding the charges brought against him. In so doing, I aim to torpedo my promising career and damn myself to a life of indentured servitude to my father, mucking shit out of his barn and stealing beer from his fridge."

"Proceed," he replied in an old, pretentious tone.

Barry turned now to face the Alafia. "Ladies and gentlemen of the jury. As you can clearly see, my client is mentally challenged to the brink of full on clinical diagnosis. I, myself, despite my outward appearance, am equally depraved and nearly insane for taking this case. Nonetheless, my intent throughout the course of this trial is to prove to you that young Karl McGregor's unfortunate and untimely death was brought about by none other than…" he paused for effect, "Bigfoot." He gave a slight bow and addressed the judge once more. "Thank you, your Honor."

At this, a slow clap suddenly grew from the darkness behind him. Barry spun around and struggled to maintain his balance.

"That was brilliant," said a voice. "Very convincing, Mr. Lawyer, sir." Ellie emerged from the shadows.

"How'd you know I was here?"

"Not too many fancy-pants Jensens in this town, Yankee. Specially not parked on the side of a bridge this time of night."

"How long you been standin' there?" Barry asked, suddenly feeling more sober than he was.

"Long enough to wanna kick your ass."

"I'm sorry, Ellie. What I said about your brother."

"What's going on, Barry?"

Silence.

"Ellie how'm I supposed to answer that?"

"Answer it like my friend."

"The friend who's also your brother's lame duck lawyer?"

"You're not a – "

"Look at me, El!" Barry swung his arms toward the indifferent river in grand gesture. "Look at me standin' here, in the middle of Nowhereville, USA, 'bout to go before a judge and tell the jury that *Bigfart* framed my client! How's about that, huh?"

"And what about that?" she asked, pushing him in the chest. "You got better things to do? Is Lonnie's life not worth your efforts? You're all we got, Barry! You're all he's got! Shit, did you ever stop to think that maybe we feel equally at a loss?"

"What'r you sayin'?"

"You know what I'm saying."

"That you don't think I can handle it?" he asked.

"You wanna tell me I ain't got reason to think that?" she kicked an empty Pabst for effect.

She was right; Barry knew it, and he was too tired and buzzed to defend himself. He collapsed in a heap, lying down on the grassy slope leading up to the shoulder before the bridge.

"I'm sorry," he sighed. "I'm so sorry."

Ellie sat next to him. "Barry, you wanna hear something?"

"I suspect that's a rhetorical question." He could see the brilliance of her smile flash through the darkness and the alcohol. She punched him in the leg.

"Go ahead," he said. "Lay it on me." He wasn't referring to whatever she had to say.

"Barry Grayson, I think you need us just as much as we need you. That's what I think brought you back here."

"Ya' know that sounds awful close to Baptist talk."

"Oh Jesus," she groaned. "Maybe it is. But I don't know how else to figure it, the two things in my life that I'd never imagined would happen."

"What's that?"

"That my brother would ever be caught up in a mess like this."

"And?" he probed.

She looked at him. "That I'd ever see you again, much less in Riverview."

He sighed and laid his head back down onto the embankment. "I can attest to that one."

"I know you can't see it," she said, tentatively, "and I can hardly believe I'm even saying this now in light of everything, but there really is beauty here, Barry."

He said nothing.

"A town like Riverview isn't much to the rest of the world, but I think it does share one thing in common with any place else: it's mostly full of people who are all somewhere between birth and death, and who are doing their best to find hope and happiness along the way. I mean for God's sake, you more than any of us know the grass isn't always greener on the other side." She picked up a small rock and threw it into the blackness, the soft splash creating ripples that they couldn't see. "In fact, I suspect the other side of anywhere is just a mirage, maybe just a reason to run."

Silence, save for the distant call of a lonely owl.

"I know you're mad as hell," she continued, "and I don't blame you. No one could."

"But?" he asked.

"But nothing," she said with emphasis, looking at him now with an electric combination of passion and pain in her eyes. "Welcome to the struggle, Barry Grayson. Look at the two of us," she said, half smiling through eyes brimming with tears, "there's enough pain between our lives to fill a horse trough, but there's gotta be hope somewhere in that murky water too, some way to heal."

Barry took off his blazer and laid it around her shoulders. It engulfed her, but she pulled it tightly around her frame.

They sat in silence.

"Ellie?"

"Yeah?"

"As your family's legal council, I believe it's my duty to tell you that I have no idea what the hell I'm gonna do."

She chuckled, to his surprise and relief. "I know," she said, "but you will."

Barry sat up slowly and looked upriver.

"What is it?" she asked.

"That damn refuge is a ten minute boat ride from here."

"Almost an hour by canoe," she said. "I hate that I know that, but some girlfriends talked me into trying to spy on you when we were practically kids."

"Wow. You had it that bad, eh?" he chided.

"You wanna walk back to your fancy car with both your legs?"

He laughed like it had been too long.

"There's something I'm missing, El. Something we're missing. In all the great wide world, what are the odds that this creature exists at all, much less that it's killing folks right here in this town? There's gotta be something else."

"Like what?"

"I don't know. Something. Anything. Drugs, smugglers, something."

"Pirates," she added.

"What?"

"Nothing."

"Why did you say that? Pirates?"

"I guess I felt like it belonged on your list," she shrugged. "Plus, you could ask them yourself in a few months."

"What on earth are you talking about?"

"The Gasparilla Parade. You know, every year down in Tampa they – "

"Holy Lord!" he stood up, stumbling.

"Whoa there, cowboy. You're gonna be a soaked rat here in a second."

"C'mon," Barry urged, climbing back up the bank to the bridge. "You gotta drive."

"What? Where are we going?"

"To ask the pirates!" he called over his shoulder.

Chapter 44

JOE drained the last of his Old Milwaukee and tossed it into a garbage can filled with equal parts oil and beer brands. Blake, who had respectfully declined earlier, carefully removed his badge and holster and motioned to the fridge.

"Please," he said.

Joe nodded. "I figured you'd reach for one of two things after all that. I was hoping it'd be the beer."

"What was the other?"

"Your cuffs."

Blake smiled, and took a long drink. "I'm not gonna arrest you, Joe."

"But?"

"But I'm gonna need some time or a lot more of these to wrap my head around everything I've just heard."

"Fair enough."

Blake held his beer and stared at the enormous plaster casts laid out before him. Ordinarily, none of them would look very interesting or convincing, but the latest addition was clearly divergent compared to the others: the edges were noticeably smoother, much more like a boot or shoe. The only oddity was that there was little to no tread where one would expect to find a sole. Blake had learned to listen to the connection between his ears and his ribs. The brain and the gut. Right now the latter was pinging like a radar blip, subtle but noticeable, and it wasn't the Old Milwaukee. Any kind of footprint from a shoe or boot without a tread pattern typically indicated premeditated purpose, attention to detail.

In a way, it was an ironic tell where one clearly intended to leave no traceable sign. In this case, however, the size of the boot alone was enough of a clue that tread was mostly a moot point. Smart, but not that smart. Which meant that whoever was out there the night Karl McGregor was murdered most likely wasn't the brains; someone else was calling the shots. Blake had been in plenty of sticky situations in his years on the force, even in a small town. He'd raided scores of rundown ranches and trailer parks. Criminal hives like these all had a seedy, dank smell to them, like mold: evident growth near a vent was only the surface of a network of filth.

That's what this was beginning to smell like, what he was sensing in his gut. Joe may very well have found the muscle, and plenty of it if this was real, but now for the brains. That discovery, he knew, would only come from detecting the motive, and he wasn't going to find that at the bottom of the beer can he was holding. However, the polar perspectives and stories of both Joe and Raymond seemed to be mixing well with the contents. He took another drink.

"So you think I'm nuts?"

Blake shook his head. "No, I don't think you're nuts. But I may not be the most qualified person to answer that."

"What's that mean?"

"It means I feel like I'm grappling with my bearings on reality my own self. I hardly know how to make sense of the happenings in this town anymore, much less the cast I'm looking at. Either suspect is something oversized, dangerous, and hardly believable."

"Did you feel like this then?"

Blake looked up, "Ten years ago?"

Joe nodded slowly.

"Yeah, Joe, I did."

The two stood in the pale glow of the single fluorescent bulb; tree frogs calling quietly in the distance, crickets chirping a cold cadence.

Joe scuffed the toe of his boot at something on the garage floor. "It wasn't your fault, Blake."

Blake tipped the can way back to retrieve the last drops. "Thanks, Joe. I mean that. Closure's part of this job, and when it's elusive it can be downright maddening for a lawman."

"Maddening for a widower, too."

"I'm sorry, Joe. I'm not proposing that I can relate. But it's hard for me to accept what feels like my inability to solve this case and then to see what that's done to you."

"What's done is done, so far as it concerns me. But it's happening again, Sheriff, and that's what you need to focus on."

Blake nodded, sincerely thankful for what felt like progress in light of years of unresolved conflict.

"Can I ask you something?"

"Sure," Joe said.

"Do you have anything to lose that anyone knows about?"

Joe chuckled with evident cynicism. "Not hardly. Cattle ain't worth killin' over."

"No," Blake agreed as he picked up his badge and holster, "but I'm wondering if that was the intent."

Joe gave the sheriff a suspicious look.

"Sorry," Blake said. "I'm trying to approach this from all angles. Probably not helpful to think out loud at this point." He extended his hand, and Joe shook it somewhat hesitantly. "I'll be in touch, Joe."

Joe waited till he couldn't hear the squad car any longer, then he made sure to tuck the frozen fingers further underneath the freezer-wrapped meat. He hadn't shown those to the sheriff, and couldn't imagine ever doing so.

Chapter 45

THE rowboat itself required at least two men, if they were going to make the kind of haste necessary for escape. The contents of the boat, however, required more. The small dispatch pulled silently out of the bay and into the mangrove-guarded river, which acted both to conceal their presence and nearly deafen the booming cannons behind them. Juan Gomez had been given simple orders by the man himself: follow the river of fire to where sapphire and pearl meet at the oaken cave. The Captain had spat the hushed words into his ear, their cheeks touching, fistfuls of his shirt firmly in the Captain's grasp.

The Floriblanca was in a panic, caught off guard by the young country of the New World, whose official standard now flew high and proud over what the pirate crew had originally believed to be a vulnerable British merchant vessel. Tricked. The immigrant nation had nerve, that was for sure. Now the crew would be forced to discover the mettle and gun power of the United States Navy firsthand. The Captain had every intention of living to report what he would learn over the next several hours, given his confidence in the abilities, experience, and bloodlust of his enterprise. However, he was seasoned enough now to know that he would be no one's captive; Captain Jose Gaspar would die by his own blade before swinging from the noose of a foreign flag.

Juan was a grateful and faithful cabin boy, and deceptively able. The Captain had witnessed his natural prowess with a Spanish rapier when his men captured him from an Indian village. The boy had single-handedly defended himself amongst a circle of angry pirates when Gaspar arrived and ordered his looters to desist. Jose took the boy in, much to the initial dismay of his captors, and treated him well. "Way of the Panther" was his given Seminole name, but he quickly became known simply as Panther John onboard. Relations were tense at first, as John would discover they were with any newcomer. A pirate outfit was a community with a strict bottom line; real estate and resources were slim at sea, and those brought to the table would have to prove that they could earn their keep. The crew came to love him, however, when they realized that Panther John was a cold-blooded survivor. Only days after his arrival they watched him fight an experienced gunner to the death over an extra loaf of bread. John attacked his harasser with such ferocity that he was soundly welcomed after the body of the loser was dispatched. Attrition by force was a way of life aboard a ship of thieves.

Under Captain Gaspar, pirating itself was driven both by monetary and political gain. From his perspective, the *Floriblanca* was a floating city of sovereign Spanish soil, willing and able to do for the good of Spain what his countrymen could not (or would not). However, unlike privateers, pirates bore no official papers from any crown, which meant that they were quite literally men without a home, as no country would offer them passage or pardon for fear of inciting war. Thus, Jose Gaspar, like many other pirates, was a man of passion and conviction, who viewed himself as one who had been unjustly driven to the margins, and yet one who was willing to accept the costs that came with the undignified or unsponsored entrepreneurship of piracy.

This sense of the suppressed or misunderstood gentleman was perhaps on no greater display than when women were found hiding amongst a captured prize. Unlike women encountered in the everyday foot traffic of life on land, women at sea were only ever of some kind of importance, which often meant that they were the most beautiful that society had to offer. Captain Gaspar insisted on treating these women with respect and safety, so long as they understood and accepted the parameters of their new reality: they would serve as pirate wives. And not only that, they would foster families for new generations. So expansive was his ambition that Gaspar and his mates populated an island community for their future wives and families. This became much more than a standard weapons outpost or garrison. However, lest the human treasure should ever forget the trappings of their new quarters, the men named the island "Captiva." The island itself still exists along the Gulf Coast of Florida. These days, though, residents visit willfully and with great pleasure as it is now predominantly a vacation resort community.

Panther John earned his first bride after a few years of loyal and earnest service to the captain and crew of the Floriblanca, a beautiful young Spanish girl. As a show of solidarity, John took her last name, Gomez, and changed his first name to Juan.

Juan Gomez is said to have been dispatched and entrusted with securing the treasure of Captain Jose Gaspar on what would be the final fight and voyage of the Floriblanca, which held no match to the volleys from the USS Enterprise, a Naval schooner eager to prove itself a man of war. For his part, Captain Gaspar made good on his word. In the throes of battle, when his ship was lost, Jose climbed the rigging of the mainmast and shouted his freedom before plunging a dagger into his *own heart and disappearing beneath the emerald waters off the Gulf of Mexico.*

***

ELLIE closed the worn cover and laid it in her lap before playfully shining the flashlight into Barry's eyes. He wasn't there. The two had been sitting across from each other, engulfed in darkness and leaning against the last aisle of the Riverview Library, while Ellie read an old article published in the *St. Pete Tribune*. It was an excerpt from a then-forthcoming biography on the local legend who called himself Panther John. In reality, there was little to no historical evidence (at home or abroad) to support anything the man claimed, even the very existence of Captain Jose Gaspar. At the moment, however, that didn't matter to Ellie. She heard the soft thump of books being returned to a shelf nearby.

"Barry!" she whispered urgently.

No response.

Ellie crawled down the aisle; the sound of the thumping had ceased. She leaned out ever so slightly and had just a split second to survey the main floor in the moonlight before something hard crashed against her head. Before she could react she was smothered under a massive weight. She screamed in panic and pain as books flew off shelves and crashed around her. She kicked herself free and scrambled toward the nearest wall before a vice grip wrapped around the ankle of her boot. Ellie spun around on the floor and was about to kick her attacker into next week.

"Jesus!" Barry shouted.

Ellie fumbled around for the flashlight and saw Barry lying facedown, buried under books, and holding onto her foot like a lifeline.

"What the hell?" he asked.

Ellie erupted in laughter. "I'm so sorry," she managed, "I got so wrapped up in that stupid story that I never heard you leave."

Barry began to pick himself up and groaned in disappointment.

"Hey, my head hurts worse than your knee."

"No, it's not that," he said, "although that's debatable. I finally found what I was looking for only to lose it again in this pile. Not to mention we gotta get this put back together in the dark."

"What was it?"

Barry pushed through the scattered books and finally emerged triumphant. "Lemme see that light." He flipped quickly through the first few pages before turning the book to her. "There," he pointed, "read that."

Ellie took the book and the light and read aloud,

The town of Riverview was founded along the Alafia River, the origins of which can be traced back to local native populations. The name Alafia means...

She stopped and looked at Barry.

"River of Fire," they said in unison.

Ellie smiled, "But you don't think – "

"I don't know what I think" Barry interrupted, "not exactly. But I told you something isn't adding up; it's not making sense. It's just not possible that this kind of...violence and uncertainty is happening here. Not without some kind of reason."

"Ok. So what are you suggesting?"

"I think you know, but I'll say it since you won't. Remember Juan what's-his-name's instructions?"

"River of Fire, something about a cave and – "

"An oaken cave."

"So what is that?"

"What do you think?"

"What? Some sort of *cave of oak trees?*" she emphasized, shining the light beneath her face for added dramatic effect. But no sooner had the words left her mouth than a different sort of light went on, this one between her ears. "A cave of oaks..." she repeated, "where the sapphire meets..."

"The springs," Barry said. "Right around the bend from our pasture. You can see it in your head. That crystal blue water running out to meet the river of fire, and all those old bay oaks standing guard over the entrance. That spring runs right through the wildlife refuge."

"No way," Ellie searched his eyes. "But the article said something about the sapphire meeting the pearls."

"That's right," Barry said.

"I can buy the springs as the sapphire, but the pearls?"

"Black pearls, El. As dark as the Alafia itself."

Ellie's eyes betrayed her reluctance.

"Look, I'm not saying I believe there's pirate treasure up there," Barry said, "but I think it's possible that someone else might. And if so, what would they be willing to do about it?"

Chapter 46

THERE are towns and villages and cities where the streets come alive after sunset. Foot traffic increases with an energy greater even than high noon. Shoppers and walkers and loud talkers. Restaurants hum with the buzz of life, street performers vie for attention and contribution, and bars and clubs begin to fill up with those looking to extend the party into the far reaches of the night.

But those scenes are a very long way from Gibsonton, Florida. The sun itself is the high king of what little commerce actually exists, seemingly powering everything and everyone with its solar energy. Thus, when it disappears every night, so do all expectations and pursuit of any kind of well-meaning human activity. The old generation of war vets had a saying that nothing of any value goes on under the moon, at least outside of your own personal residence. They were wrong, according to the Baby Boomers. Yet on this night, the exact kind of activity their parents railed against was going on right underneath their noses.

A single lamp burned in an abandoned cinder block gas station, two blocks off of U.S. 41, which may as well have been two miles away from any kind of potential traffic. Two figures filled the room: one with his urgency and anger, the other with his sheer size; he was enormous.

"This has gone sideways, again, and this time we're in danger of losing it altogether. I hire you for the one goddamn purpose you could possibly provide to this earth, and you wreck it so badly that it may very well be irreparable!"

"I told you," mumbled the large man, "it wasn't me. I was there, but it wasn't me." He sat on a chair that labored under his load, and he was still taller than the angry man.

"Oh spare me the bullshit. If you're gonna stick to that story then – "

"I know what I saw. What I heard. I ain't afraid of you or any man," his voice trailed off. "This was something else."

"Are you out of your mind? You expect me to believe that you stumbled upon the real thing?"

"I never said I know what it was. I know what it wasn't. It wasn't me, and it wasn't another man."

"For Christ's sake. I oughta cut you loose now."

"Then do it, little man!" The Giant stood now, as quickly as the large trunk of his body would allow. "I got nothing to lose. Besides, you ever stop to consider whatever happened to those two other fellas you sent into the refuge? The ones we never found?"

The little man chuckled without missing a beat, malice in his tone. "You? Nothing to lose? Your memory fails you. You and I are forever linked, for better or worse. Trust me, there's a very clear trail of crumbs leading from me directly to you. I've made damn sure of that." He took a few steps closer to the Giant. "And I ain't worried about those other two clowns. Probably gator bait for all I care," he snarled. "So whatever else may be stumbling around in that massive skull of yours, just know that it's not possible for me to go down without your oversized ass right behind me."

The Giant's brow softened, the corners of his eyes hung heavy.

"We finish this, you and me." The little man stormed out.

The Giant slumped back down in his chair. He sat there for a long time. Finally, he rose and walked slowly around the corner into the main open floor of the station. It was dark, and cold. He double-checked the doors, then walked behind what used to be the register counter, and lay down to sleep.

PART IV

The Giant

Chapter 47

New Jersey, 1922

SCHOOLYARDS are intended to elicit joy and fun through activity and social engagement. But the Darwinian brain of human nature will always resort to survival when it feels threatened. Factor in the reality that children and adolescents are extremely prone to the momentum of tribal leadership, and you have the foundation of understanding every kid's nightmare: standing out. Al Templeton stood out, literally. Before the age of eleven he was over six feet tall, and in the suburbs of New Jersey in the early 1920s, that was freakish. Unfortunately for Al, influence isn't always measured in inches, especially amongst those in his elementary class. The bullies hated him, jealous of his uniqueness and threatened by his potential. They invented and propagated every manner of lie and explanation for his stature. In truth, Al's height was virtually useless at that age. He was too big to engage in any playground device, and far too uncoordinated to be chosen as an asset for any game. Worse still, he found no refuge in his own family, at least regarding his appearance. Al had four brothers and three sisters, and the height difference between himself and the other seven could be measured in feet, not inches. Al seemed destined, or doomed, to stand alone and above the world.

And the growing didn't stop. By the time he was fifteen he had eclipsed seven feet, a stature almost unheard of at any age. Everything he wore had to be custom made, which meant two things: an added financial burden on his family, and very little variety. Finally, his parents found a specialist through a family friend who determined that their son suffered from an overactive pituitary gland. From his experience, the physician warned that continued growth presented significant health concerns, specifically regarding blood flow throughout the pathways of his enormous frame. By that time, the prospect of death felt like a welcome relief from a life of incessant chiding and gawking.

But that doctor's visit proved to be a watershed moment for the young teenager's life. Al woke the next morning and informed his parents that he wouldn't be returning to school. If he were going to grow his way into a coffin (custom made, at that), then he sure as hell wasn't going to spend another moment around the morons at school, for his sake and theirs. His folks were indignant at first, but only for a moment before they realized that they certainly couldn't make him. When asked what he would do, Al replied with the only thing he could imagine. He'd seen a flyer on a bulletin board for the circus, which prominently featured a living half-woman (she had no legs, after all), and a variety of other characters. "The World Famous Sideshow," they were called. A boy in his class earned a good laugh from the hallway when he dubbed them "The Freakshow." Al realized then and there that this may very well be the only home on this lonely earth for him. What others saw as freaks, he saw as comrades.

Al Templeton looked down upon his mother and father; he conjured all the confidence in his giant person and told them he intended to join the circus.

Chapter 48

Gibsonton, 1950s

AL Templeton stared at his hands, strangely aware of their size in the fading sunlight. He'd shaken countless others in his days. Despite his start in life, he had good reason now to believe that he'd gotten the better end of the giant sentence. He was grateful. Still, his hands were no match for the Florida mosquito. He smiled, taking a rare moment to pause and reflect. He'd gone to the circus that afternoon so many years ago and never looked back. Al learned a valuable lesson that became a mantra he repeated often: *no one's going to build the life you want for you.* He met that half-woman in the sideshow and married her, much to the approval of the circus manager. For all of her thirty inches in height, Jenni Bromfield was like a beacon of hope and joy for Al, something he'd never known or experienced before. Shortly after their marriage, the two were branded as

"The World's Strangest Married Couple," and they embraced it, turning their eyes to comedic moments throughout the act.

The circus was everything Al had ever hoped for, and more. What was once the source of ridicule became the bedrock for celebrity on the stage. Jenni and Al virtually transcended the main event and certainly the rest of the sideshow. However, they were always careful to spread the limelight wide enough to encompass the entire cast, an act that endeared their fellow sojourners to the couple, and essentially galvanized the misfits into something of a family. Thus, when the Templetons built a home in a small, unknown town outside of the Barnum & Bailey headquarters of Sarasota, many of their co-workers in the human entertainment industry followed suit. It wasn't long, then, that the town of Gibsonton took on a life of its own with their strange new residents.

Al led the way toward not only acceptance, but integration within the daily life of the town. Most folks were surprised, in fact, to discover that his heart was every bit as big as his frame. Since coming off the road, he found a new purpose as the town's fire chief and president of the Chamber of Commerce. He volunteered countless hours at the children's hospital in Tampa, dusting off his stage uniform several times a year, much to the pleasure of the staff and patients.

It was Jenni, though, who had the eye for branding. She saw the potential for everyone to capitalize on their community, to bring the paying customers to them, in a fashion. The Templetons built a restaurant and a fishing camp, both erected along the slow, quiet stretches of transportation between U.S. 41 and the Alafia. Still, despite their efforts, the novelty of what they envisioned for Gibsonton could never really outweigh the hushed legends and sideways glances. Teenagers from nearby towns rolled through at night on the whims of a dare, and pressure was placed on school boards to isolate their once-overlapping districts. Jenni was disappointed, but none of it even came close to what Al had lived through in his previous life.

He stood on the dock of his fishing camp now and watched the shrimp begin to rise to the warmth of the searchlight. Soon, large snook would begin to lurk just beneath the shadows, taking turns inhaling mouthfuls of the little crustaceans. Maybe he'd fish tonight, despite the mosquitos. He turned and loped back toward the camp where their cabin home was built. Suddenly, he remembered that it was Saturday. He should stop in the restaurant tonight and make an appearance.

Chapter 49

GIVEN the nature and degree of their physical differences, Al and Jenni Templeton weren't able to have children of their own. However, that didn't stop them from adopting and creating a family. As a father, Al found that being a child of a giant was far more advantageous than his own experience at their age. He and Jenni were doting parents, and their children grew to acquire a perspective of the world far beyond their years. Jenni took the lead on managing their business ventures, and Al did his best to pack little lunches and track their school progress in between public appearances of various sorts. His passing, then, in 1965, was sorely felt throughout the community; he was beloved by both family and neighbor. Just over fifty years of age, he'd long ago outlived the prognosis of his condition. At the time of his death he was measured at eight feet, six and a half inches tall.

There was a huge parade through town, and Barnum & Bailey issued its own glowing remembrance. A proposition to erect one of his massive performing boots onto a platform in front of the fishing camp was warmly accepted. The small, rather insignificant town of Gibsonton mourned and honored the loss of *their* giant.

Then life does what it always does, and it got on with itself. The restaurant closed within a few years, unable to attract customers who didn't have a chance to see the legend in the flesh. Jenni wouldn't allow it to be torn down or renovated, however, so it sat there much like herself: an aging monument to what was once so full of life. The fishing camp limped along, capitalizing on more dependable traffic and far less overhead. Finally, Jenni herself passed away toward the close of the sixties. The town celebrated her memory in kind, though her presence had long been gone. And once again, time moved on, with the younger generation telling their own children stories of The World's Strangest Married Couple.

Gibsonton, 1978

WITH the stories and legends circulating in her small town, it wasn't altogether surprising when Bridgette Marigold dumped her bike excitedly in the garage and went running inside to tell her mother she'd just seen the Gibtown Giant.

"Oh you did, huh?" her mother was accustomed to going along with her imagination.

"No, Ma', I really *really* saw him!"

"Has your father been spinnin' those yarns again?"

"No, why? Ma' I saw him, I saw the Gibtown Giant. He's alive!"

"Honey, Mr. Templeton went to be with Jesus a long time ago. We told you that."

"Well, Jesus must've sent him back."

"Bridgette," her mother looked up from the pot on the stove, "let's not say those things."

"Ma'?"

"Yes?"

"Do you think Jesus sends people back because they did something bad up there?"

Mrs. Marigold stopped stirring and set the spoon down with a degree of finality. "Bridgette, that's quite enough of this. Why on earth would you ask such a thing?"

"Ma' he had blood all over his shirt."

PART V

Legend

Chapter 50

DAWN came with a rare bite of winter sting. Joe Grayson walked back to the truck to get his second flannel; the activity of pitching hay alone wasn't enough to warm his core. He thought of the Goodson family down at their strawberry farm; he knew they'd be scrambling this morning to keep their future harvest from ruin. He pulled the bench seat forward and rummaged around for a spell, certain he'd tossed a shirt back there a few days ago. Despite the urgency of his search, and the growing frustration at the prospect of staying cold, he felt the indescribable presence of someone in the vicinity other than himself. In a split second, he gave up on the shirt and grabbed the large flashlight from the floorboard as he whirled out of the cab in a single motion.

"Whoa, Jesus!" Barry said, holding up his hands, one of which featured the extra flannel. "Thought you might want this."

Joe exhaled, a trail of breath showing his frustration. "What the hell are you doing out here? Aren't you supposed to be lawyering or something? Anyway what time did you get in last night?"

"Hey, thanks, son, I was freezing my ass off out here," Barry mocked, in a gruff impression of his father.

Joe sighed. "Sorry. Thank you," he said, snatching the shirt out of Barry's hand.

"You're welcome, old timer."

The father feigned a punch; his son didn't flinch.

"One of these days…"

"Yeah, I know, you won't stop."

Joe buttoned the second shirt all the way up. "You come all the way out here to finish my sentences?"

"I came out here to think. And to ask you a few things."

"Too early and cold for either of those."

Barry was already climbing up to the loft. "Since you asked, I got in late. But I could hardly sleep anyway."

"Doesn't your trial start today?"

"Yep," he called from the back of the loft.

"So I ask again: What the hell are you doing out here?"

Barry reappeared from the loft with a pitchfork full of hay. He tossed it into the bed of the pickup and said,

"How much do you really know about that refuge across the river?"

Joe looked stunned. "And here I thought we were gonna talk about birds and bees?"

"What?" Barry stopped working at the pile of hay.

"Don't think I haven't noticed you and Ellie McGregor hanging around."

Barry decided to be the aggressor and turn the tables. "Wanna know what we did last night?" It worked.

"No, I do not. But – "

Barry threw another load into the truck and leaned against the fork. "Then what can you tell me about that tract of land over there?"

"Well, not much," Joe pondered.

"Who owns it? Who can I talk to about it?"

"I'm not completely sure. I think – listen, what's that got to do with anything?"

"Maybe everything. Maybe."

"How's that?"

"I can't say just yet," Barry said, returning to the task at hand, "but I suspect that somebody thinks there's something valuable over there."

"Valuable? In that *swamp?* You mean beyond what you and I have experienced?"

"I'm not certain yet how that fits in, but it'll come. So who owns it?"

"I told you I can't remember. There are signs posted around, sparsely. Seems I can remember it being a company with a short name, like Bow or Bell or something. Maybe a phosphate company, now that I think about it."

Barry heard Joe's attempts and kept heaving hay out of the loft. Neither of those sounded familiar, and they may not even be accurate. He was going to have to go over there himself. But that would have to wait until after – he stopped suddenly, mid-thought, as though his pitchfork had struck a buried chest. Maybe it had.

"Tell me those suggestions again? What you thought the name of the company was?"

"I told you I'm not sure, but I think it's something like Bow or Bell."

"Bell," Barry interrupted. "Do you remember how it's spelled?"

"For God's sake what does it matter?"

Barry jumped down out of the loft and took off toward the river. "It matters," he whispered to himself.

***

BARRY rounded the corner of the barn in such pursuit that he nearly ran through Ellie. He scooped her up to prevent falling on top of her and spun her against the side of the barn. "For God's sake," he heaved, nearly breathless from the sprint and the shock, "do you just wait out here for me to come running out to scare the hell outta me?"

"I work here!" she scolded, making no effort to escape his embrace. "What's going on? Wait, shouldn't you be getting ready for this afternoon?"

"I am," he smiled. "C'mon." He dashed away toward the house and called over his shoulder, "Meet me over by the canoe!"

Barry was out of the house again and racing toward the canoe only moments after Ellie arrived, who seemed perturbed to be out of the loop of whatever was going on inside his head.

"What's this all about, Barry?"

"You'll see. Literally. If I'm right. I don't wanna say anything just yet." He slipped the canoe into the liquid glass of the Alafia, fog resting quietly just above the surface of the water in the early dawn. Despite the urgency, the scene before him caught his sudden attention like a sucker punch. He rose slowly from kneeling on the bank and looked across the river, focusing on nothing in particular. These waters had outlived a million men, and they would whisper silently on long after him. No doubt they held many secrets in the darkness beneath their mirror. But Barry Grayson intended to leverage at least one of them from their grasp.

Strangely, though, he didn't sense resistance; rather, a subtle collaboration, as if the river itself knew it was time to draw back the curtain.

"Barry?" Ellie interrupted.

"Yeah, sorry. Here, let me see those paddles." He laid them gently into the canoe and helped Ellie in. She didn't need to take his hand, but she wasn't going to miss an opportunity.

They paddled slightly east up the river and pulled the canoe around a small lip that jutted out, thus concealing the vessel.

"Can I ask again what we're looking for?"

"A posted sign for whoever owns this."

"What for?"

"You'll see. I think."

Barry took her hand again and led her through the thick growth, brushing aside rows of proud palmettos and lazy Spanish moss. Finally, they emerged on the service pathway. It was too overgrown to be considered a "road," but a four-wheeler would be able to pass with ease. Barry pulled out a flashlight; whatever early rays of sunlight had pierced through the horizon were no match for the canopy overhead. Together they walked down the center of the pathway for the better part of an hour. Barry hadn't let go of her hand, and she was glad.

A crow broke the silence; it was hard to tell if the creature was welcoming or cursing the arrival of daybreak. Barry swept the beam steadily from side to side, suddenly remembering that he had not thought to bring a weapon. His eyes worked even harder to find the reflective gleam of rectangular metal composite.

Finally, he caught a familiar flash maybe thirty yards ahead, nailed into a forgotten oak. They walked quickly toward it, without speaking. The sign was nearly covered in the muddy residue that seemed to fall with the rain in such environments. Barry wiped it clear with his large, flat palm, his heart racing.

The laughter of stress giving way to joy was already emerging from his mouth when the distant snap of splintered wood cut it short. Barry and Ellie instinctively spun around. It was still far too dark to see, and Barry knew the sound had come from much farther beyond the reaches of his light.

"Probably a 'possum, or an armadillo?" Ellie asked, unable to fake any confidence in her suggestions.

Barry didn't answer. "Here, look at this," he said, turning back to the sign.

Ellie read the words aloud. *"Posted. Private Property. Trespassers will be prosecuted. Bel, Inc."*

"What about it?" she asked.

"Look at how it's – " this time they spun to their right. Another snap, though this sound resembled more of a smash. It was closer too, easily within one hundred yards. That was disconcerting enough, but what followed was altogether shattering. A second sound erupted from the darkness, this one in the direction of the first they had heard, and in a manner that felt like their position was being triangulated.

"Let's go. Now!" Barry grabbed her hand and sprinted hard, his long athletic strides forcing her to run nearly to the brink of her own ability. Trees and brush passed in a blur, their legs were soaked from sweat and dew. He practically threw her down the slope to the canoe; she had only a moment to sit down before she felt her body thrust backward by the sudden surge of the launch. Barry was splashing up to his knees before he climbed in, and for a split second she thought both of them would end up swimming across.

The momentum from that final push carried them out into the middle of the river, which may as well have been the middle of the stratosphere. Fog wafted across the surface like the homegoing of raptured souls; the river itself stood as if it were on strike from the moon's demands, unwilling to move in either direction. In the silence that engulfed them, Ellie started laughing. First at a chuckle, then a full on fit, doubled over and clinging to the side of the canoe for support.

"What are we, teenagers again?" she could barely speak.

Barry sat heaving from his efforts, and then started laughing at Ellie's own hysteria. "God," he said, "I guess I needed that."

The moment was fleeting, however, as the gravity of their reality soon set in. Barry had a pre-trial hearing that afternoon and Ellie's brother was suffering God-knows-what in prison. But before dismay snuffed out all hope, Ellie leaned over and kissed Barry, gently at first, as an expression of thanks, then firmly as something more. Barry returned the intent.

"I'm sorry," she said.

"For what?"

"For everything. For all that piece of property over there has done to your life, and mine."

"It doesn't seem so bad right now, or at least without reward."

She smiled, thankfulness and weariness mixed in her eyes.

Barry's eyes widened suddenly.

"What?" she asked.

He reached behind his back and sighed with relief as he pulled a small book from under his shirt.

"This," he said. "This is why we came over here."

"You took that from the library?"

"You're not gonna tell on me, are you?" he smiled. Barry flipped through a few pages, then turned the book to face her as he passed it over. "Here, read this."

Ellie took it reluctantly. "I have no idea what we're chasing here, or what's chasing us, but this had better shed some light on it."

"You'll see."

Ellie found her place at the top of the page and began reading:

Despite the lack of overt historical documentation regarding the personal life and times of Jose Gaspar, there are several examples of local Florida lore that still bear the marks of his legend. For example, strong anecdotal evidence suggests that a crewmember close to Gaspar was allowed to take a captive for his wife, an action that was uncommon for most pirate outfits, though not for Gaspar's. A local elderly fishing guide by the name of Juan Gomez claimed to be that man. Near the turn of the twentieth century, Gomez was known to have told many journalists that on one occasion he rescued Gaspar from a close encounter with a shark. To express his thanks, the pirate captain permitted Gomez to name one of the many intercoastal islands that served as their operational outposts. He chose one in particular, and named it Sandybelle, after his first wife, Bel. The island exists to this day, ironically as a popular tourist destination, with the name only slightly modified to Sanibel.

Barry paddled slowly while Ellie read.

"Bel," she said. "That's what this is all about?"

"That's why we came over here, anyway. And it doesn't feel like a coincidence."

"C'mon, Barry."

"Gimme something that makes any more sense, El," he protested. "We've been over this, right? I haven't connected all the dots, but something's going on over in that God-forsaken jungle and it's too much to chalk up to some kind of monster."

"But we *can* chalk it up to pirate lore?" Ellie protested.

"I didn't say I believed it."

"So you think this *Bel, Inc* is involved?"

"No idea," Barry shook his head, "but what lengths do you think someone would go to if they thought *Bel* was a connection to some pirate payload buried over there? I'm betting the kind of fool who would buy into that would be willing to kill for it."

Ellie was silent for a long moment, the sound of the paddle pushing the water eclipsed only by the cry of a hungry kingfisher. Her eyes rose from the floor of the canoe and looked directly into his.

"What?" Barry asked.

"I guess I never thought of it that way."

"Thought of what?"

"That *someone* in this town has taken from both of our families."

Barry stopped paddling.

"Life hurts a lot more when it's gutted of the mystery."

Her eyes were heavy and sad, as though an innocence had just been dumped over the side of the canoe.

"I'm sorry," he said. "What were you hoping for?"

"I don't know," her voice trailed. "Maybe it felt easier to believe that something was to blame."

The nose of the canoe nudged gently against the bank. The sun's rays had finally broken through the clutches of twilight. Ellie got out carefully and pulled the craft up to where the riverbank transitioned to meet the pasture grass. Barry lifted it easily over his head and returned it to the racks Joe had built.

"There is no 'something else,' Ellie. Never was. We're all a lot more alone in this world than we ever wanted to believe. *Someone* did this, and I'm gonna find out who. I've got another hunch to check out, but I'll see you this afternoon." He turned and walked toward the house.

Chapter 51

A TIRED truck pulled quietly into an auto shop off U.S. 301, immediately turning out their lights upon entering. Several minutes later, a second followed suit. The driver of the second truck walked into the management office, where the first driver was pacing quickly, vainly attempting to corral energy despite the early morning hour.

"This isn't going to work, Tom."

"It will and it is, but not so long as you're strung up tight as a rodeo bronc."

Ritchie McGregor stopped and looked at his brother. "What do you think this is? We're going to a real courtroom today, Tom. With a real judge. My son's real dead and yours is on trial! And don't forget about those other two goons who disappeared in that swamp."

Tom took a step closer to his brother, and spoke quietly, but not without power. "What do I think this is?

I think it's called doing whatever it takes. I think it's called seeing the long play. Someday you're gonna be sixty-five, brother. Do you wanna still be turning wrenches in this hell-hole or living on a private island where the tide is cleaner than a swimming pool?"

Richie slumped.

"What we do now matters tomorrow. What we do today creates our tomorrow. And ours is gonna be a helluva lot brighter and richer than everyone else's."

Chapter 52

15 DECEMBER, 1821. I am alone; all is lost. The Spanish standard burns on the mainmast; captain and crew have fallen beneath American steel and cannon. Plumes from the Floriblanca are visible even from our distance; the gulf runs red along with its green, as does the river of fire. Our secret dispatch has been torn asunder; the foul fruits of greed have awoken an ancient evil that prowls this tropic of death. I alone have escaped, but I suspect even now that my days are few. I am dismayed at the weight of all my sins. May God have mercy on my soul, in this life, and most especially in the next, for I believe that I shall pass into it soon.

The librarian gently laid the protective covering back onto the yellow, wrinkled parchment.

"And that's it?" Barry asked again.

"That's it, unfortunately."

"No idea who wrote it?"

"None," she shook her head. "But you're looking at virtually the only *historical evidence* (she made air quotations with her hands), supporting the actual existence of Jose Gaspar and the whereabouts of his treasure."

"What about the alleged confrontation with the United States Navy? There's gotta be something on record."

"One would think, but not to our knowledge; and we've submitted numerous requests to Washington."

Barry leaned off the table and stood erect, folding his arms across his large chest. A dead end, maybe. But not yet. The University of Tampa boasted a vast and varied collection.

"What about the evil he speaks of here? What's that referring to?"

"Ah, I'm glad you asked. For a long time we knew nothing about that. As you know, our Sunshine State is full of all kinds of critters that might qualify as evil," she laughed, "especially for someone without shelter or what we enjoy about our modern comforts."

Barry rolled his eyes in agreement. Florida could kill you through a different means every day of the year and still not scratch the surface of its armory.

"But not long ago we received a document – in a rather mysterious manner I might add – that might shed some light onto this passage. It took some time to authenticate, but we do believe that it's at least as old as it claims to be; I can't say the same for the subject matter, of course."

"Does it address Gaspar?"

"No, not at all. The origins are Native American, not Spanish."

"Whoa, what's it say?"

She chuckled again. "I think I'd be better off letting you read it."

The librarian led Barry across the room. It was large, for a historical archive, and appropriately lit to preserve the fragile documents. The corner farthest from their entrance held a small door tucked a few inches back into the wall. A single word stood at eye level: Staff. She fumbled through a pile of keys. "I know this is the one because I was just in here." She was right. The door opened the way Barry rolled out of bed these days, with pain and effort. "Oddly enough someone was just here recently looking at this piece." Before he could think of a way to craft a question about that person's identity, she was once again carefully removing a protective covering. She handed him a magnifying glass. "Here ya' go."

Barry placed the glass over the page and allowed a few moments for his eyes to adjust, not only to the light, but to the nuance of the writing and language.

My sons, you must know this now, and you must be vigilant to do even as I do in passing this knowledge on to the arrows in your own quivers. What I speak of is the ancient Guardian over the Earth. The winter moon rules over the song of the chickadee, and so the Tall Song moves over the land; a darkness like war paint against those who would bring it harm.

"Oh my God," Barry whispered, momentarily dropping the glass.

"Excuse me?" the librarian asked.

"Oh nothing, sorry." He continued.

You must be wary to never give cause to the Tall Song; its wrath knows no bounds. You will know the possessed by the darkness in their eyes, and they must serve the Song for as many cycles required. Their purpose is worthy and not without honor, but the chosen will carry the weight of their actions. I received these words from my father, and I pass them now to my sons.

I have seen the Tall Song only once in my lifetime, like a tree that rages in the fury of the hurricane, with the talons of an eagle and the strength and span of two bears. It roams the earth, taking possession of a willing warrior, like a hungry, vengeful guardian.

Barry read it all again, then he stood and sighed and handed the glass back to the librarian. "Any ideas what it means?"

"I didn't have any myself, no. But part of our authentication process was to bring this before several people of influence within this community."

"And?"

"And we noticed two things. First, they all individually affirmed the same interpretation, from here to Tallahassee. Second, they were all very hesitant to do so, like they themselves were guarding some sacred knowledge."

"What's the general interpretation?"

"Well, basically that this ancient spirit's role is to protect the land, or the people on it – from what we don't know – and it does this by taking possession of a man and transforming him into some kind of huge, terrifying...creature."

"Creature?"

"That's what it seems like," she chuckled. "All of our sources affirmed the general description in this artifact: sharp claws or talons, the dimensions of a giant bear. Sounds crazy, I know," she said, replacing the protective covering onto the document.

Barry stood with wrinkled brow for a long moment. "You alluded to a story behind how you came to receive this in the first place."

"Oh, yes, that is interesting. Not so much how we received it, but what was written on the package. We don't know who sent it, but the inscription on the package was of particular interest." She sifted through a pile of papers on the table and brought out a standard brown folded paper, carefully laying it flat on the table so that Barry could see what looked like a word or short phrase in an unknown language.

"What is it?"

"Turns out it's Cherokee, from what all of our sources identified."

"What's it mean?"

"That's the most interesting piece. The closest interpretation is, 'Forgive me.'"

Chapter 53

THE Riverview Courthouse stood like a monument to the hands that built it: steady, stable, absent of anything but necessity. Pale brown and yellow brick rose up from the greedy ground, their utilitarian colors fading further by the day in the virtually endless Florida summer. Barry had been here before during various intern projects for research. It didn't impress him then, and it certainly didn't now. Today was no project, though; today was the beginning of a pass or fail: either he would lay the groundwork for a man's freedom, or that freedom would already begin to slip through the cracks of a fragile opening statement.

Barry arrived early and parked in the back. He wasn't nervous, but he still couldn't quite appreciate the information coming through his windshield. A criminal trial was about to begin, and he was the defense attorney for the town simpleton. Four months ago he was gainfully employed in a prestigious law firm, raising drinks to the Yankees as they marched on to the postseason. He chuckled at the irony of feeling out of place in his hometown.

But the silent vow never to return had haunted him for years, and in his more honest moments, he couldn't say he was surprised to be back. The same couldn't be said, however, for what he was about to do. This was madness. *What the hell am I doing?* he asked as he climbed out.

He took a moment to inspect his reflection in the driver side window. Not bad, surprisingly. The mustache and stubble were gone, and he could make out more of a jaw and chin line than he could recall. Maybe that explained why his shirt collar was loose, even with a tie. Still, even his hair looked thicker. *Now you're reaching,* he laughed. Barry inhaled deeply, adjusted his tie once more, and grabbed his briefcase from the passenger seat; he wanted to be waiting inside when Lonnie arrived.

Only family and those with special permissions were allowed into this early stage of the trial. Barry opened the tall pine doors to what he generally expected to find: a family divided. Ellie and Maryl sat on the left side of the aisle, with a small collection of distant family supporters; Richie sat alone at the front on the opposite side with the prosecutor. The two were speaking in hushed tones and looking sideways at him.

Barry walked the length of the room, through the swivel saloon doors, and took his place at a designated desk on the left. He looked back once at Ellie while he was rifling through his notes; her eyes were longing for answers, for hope. The back doors opened once again before he could give her any kind of response. Three men were walking toward the front, two of them together, and one further back. Blake Martin was carefully leading Lonnie McGregor, with a posture and expression that resembled more of a therapist than an officer of the law: firm, yet not without a deep empathy. Barry was expecting them; they all were. But one glimpse of the third man, who evidently caught the door before it closed behind them, instantaneously sent everything in Barry's collected mind straight into the chute of a stump grinder. It was the stranger he'd met at the giant boot in Gibsonton, and he was sliding into the pew next to Maryl McGregor.

***

BARRY Grayson knew that whatever confidence he had managed to summon was now firmly collapsed around him; he could see the concern in Ellie's eyes, and the momentary question in those of the sheriff as he handed off the defendant to the bailiff. Far more telling, however, was the fact that when Barry caught eyes with the stranger, the man withheld even the slightest indication of any knowledge of their prior meeting. Barry peeled away and had to remind himself to at least acknowledge his own client. Lonnie did look better, compared to their last visit, but his eyes were wide and hollow with the awful elixir of fear and lack of sleep. Barry snapped out of the shock and clasped Lonnie on the shoulder.

"You ok?"

"Yessir. Yessir, I'm ok."

Lonnie seated himself and picked at a corner of the table. The gravity that had escaped him in the last few seconds came rushing back to Barry. There are people who have, and there are those who don't, and even more who won't ever. Whatever else may happen to his marooned career, and whatever else Lonnie was going to do with his life, Barry was going to get this young man out of this predicament.

The judge entered from his chambers and took his seat on the bench; members of the jury straightened in their chairs. *No backing out now,* he thought.

Chapter 54

1940

THE boy "celebrated" his birthday with a new pair of slacks; they were hand-sewn and two-toned, just like the new pair he'd been given only a few months ago that no longer fit. His mother would purchase old slacks at the Five and Dime and then sew denim fabric onto the legs to add length. This time she added enough so as not to be bothered by the task for several months; the boy had to double cuff the bottoms just to keep them from covering his boots. He was already over six feet tall.

When most kids his age were still enjoying the naiveté of their youth, his was an existence of profound awareness, and an equal measure of pain. The boy knew that he was anything but normal, and worse, that he would never be so.

Every day felt like a being that was trapped between life and death, the loneliness of a phantasm cursed with the reality of flesh. He couldn't hide. He longed for isolation despite a constant sense of already being isolated.

By the time the young man entered his teenage years, he was seven feet tall, and the lonely eyes that watched his boyhood from afar were now filled with a resentment and anger that hardened like sunbaked cement. Theories of his condition were in no short supply, and his mother offered no relief.

But he would never forget the day that shaped the rest of his life, the day he found both answer and purpose, the day he almost killed a teacher.

Mr. Fitsomes' class began that morning like any other, with his subversive, arrogant demeanor cleanly undercutting any student who happened to feel even mildly happy or optimistic about life. Even now after all these years, the young man couldn't recall a day in his life in which he'd ever experienced either of those emotions, which meant that he was low-hanging fruit for the likes of Mr. Fitsomes. He was bound to snap some day, and maybe that's what the old bastard had in mind all along. The watershed moment finally happened, the moment he was pushed too far, the moment that the breaking of bones felt like finally breaking out. He wasn't sure if Mr. Fitsomes would ever walk again, and he didn't care.

What he did know, however, and what helped to fuel his flight as he ran out of the schoolhouse for the last time, was that he wasn't alone. Mr. Fitsomes had produced a flyer for a travelling circus featuring "The Tallest Man On Earth," which then led to the remarks that triggered the burst of rage.

Perhaps Mr. Fitsomes suspected the flame that would light from his sparks, though surely he couldn't have guessed the inferno that would engulf and ruin him. But what he had inadvertently lit was something the young man had never known in all his troubled years: purpose. The teenage giant was committed now to finding this fellow freak. He didn't know it that afternoon, of course, but he would spend the next ten years of his life looking for who he'd come to believe must be his real biological father.

His search and toil led him through all manner of odd jobs along the eastern seaboard and into the Deep South, eventually dumping him in Gibsonton, alone and nearly soulless. He was furious, then, to find the man he'd been chasing for so long to be deceased.

Still, a hollow vessel is nothing if not receptive, and the short man he met at the bar had a tall tale and a silver tongue. More importantly, he showed an apparent appreciation for the visitor's unique, natural talents, as well as a promise of untold riches in exchange for the use of them.

Chapter 55

THE judge rapped his gavel as a formality, signaling the completion of this first stage. He stated the upcoming recess along with the next appointed time for the hearings to begin, then disappeared through a back door. Barry stood and buttoned his suit, and helped Lonnie out of his chair. As Sheriff Martin was making his way forward, Barry leaned in close and whispered, "On my own life, I will get you out of this."

Lonnie looked well past the depth of Barry's eyes and held his attention for a moment. "You gotta talk to the Chief, Mister. He knows."

"Wait, who is – "

Blake Martin was already leading Lonnie away, but not before the stranger beat them to the door and rushed out.

Barry gathered his notes, shoved them into his case, and approached Ellie and her mother.

"We need to talk, immediately," he whispered. "I'm parked in the back."

His tie was hanging loosely around his neck by the time the two McGregor women reached his car.

"Barry, you were great in there," Maryl began. "We can't thank you enough."

"Who was that sitting next to you?"

She looked at Ellie in confusion. "You mean Tom? My husband?" she emphasized with disgust.

"What's going on, Barry?" Ellie asked.

"Believe me, that's what I'm trying to figure out. I was down in Gibsonton a few days ago, just poking around. I walked up to that giant boot, the one right off U.S. 41 on that platform. Suddenly I'm being questioned by a man who gave me a funny look, but he wouldn't share his name."

"I'm not following you," Maryl said.

"That man was your husband."

"Tom? That's impossible. He only got home from his trucker route yesterday, just in time for the trial."

"Trucker route?" Barry asked.

"Tom drives long haul routes; he's gone for weeks at a time."

"Let me tell you two things," Barry said. "First, Tom McGregor was in Gibsonton three days ago. No question about it. Second, I got the distinct feeling that he was there on business, and whatever it was, it had nothing to do with trucks."

"I don't understand," said Ellie. "That doesn't make any sense."

"At least not yet," said Barry.

"What's that mean?" Maryl asked with a suspicious look in her eyes.

"I'm working on it," he replied, "but I've got something more immediate that I need your help with."

"Anything."

"Just before we left in there, Lonnie told me that I needed to talk to the 'Chief,' that this person would apparently be a help to our cause."

"God," Maryl mumbled. "He's been calling him that since his first Scout campout."

"Who?"

"Raymond Muskee. He works in the diner."

"Why would Lonnie send me to meet him?"

Maryl rolled her wheels back a few inches and began to scoot slowly toward her car. "I'll do you a favor and let the man speak for himself."

Chapter 56

"WE got a problem!" the little man shouted into the abandoned gas station. Even at midday the space had a soul-sucking presence, not that it was noticed by either man. Tom McGregor kicked empty bottles against rotting walls on his way through the back entrance.

"Get up, you sonofabitch." He rounded a corner and ran straight into the navel of his accomplice.

"Jesus!"

"Why you shouting, little man?"

"Plans just changed. We've got to accelerate; no more long game."

"What happened?"

"I caught someone snooping around here earlier this week, someone outta town looking at that damned boot. More than a tourist; someone up to something. I could smell it on him."

"And?"

"And turns out I saw him again today at Lonnie's trial. He's the goddamn defense attorney. His jaw about hit the floor when I walked in."

Tom's partner was never mistaken for a smart man, but even he realized the gravity of the events. "So what do we do?"

Tom lit a Pall Mall and inhaled deeply, forcing smoke out of his mouth and nostrils. "We move," he said.

Chapter 57

BARRY gripped the steering wheel with both hands like he was earning his learner's permit all over again, his fingers connected to the vinyl wrap by sticky perspiration. He was trying to keep a lid on everything racing through his head. He had been no stranger to Hester's Diner in his day, and he'd only met Mr. Muskee a few times through the Scouts, but something about the desperation of Lonnie's plight had driven him to the iconic eatery straight from the trial. Still, he had no idea how he was going to navigate this conversation.

Barry pulled the glass double doors open and was welcomed by the smell of bacon grease and pancake batter. The pale orange seat and bench cushions sat empty, staring back at him like unexpected holiday guests.

"We're closed, honey. Six to two-thirty. Missed us by that much."

Barry looked across the expanse to see an elderly but capable woman thumbing through old ticket orders, grey curls hugging her head in neat rows. "That's ok," he said, "I'm wondering if I can speak with Mr. Muskee."

"You and me both," she said.

"Excuse me?"

"Ray hasn't been to work in three or four days. Can't anyone get 'hold of him."

Barry stood there, his mind working faster than he could keep up.

"Hon?" she asked.

"Sorry," he said, "Can I use your phone?"

***

BARRY made two calls, careful to keep the receiver tight to his ear and his eyes watching his back. The first was to his old wingman, Ben Ford.

"Y'elo," came the familiar welcome. Barry smiled. Somehow Ben was always near a phone.

"Ben, it's me."

"Barry? Listen I don't wanna – "

"You're coming with me."

"Ah, man," he groaned. "Look we had some times, Barry, but things've changed, ya' know?"

"Yeah, like what?"

"Well, man...ya' know."

"Maybe some things have, but what's important hasn't."

"What's that?"

"You think you can sleep with the knowledge of an innocent, handicapped man getting his ass kicked in prison?" The line was silent, then Ben let out a long, resigned sigh.

"Come on over then," he said.

"I'll be there in ten."

Barry hung up. The most important things hadn't changed. Then his face grew serious as he flipped through the phonebook Miss Hester had given him. His next call would be to the University Library.

Chapter 58

RAYMOND Muskee didn't hear the gravel crunching underneath the tires of the truck that pulled onto his one-lane driveway. Partly because the gravel he'd laid down so many years ago had now nearly sunk down into the natural sandy bottom. But he also didn't hear the early alarm due to factors regarding his own exhaustion. The truck pulled confidently into the grass next to his own pickup. However familiar the driver was with the terrain, though, they stepped slowly out of the cab and took a long moment to survey the scene. They closed the door with care and caution, seemingly avoiding detection.

Raymond didn't hear the doorknob turning either, or the hushed sounds a person makes when snooping around.

He only barely heard the scream, and even then struggled to regain consciousness when he was shaken awake.

Chapter 59

THE same librarian Barry met earlier picked up the phone. "University Library, how may I help you?"

"Hi there, this is Barry Grayson, how are you today?"

"Good, thank you Mr. Grayson!"

"We spoke earlier this morning, didn't we? I was looking at old historical documents."

"Yes, that's right, that was me."

"Excellent. Thank you again for your assistance."

"Oh, you're most welcome."

"I was wondering if I could ask one more favor of you."

"Sure, what can we help you with?"

"As I mentioned I'm working as the legal council for a trial held in Riverview, and oddly enough I believe some of the information surrounding those documents may be helpful."

"Yes, of course. Do you need access again?"

"No, not yet, but I'll let you know. I have a small army of paralegals and interns collecting information for me on other aspects of this case; we're trying to maximize our reach and efforts."

"I understand."

"I want to be sure we're not retracing each other's steps here. I do need to head back up there, but not if my assistants have already visited. Could I ask you to check the guest log for me?"

"Sure, who are you looking for?"

"Oh gosh, I hardly even know their last names yet. Could you maybe read me the last several entries?"

"Ok, give me just a second." Barry could hear her holding the phone with her shoulder and shuffling papers. "Normally we wouldn't offer this kind of information, you understand." Her voice was sweet and timid, as though it pained her to say that.

"Yes, of course, and I very much appreciate your help with this matter."

"Ok," she said absently, "let me see. I have a Shaun Roberts, Lacey Birch, John Ackers, Al Templeton, Susan – "

Barry's mind snapped like a hot spark plug. A vision of the gothic boot altar in Gibsonton suddenly forced itself to the forefront of his thoughts. "That's the one," he interrupted.

"Susan?"

"No. It's Al. Poor guy," he fumbled, "I can never remember his name. Thanks so much."

"Happy to help," she chirped.

He replaced the phone behind the counter by the register and stood looking at the clock in front of him.

Back from the dead, he thought.

Chapter 60

BEN Ford was sitting on the corner of the front porch of his trailer, wearing a black ski cap and a dark blue sweatshirt featuring two faded wolves howling at a full moon. The cap looked brand new; the sweatshirt barely fit over his meaty forearms.

"Hey," he said, "got my lucky shirt on."

"And what do you call the beanie?"

Ben looked incredulous. "Well, excuse me, Mr. 'Sunday Best,' but seeing as how I wasn't told a damn thing I figured I'd come prepared."

Barry smiled, and he was grateful for it. "Got one more favor to ask you, buddy."

"You're very near your limit, Malorie."

"Can you drive?" Barry gestured toward the nondescript El Camino.

"You wanna take Bertha, huh?"

"The Jensen sticks out like your mom in church. No offense," he added with a wink.

"Some taken," Ben shrugged. "All right pal, but you're gonna owe me if anything happens to her."

The two climbed in, and Ben winced as the old girl labored to turn over. He backed out of the worn grass lot. "Where to?"

"You remember your nursery rhymes, right?" Barry asked.

"Yeah, like Mother Goose and all that?"

"Sure," Barry said, "let's head south on 301."

"South as in one of them body beaches in Miami?"

"Hardly," Barry said. "We're gonna go climb a beanstalk."

"Jesus Christ…"

***

DANCING Brook wedged a pillow under her brother's head, careful to make sure the damp cloth on his forehead was cool enough.

"I'm ok," he moaned.

"Raymond," she scolded, "you are not ok!" Her voice was frightened and angry, and her eyes and brow worked in unison to fight back the tears.

Her brother saw this, and sighed. "I'm sorry," he said. "I should have told you sooner."

"Tell me now."

Standing Oak held her stern focus for several moments. The ceiling fan hummed quietly above, maintaining a consistent rhythm.

"I've been summoned," he finally offered, watching the fan blades spin.

Dancing Brook flexed her jaw in fortitude. "For how long?" she asked.

Ray shook his head gently. "I can't be certain."

"Onto the refuge?"

"Yes."

The two of them were quiet, Raymond lying on the floor and his sister hovering over him. Finally she leaned back and sat next to him, pulling her legs up to her chest.

"Is it safe?"

Raymond nodded. "For now." He sat up slowly, thwarting her resistance. "But you shouldn't be here tonight."

"I'm not going any–"

"No," he interrupted. "I feel the conclusion is very near."

***

BARRY pointed to a left turn off U.S. 41 just before they entered the main stretch through Gibsonton's downtown. "Let's see if we can patrol parallel to 41."

Ben obliged and turned two blocks east before returning to their original heading. He slowed to a more appropriate cruise through neighborhood streets, and even he was glad to be riding in anything other than Barry's import. The Florida jungle was launching a fully funded campaign to reclaim the land taken from its grasp. Fences labored under the weight of rust and vines; weeds grew tall around broken playgrounds; spare tires and assorted auto parts seemingly gasped for air under the patient advance.

Dead pine needles poured out of gutters like river logjams, effectively creating the foundation for other seedlings to grow up vertically from their base, fueled by sun and rain and neglect. It was easy to imagine the scene before them as some kind of long forgotten, low budget movie set.

"What are we looking for?" Ben asked.

Barry didn't answer. They drove on, crossing streets with names like Tent Top and Grand Stand.

"That," Barry said, leaning forward with sudden interest. "Slow down."

Barry was pointing to a building that somehow made the rest of the surrounding structures look almost admirable. The concrete walls stood perpendicular to a barren patch of asphalt that not even the weeds seemed to care to invade. Iron bars covered every pane of glass, which wasn't much, and the large garage door at one end was halfway covered in cinderblocks. The corner nearest the intersection featured a marquee that had long since been drilled through with rocks, no doubt a pastime for local teens at some point. The lot had once been a gas station.

Barry tried to imagine a day when it was alive with neighborhood commerce and chatter, but it was nearly impossible to penetrate the shroud of hopelessness and despair that seemed to resonate from the property.

"Circle back around and pull over there."

Ben was willing enough to follow these instructions, parking a few blocks away from the front entrance under the cover of a gnarled oak.

"Listen," he said, "I know we had some times back in the day, but there ain't no amount of nostalgia that's gonna get me to follow you in there."

"Relax, we're not going in."

"We're not? I mean *you're* not?"

"No."

"Then what are we doing?"

"We're looking to see what crawls out."

Chapter 61

TWILIGHT quietly thanked the afternoon for the turn and began the nighttime negotiations. Sheriff Blake Martin had witnessed the same celestial song and dance thousands of times. Early in his career it meant the beginning of a shift; he was thankful that now it heralded a hot meal and a cold beer. *Maybe two,* he thought.

Trial days were always long; prisoner transfer required as much paperwork as it did emotional calories. Driving the better part of two hours round trip with a felon in the back seat was inexplicably taxing. The drive to the courthouse was always a troubling dichotomy: the first taste of freedom tainted by the looming trial awaiting. The return trip was downright depressing, almost regardless of how the events unfolded before the jury. There was an awful, invisible yoke heaved around a man's shoulders when they drove into the Hillsborough

County Jail. Blake could see the effects in his rear view mirror even before he parked the car, like the force of gravity had suddenly been doubled down upon the inmate. The brow, eyes, and shoulders would all sag under the mental and emotional strain, presenting the man in something of an upright fetal posture. Sometimes they would begin to cry; once he had a transfer puke all over the back seat. Moments like these made him remember that beneath whatever they had done, there was still a human soul held in those cuffs.

But Lonnie McGregor did none of those things. Instead, he moved his tongue quietly from one side of his mouth to the other, rocking gently to an unknown beat. Blake watched him for a few miles through the rearview mirror. Of course, he knew the protocol, but he couldn't help himself.

"Lonnie?" he asked.

No answer.

"Lonnie?"

"Yessir."

"What's on your mind, son?"

Lonnie reached both hands up and rubbed his clean-shaven scalp, checking his hands occasionally.

"Lonnie?"

"Yessir."

"What are you thinking about?"

He checked his hands one last time, then looked directly at the sheriff in the mirror.

"I want him to be all right. Tonight. I want him to be all right tonight."

"Who?"

No answer.

"Lonnie?"

"And you, too," he said.

***

JOE Grayson stood silently at the kitchen sink, slowly drying his hands as he watched the last suds disappear down the drain, entranced by their helplessness. They were going to get sucked under, all of them, and there wasn't a thing they could do about it. He could put the stopper in, and he imagined them grateful. But he didn't.

Some days were harder than others; this had been one of them. He didn't know why, but he knew he needed another beer tonight. He drank alone, ate alone, worked mostly alone. Joe couldn't remember if he'd always been like that or how much the tragedy had affected him. Essentially, he couldn't remember who he was before that fateful night so long ago. It rarely bothered him, but he thought about it now, and he thought about the future. He thought about the beer outside, and about the other contents hidden behind the six packs. In that moment, a new thought became abundantly clear. Joe hung the towel carefully over the hook, and he knew that his only chance of dying with any amount of contentment was if that fridge in the garage was stuffed with the rest of whatever or whoever had ruined his life in the first place.

Beer wouldn't do the trick tonight, not nearly economic enough for the job. Joe reached over the small cabinet doors above the fridge and pulled down a nondescript jar of clear liquid. Then he walked back across the kitchen to the far cabinet for the appropriate glass. A taller one.

Joe stopped suddenly and reversed his last two steps. His position offered a view straight through the living room and out through the window to the right of the front door. In the daylight, the barn rested neatly in the upper frame. Joe dropped the jar and ran for the phone.

The scene beyond the window showed a blazing inferno.

Chapter 62

NOTHING challenges your patience and attention span like a stakeout. Some people are better at it than others, but no one likes it. Sitting in a vehicle for endless hours waiting for any kind of useful information to come across your windshield is like being tied to a chair and forced to watch midday television. Barry looked straight ahead and studied the building in the fading light. He could almost feel the foul spirit that guarded the premises like a phantom. Barry wasn't exactly sure what to expect, but he about jumped through the roof of the El Camino when Ben tapped the window and motioned to unlock the door.

"Whoa there, Jack, I ain't your giant," Ben laughed as he climbed in.

"Yeah, all right funny man. Whatcha' got there?"

Ben proudly produced a large carryout bag, already wet with grease on the bottom.

"Coupl'a Cubans, fried plantains, and a deviled crab for each of us."

"Hmm," Barry grunted, "should I be thanking you?"

"Hey man, we can't all be Times Square ya' know," Ben retorted. He settled behind the wheel and set the bag down between them. "Listen," he said, "I know you've been to the mountain and back, and that all of *this*," he motioned through the windshield, "is a helluva long way from anywhere near 'upstate,' but you gotta dial back the smack, know what I'm sayin'?"

The two men sat quietly; the aroma from the bag whispering to their hungry stomachs like the serpent of Eden.

"I'm sorry, Ben," Barry sighed. "You're right. I've been an asshole."

Ben gave his friend a knowing rap on the shoulder. "You've been under a lot of pressure, buddy; go easy on yourself. I don't mean to come down on you. Maybe I'm partial or even delusional, but I think there's more to these swamps and back roads than maybe you're giving us credit for. Like the food, for example," he smiled, digging into their takeout.

Barry picked up the first half of his sandwich and ate almost a quarter of it in one bite. The mixture of sultry spices and flaky texture that filled his mouth felt like instant relief to a nagging wound. "Jesus," he whispered, slouching down into the seat, surrendering to the satisfaction.

Ben was right to call him out; he was probably overdue for that. In fact, he knew that his own soul needed mending as much as his stomach was craving another plantain. And like the greasy bag of goodness sitting next to him, maybe the distance between the pain of the past and finding peace in the present was a lot closer than he realized.

"So I gotta ask," Ben said with a mouth full of crab, "what's your theory here? I mean what do you really think is going on?"

Barry swallowed hard. "You'd laugh all the way back to Riverview if I told you."

"I just want to get back in one piece, laughing or not. I figure I deserve to hear however far gone you are."

Barry finished the first half of the sandwich and took a long pull from the fountain drink. "All right, fair enough." He took a deep breath. "You remember that cast my dad showed us that day at Dan's. I was down several days ago looking around at that boot memorial you mentioned. This fast talker appeared outta nowhere and grilled me up and down, basically refusing to give me his name. A few days later I ran into him again."

"Yeah? Where?"

"At Lonnie McGregor's trial."

"What?"

"He's their father. Lonnie and Ellie."

"No shit!" Ben was silent for several moments, holding his Cuban sandwich away from his mouth as if he were frozen. "Ok," he finally spoke, "but what's that got to do with why we're here. You think their dad and this super freak are in cahoots? For what?"

Barry sighed. "That's where it gets tricky, as if it weren't already. You ever been to the Gasparilla Festival?"

Ben wrinkled his face in confusion. "What? Yeah, a few times, but how's that – holy hell what is that?!"

Ben was staring straight ahead, one hand on the steering wheel, the other holding the wrapper of a sandwich that now sat in his lap. He didn't notice. Neither did Barry. They were both pressed hard back in their seats, looking at a little girl who stood squarely in front of the car, glaring at them through the windshield.

***

"OH my God she's saying something!" Ben shrieked. He glanced down at his lap and swore as he picked up the fallen sandwich. Barry started to roll down his window. "No no no no!" Ben howled.

"We need to hear what she's saying."

"Don't let that she-demon anywhere near us!"

"She's already near us," Barry said, gesturing toward the hood of the car.

But she wasn't there.

"God almighty!" Ben jumped back and stared over Barry's shoulder. Barry turned slowly and was met with a dirty white lace dress covered by an oversized black jacket. In a split second the body bent over and the serious face of a young girl was pressing against his window.

"They ain't here," she said.

Barry rolled down his window halfway.

"Who?"

"The two yer lookin' for. The Giant and the other one."

"How'd you know we were – "

"Why else would you be *here?*" she emphasized.

Barry nodded in agreement. "How long have they been here?"

"You mean today?"

"Yeah. How many days?"

"Months. On and off. At least since I turned eight."

"How old are you now?"

"Ma' says I ain't supposed to talk to strangers, but then she don't believe me about the Giant. My name's Bridgette. Anyway they left just before you got here."

"Ok, thanks." Barry dug in his pocket and pulled out a few dollars. "Here," he said, passing them out the window. "Thanks for your help."

Bridgette counted the bills and shrugged slightly, as if the offering was marginally fair market value for her services. "Two more and I never saw you here."

Barry paid up and she disappeared into the darkness, content with her bargain.

Ben let out an exaggerated sigh.

"C'mon," Barry said, "I need a drink."

Chapter 63

BLAKE Martin sat in the squad car outside Hillsborough County Jail for a long minute. *What on earth was Lonnie talking about?* In his line of work, Blake wasn't one given to much beyond the realm of facts and hard evidence. Hunches had to be tested, theories required proof. Lonnie was something else altogether. This whole twisted case was trending toward the furthest parameters of reality.

He pulled out and headed back to the station to file necessary paperwork. Kathy would be upset at his late arrival, but he hated starting his day staring at blank documents that demanded his memory of the past. As tired as he was, he'd rather get it over with today and go home with a quiet mind.

Blake drove the speed limit down U.S. 301, suddenly aware that night was overtaking without a proper sunset, like some secret plan was finally unfolding and couldn't be thwarted.

He stopped at the red light at the intersection of Balm Riverview Road, just in time to see two fire engines come screaming out of the station on the corner, lights and horns blazing like a circus on wheels.

Safe home, fellas, he thought.

The light turned green and he moved off the line, slowly gaining speed toward his destination.

His CB radio crackled to life, and Maryl McGregor's voice broke through the static; it was unusually urgent.

"Sheriff Martin?"

He picked up the handset. "Go ahead."

"There's a fire at the Grayson ranch. A bad one. Two units dispatched and more coming from the county."

"Copy that," he shouted as he whipped the squad car around and threw on his own lights in one smooth motion. "I'm on my way!"

***

JOE Grayson didn't bother to hang up the phone. He grabbed his coat and fumbled for a flashlight in the kitchen drawer. Then he ran to the front door.

Something caught his eye. Something out of place. Something that wasn't there before. Something that stood out.

There in the single window pane, the one that framed the chaos outside. A new image.

Even from that distance, Joe could clearly make out the silhouette of a figure standing in front of the roaring flames. It was huge.

"Sonofabitch," Joe whispered in awe. He yanked his rifle off the rack and launched out the door.

Chapter 64

BEN eased the weary El Camino into the unpaved lot of Dan's Three Corners Bar. Familiar territory. Barry had been quiet the whole drive. The two men walked in and felt their shoulders relax in the embrace of flickering neon and the low fog shelf of cigarette smoke. They took their places on a pair of weathered stools and each ordered a beer.

Ben set his glass down on a salted napkin and looked over at his friend, who was patiently offering a Lucky Strike. "All right buddy, you win."

"How's that?" Barry asked, pulling a stick from the carton.

"I'm all out of guesses. What's the Gasparilla Festival have to do with any of this?"

Barry smiled into his half empty glass. "Trust me," he started, "the deeper we get into our cups the better this is all gonna sound. Maybe I need a few more to see if I still believe any of it myself."

"Nah, c'mon. Out with it. Don't forget that you're the one who's been gone for so long."

"What's that got to do with anything?" Barry asked.

"It means that I've been here for the last ten years listening to everyone's crazy shit."

Barry chuckled. "That's fair enough." He stared ahead into the mirror at the reflection disrupted by rows of old trophies, small mammal mounts, and the occasional bottle of hard whiskey. "It's gotta stay here, Ben. And you at least need to hear me say that my telling you this means that you're involved, probably even liable to some extent. If I'm right, then the kind of characters crawling around that old gas station are not the common kind of trouble that a person can just shrug off or ignore."

"You mean Ellie's dad?"

"Unfortunately. Though I don't suspect there's much more than blood relation there anymore."

"All right," Ben said, "hit me with it."

Barry sighed. "Well, what do you know about Gasparilla?"

"Only that there's no point going down there without a fist full of beads."

Barry laughed. "What do you know about the history of the festival, the pirate lore?"

"Nothing, really."

"All right," Barry said, "long story short, before the beer starts talkin'. Jose Gaspar was an alleged Spanish pirate who raided the Gulf of Mexico and apparently had headquarters along the intercoastal waters not far from here."

"Ok, I'm with you."

"It gets better. There's rumor that he met his end in a final battle in Tampa Bay, but not before dispatching a small crew to safeguard a treasure."

"And you think you know where it is."

"No. Well, not exactly."

"Then I don't follow."

"I think someone else believes they know where it is."

"So what's any of that got to do with your case, or your client or whatever?"

"Initially only as collateral damage, though now he's at risk of becoming the scapegoat altogether."

"So let me get this straight – "

"Quietly," Barry interrupted.

"Sorry." Ben cleared his throat. "As of right now, you're leading theory is that Ellie's old man is after a pirate treasure and is somehow responsible for the death of his nephew?"

"He's not working alone."

"Ok. Any ideas? Wait," Ben said, putting the pieces together as he spoke, "the beanstalk…that cast your dad got at the crime scene."

"Yeah, something like that," Barry swallowed the last of his beer.

Ben sat lost in his thoughts. Barry flicked the ash of his cigarette and ran his hand across his face. He was trying to decide just how deep to go down this road, even with his friend.

His theories would have to wait.

The door to the bar suddenly slammed open and both men turned to see a tornado of emotion: eyes wild with urgency and fear, jaw set with concern and focus. Ellie McGregor shouted from across the room, "Barry you've got to come now! There's a fire at the ranch!"

Barry jumped up so fast that he nearly knocked Ben off his stool. All three of them came crashing out of the door just in time to see the sheriff's car pull a screaming 180 degree turn in the middle of the highway before speeding down Balm Riverview Road, presumably toward the Grayson homestead.

***

NO ONE spoke as they ran toward Ellie's truck. Barry instinctively climbed into the passenger seat, and Ben dove headlong into the bed, swearing loudly when Ellie punched the gas before he was able to sit up.

"What do you know?" asked Barry.

"Not much. Mom's on the switchboard tonight, and your dad called about a fire in the barn. But I know it's big enough for the county trucks to be involved."

"Shit."

"There's something else, too," she said.

"What?"

Ellie gripped the wheel tight with both hands, leaning slightly forward, eyes moving quickly.

"It's all right, El, I already know."

She looked over at him so fast that she nearly ran the truck off the frail, two-lane road. Ben swore wildly from the back. In that brief moment, Barry could see her face full of guilt, shame, and fear.

"What are you talking about?" she said.

"Your dad."

Her voice quivered and her face began to cringe.

"What about him?"

"I don't know exactly, but I've figured he's involved somehow."

"Damn sonofabitch," she whispered through a controlled sob.

"You had nothing to do with this, El. Let's get to the farm and start to figure this out."

Ellie reaffirmed her grip on both the wheel and her emotions.

"Ok," she said, "but if we find him out there, he's mine to deal with."

Chapter 65

ELLIE'S pickup achieved liftoff coming over the small dune that led down to the Grayson ranch. Ben's vulgar tirade was cut short by the wash of flashing lights; the scene before them looked nothing short of apocalyptic. Fire crews surrounded the pasture to contain the flames spreading out from the barn.

Ellie hit the brakes hard next to the house, and Barry was out the door before she could advise his caution. He cleared the barbed wire fence in a single leap and headed for the barn on a dead sprint; Ellie and Ben (who was now riding gratefully in the front like a spoiled dog), tracked him along the perimeter in her truck.

Barry could feel the heat from a hundred yards away; at half the distance he had to stop and shield his face, backing up several paces. He felt himself bump into someone behind him and he turned abruptly to find Sheriff Martin. Blake looked like hell, sweat drenching the front of his uniform, steam pouring from his head and shoulders in the cool night, dirt and ash smeared across his face.

"Barry, it's me. It's ok. The crews have it contained."

In the glow of the flames and lights, Barry could see something more than mere information in the sheriff's eyes, something like restraint. Blake, in turn, could feel the singular question bearing down on him. He'd felt it many times before in the wake of emergency.

"Joe," Barry said, "Where's Joe?"

A younger deputy would've fumbled the moment, making it worse. God knows Blake had a long list of his own mistakes in such situations during his early years: dropping the eyes, offering condolences, failed attempts at redirection. Now, he looked straight into Barry's earnest stare and met it with an honesty and confidence that kept the emotions from escalating worse than the flames.

"Barry, we don't know."

The younger Grayson's eyes were hungry and wild; they moved in short, rapid bursts as he processed the response and all possible implications. "What about the horses?" Barry asked.

"The crews can't get in on account of the heat; they can hardly get near it."

Barry felt his world spinning, his stomach dropping, and the metallic tinge of acid on his tongue. The free-fall was mercifully interrupted by the fire chief. Like Blake, he was seasoned enough to choose his words and tone carefully.

"We've got this contained, so there's no further damage to the pasture, Mr. Grayson."

The guy must've been at least ten years older than Barry.

"Dad," he said. "Where's my dad? Is Joe in there?" He began to walk toward the flames and both responders restrained him: Blake from the rear, the fire chief scuttling out in front.

"Now hold on Barry, we're – " a single rifle shot rang out over the controlled chaos. All three men stopped abruptly and looked in the same direction.

The refuge across the river.

The flames cast strange, alien shadows that disappeared into the black water, but there was light enough for Barry to notice a critical detail: the canoe was gone.

He broke through the sheriff and fire chief like they were children and felt the adrenaline rush of an open-court fast break. Ellie and Ben entered his peripheral vision, but they were behind him as soon as they appeared.

Barry leapt off the grassy ridgeline without breaking stride and never stopped, plunging headlong into the darkness. The water was cold, much colder than he anticipated, and he felt its greedy fingers soak through every article of clothing and pierce the skin beneath. The experience had the opposite reaction from what he feared. Rather than an energy-sapping numbness, Barry burst through the surface like a newly baptized saint. His lungs burned with the flush of winter air, and he suddenly felt alive and focused, as though the inferno at the barn matched the fire in his soul. With any luck or divine favor, he would be the Good Lord's righteous rod of vengeance tonight.

Chapter 66

ELLIE and Ben jumped down onto the damp sand. Sheriff Martin was closing fast and called for them to stop. Ellie shoved off her heavy jacket and ran toward the water's edge.

"Wait!" Ben grabbed her arm. "Maybe Sheriff's right. Maybe we should let him handle this."

"You'll never forgive yourself, Ben. And I sure as hell won't. Now get your ass in that river."

She was diving in before he could counter.

"Dammit," he hissed, reluctantly rolling up his sleeves, "I miss not having any friends." He lumbered into the low tide, shrieked when his toes touched the water, and finally flopped in just as Blake was nearing the end of the pasture.

***

BARRY hoisted himself up with the help of a cypress knee. His legs were heavy and his feet sank into the sediment. He suddenly remembered watching otters and manatees play and feed on this bank as a boy. Summer days along the Alafia; a million memories away. He snapped out of the lapse and turned to find Ellie pulling hard toward him, and Ben floundering in the middle of the river like a grocery bag.

"You shouldn't have come," he said as he reached out his arm.

"Like hell," she said, coughing.

"El, I don't know what we're gonna find out – "

"We?" she interrupted.

"What?"

"You said 'what *we* are gonna find.' Now let's get going." Barry looked at her sternly; she returned his concern with an iron will, ignoring the fact that he was holding her in his arms.

"Wait! No! Don't let me die here!" Ben's head struggled to remain above the surface, as though the secrets of the fire river sought to add him to their coffers.

"Ben," Barry called, "stand up!"

"No...I can't...what?"

"Stand up."

"Oh God, thank you Jesus," Ben sputtered.

Barry and Ellie helped their friend gather his balance. "Ben…" Barry began.

"Shove it," Ben spat between gasps for air. "Besides," he said, "I sure as hell ain't swimming back."

The two old friends exchanged nods and started through the palm fronds when a long, terrifying scream erupted from the throat of a man somewhere deep in the refuge. Barry crashed through the line of foliage, barreling headlong toward the cry. Ellie started after him.

"Ellie, wait!" Ben called; the sudden tone of authority halted her more than the instruction itself.

"I'm not leaving him, Ben."

"But you wanna help him, right?"

"Of course."

"As kids Barry and I used to run all over these roads."

"So?"

"So it's basically one big circle, with two exits about a quarter mile apart out on Bloomingdale and 301."

"Ok?" she asked, making no attempt to hide her frustration.

"You saw him take off just then. We'll never keep pace with that horse. Best thing we could do is cover the exit this way if Barry ran that way."

Ellie hesitated, frustrated at Ben's stalling but unable to argue with the logic.

"All right," she huffed, "but if anything happens to him…"

"Have you actually even seen your boyfriend lately? That guy could run through a house tonight."

Ellie smiled weakly, and the two started off in the other direction.

Chapter 67

THE moon was full and his eyes were wide, charged with the vitality of something long awaited. Barry was amazed at how well he could see in the darkness. He stopped after what must have been a few hundred yards, controlling his breath and listening hard. The scream had come from this general vicinity, but there was no possible way to pinpoint the precise location. As his breathing slowed, however, he heard a different sound: the muffled groan and blunt thump of flesh being beaten. He walked hurriedly down the path and stopped immediately upon rounding a bend. There, through a break in the canopy, he could clearly make out a massive frame kneeling over another that could've been half its size.

"My God," he whispered. The Giant.

Barry could see Joe's fallen Stetson off to the side; whatever struggle his father had put up, he wasn't moving well under the Giant's assault. He wasn't moving at all. The Giant smothered him now like a huge demon mantis.

Barry closed the fifty-yard gap in seconds, the balls of his feet barely touching the ground as though he was sprinting across hot coals. He had been a three-sport athlete in high school before committing to basketball in college, and he lowered his shoulder into the Giant's rib cage like a punishing linebacker. Barry lifted upon impact and ran several more steps, driving fully through the target before crashing down on top of him. He felt bones crack beneath the force of his momentum, and he heard the telling moan of breath being suddenly forced out of the lungs. In his experience, the sound was an involuntary song of surrender, like landing on your back after going up for a rebound. Typically, a player would need at least several minutes to even consider returning to the game.

But the Giant was no freshman quarterback, and he was no kind of quitter. He rolled onto his stomach before Barry could swing on his face, but that didn't stop the younger Grayson from landing a barrage of punishing blows to his kidney and newly broken ribs. The Giant countered by jerking an enormous elbow backwards that caught Barry just above the ear. The blow itself landed hard, like the focused fury of a tornado unleashed in just a few seconds. Barry was stunned at the quickness and agility of such a clumsy frame, but this was no time for admiration. The Giant was on his feet and launched a kick that would've punted Barry's head into the next county. He dodged and sprang back, grasping his opponent around the waist from behind.

Barry lifted him off the ground, and spun in a sort of pirouette to garner momentum before falling backwards and slamming the Giant into the unforgiving earth. He could feel the Giant's head succumb to the whiplash and hit hard and long after all of the other body parts. The Giant groaned again and rolled over holding his head.

It was Barry's turn to line up the winning field goal, but a momentary distraction caught his attention for the split second that the Giant needed to swing suddenly and smash a rotted limb across his shoulder. Barry's balance gave way under the unexpected blow, and he fell sideways clutching his arm. The Giant was on him before he hit the ground, using the limb with both hands to drive him back and pin him against a tree. Barry's neck and shoulders were strong enough to keep his head from snapping back and denting the bark, but he stood no chance against the physics of the Giant's weight and the angle against his own body. Barry had the sudden, sickening realization that he would die in the same swamp as his mother, and likely by the same hands. With the effort of a man who knows his last chance, Barry simultaneously collapsed his lungs and drove both of his hands inward toward each other along the branch, then gave a swift, hard jerk outward with all the effort he had left.

It worked. The weight of the Giant's pressure on the outsides of the branch caused it to splinter in the middle, where Barry had focused his efforts. The Giant fell forward and Barry met him with a clean head butt. The blow was weak, given the energy he had already exerted, but it was enough to turn the tide and allow him to drive his attacker toward what had distracted him a moment ago.

Barry landed a left and right jab as the Giant continued to backpedal off the path; then he drove forward and pushed him directly in his massive chest, careful to release and wring his own arms free from any flailing grasps.

The Giant flew back and slammed against an unexpected obstacle.

The hanging slab of cow ribs.

In the next blink, the thirsty, iron jaws of the bear trap slammed shut with a metallic growl. The tortuous scream that erupted might have woken the entire town. The Giant collapsed, writhing in agony. He vomited once, and then passed out in shock.

Barry stood there, heaving. The guy might bleed out, he realized. A fleeting moment of human sympathy passed through his mind, and then it was gone.

Chapter 68

ELLIE and Ben stopped dead in their tracks; the cry they'd just heard was enough to turn even the strongest stomach. "That wasn't Barry," Ellie finally said, half trying to convince herself. "Couldn't have been."

"No, but God knows what happened to the other guy."

The other guy. Her father, maybe? She suddenly felt a strange sense of betrayal in the form of empathy from the distant biological connection to her father. She attempted to stifle the emotion by refocusing her thoughts on all that she hated about him, but something distracted her. Something quiet, yet clearly getting closer.

"You hear that?" she asked.

Ben straightened up and held his breath to keep from panting. There it was. An urgent muttering, almost whimpering, and it was coming down the path toward them. Ellie grabbed Ben's sleeve and pulled him off the shoulder and into the thicket. They were only a few feet from the path as hurried footsteps grew closer. They ducked beneath a suspended cloud of Spanish moss. The silhouette of a short, worried man shuffled by. Through the stillness they could hear him whispering, "Jesus, oh Jesus, oh God no…"

Ellie stepped out.

"Tom?"

The man jumped at the sound and whirled around. "Who are you?" he demanded, his voice shaking.

"Is that you, Dad?"

"El-Ellie?" he stammered. "Jesus, thank God," his voice sounded relieved and he strode over to her.

Ellie opened her arms, "Dad, you're ok," she sighed, "what are you doing here?"

Father and daughter embraced. Ben stood by, speechless.

Tom began, "I came as soon as I – " He never finished. Ellie's knee was driving through his groin and slamming to a halt at his pubic bone. Whatever gas sat idle in his lungs was forced out over his daughter's shoulder, along with a mouthful of bile. The man collapsed in her arms before she let him fall to the earth in a heap, like a heavy old saddle.

Ben came crashing out from their hiding spot and stood next to Ellie. She held a cold, exacting stare as she watched her father writhe on the ground. Tom tried to pull himself to his knees, but she planted her foot on his back and pushed him back down.

"Ellie, what in God's name?" he groaned.

"Don't you call on God's name, *Daddy*."

"What are you doing?" Tom was lying in the fetal position, panting and moaning. "We have to get outta here." He winced. "There's a...a…"

"There's a *what?* A monster in the swamp? None more so than your own sick self."

"No," he moaned. "Something else," he rolled over and Ellie made another motion with her leg. "Wait, wait, goddammit!"

She hesitated.

"All right," he sighed, "I deserved that."

"And why's that," Ben asked.

"I never meant to hurt anyone. Never meant for it to come to this."

"Who did you hurt?" Ellie took an aggressive step toward her father, who was now resting on his knees.

"I never could get your uncle to let it go. Richie wouldn't let it go. He was gonna pay for Karl's education and get himself all set up. He found something in some damned book and spun this wild treasure hunt."

"What treasure?" Ben asked.

"Oh Lord," Tom sighed, standing up with considerable effort, "some nonsense about Gaspar's treasure buried out here."

"That big festival in Tampa?"

Tom nodded. "He was a pirate captain. I don't know. Richie hatched this whole plan to just scare off the old Grayson fella and then buy the land himself so that we'd have unfettered access to this swamp."

"So how'd you two work it out, Dad? Richie did all the scaring while you did the digging?"

The mettle returned to Tom's eyes now, and he gave the two of them a small wink.

"I think they found help, Ellie," Ben offered, "of a certain kind."

"What are you talking about?" Ellie asked.

"Smart friend you got here, Ellie," her father smiled. He seemed taller now, and beginning to savor the moment, though not without flashes of pain.

"What's he talking about?"

"Let's just say that your uncle found a friend with a unique skill set. A giant."

"A what?" she asked.

"He's right, Ellie," Ben whispered in a guilty manner. "Barry's dad found prints at the crime scene."

"Ol' Joe," Tom chuckled. "Poor paranoid widower."

Ellie's mind was racing, spinning wildly to connect the dots. Tom wasn't going to wait for her.

"Some men on this earth have an uncanny similarity to monsters. I was against it from the start, but Richie turned that sonofabitch loose, and there was no reeling him in."

"What about Karl?"

"Like I said, there was no stopping him." Tom said, eyes suddenly heavy with shame. "Not again. Not this time."

"What do you mean, *this time?*" Ben asked, timidly.

"Well, we all know Karl ain't the first body pulled from this swamp."

"Jesus Christ," Ellie gasped. "Barry's mother. You bastards."

"Now hold on a minute, Ellie," Tom pleaded. "Richie said he was gonna make his final move tonight. I saw the emergency units coming this way, and thought I might be able to intercept either one of them out here."

Ellie scoffed. "My dad, the hero." She balled her fist and took a strong stride forward when the piercing sound of snapping twigs startled her from behind. The path was empty for the length of their visibility.

"Ellie?" Ben whispered. Something in his tone was different. She turned to find her father pointing a pistol right at her, motioning her over to Ben.

"Oh, Ellie," Tom smiled. His eyes were suddenly clear and vibrant, absent of any guilt and filled with a strange combination of malice and fear. "Daddy's little bastard," he said in a mocking tone.

Chapter 69

BARRY dropped to his knees next to his father. Joe was breathing, but little else was going on in the way of voluntary motion. Barry rolled him onto his side, positioning him so that nothing would clog his airways. Joe coughed and groaned softly, and made a faint whisper. Barry leaned over.

"Dad," he said, and put his ear close to his father's mouth.

"I had him," was all Joe could manage. The old cuss wasn't about to go quietly.

"I'm sorry, Dad," Barry whispered, "I'm sorry about everything."

The two men rested in a quiet chorus of cicadas, both lost in their own kind of pain. Barry's shoulder was throbbing, and he could feel his body succumbing to the chill of the night air as the adrenaline faded. He wondered how all of this would play out, what they would discover about the man locked in the bear trap and how he was connected with Ellie's father. He wondered how they'd rebuild the barn, and how long Joe would be laid up. He winced at the throbbing sensation in his head where the Giant's elbow had connected; his temples still felt as though they might explode.

Suddenly, he felt something else, something ripple through the invisible molecules and atmosphere of their perimeter, something distinctly present. He couldn't pinpoint the sound or the direction, but he knew with alarming clarity that they were no longer alone.

Joe whispered, and Barry leaned closer.

"Son," it sounded like, "son."

Barry was beyond exhausted, but his mind was trying to focus his available senses on locating whatever threat had joined their present company.

"Son," Joe muttered.

Barry hushed his father and raised himself to one knee, not daring to turn around. He noticed for the first time that the cicadas were silent. All ambient noise, in fact, had utterly ceased, leaving him standing in something of a raging vacuum.

"*Song,*" Joe whispered, and closed his eyes.

***

ELLIE wrinkled her face and stared at her father in disbelief. "Daddy's little bastard?" she repeated.

He laughed. "Maryl's got some explaining to do, then. Oh, your mother can spin a yarn from here to Okeechobee. But she won't get the chance, and I'll spare the truth from your last memory."

"What the hell are you talking about?"

"A terrible tragedy, they'll say. Joe Grayson, the widower who lost his shit, burned the farm, and pulled the trigger. They'll find you all in due time, and I'll be sure to cry my little heart out at the funeral. But by then I'll be – "

For the second time that night, Tom McGregor's performance was brutally interrupted. From Ben and Ellie's perspective, all they saw was the top of his head jerk instantly sideways and downward. But their other senses filled in the missing pieces. They both heard a thunderous crack, like two wooden baseball bats being swung against each other with the express purpose of smashing their barrels together into splintered shards. They also felt the sensation of tiny droplets splattering their faces and garments, which would later be identified as blood and brain matter.

And so, once again, Tom McGregor's human form was forced to reconnect with the dust of the earth. His body collapsed as if it were suddenly absent of all muscular purpose and skeletal structure. This time, however, there would be no rally of strength, no refortification, no return to the stage. Tom McGregor fell dead where he lay. In fact, the medical examiner would later guess that he was most likely dead even before he hit the ground. He may as well have fallen directly into his grave.

Ellie and Ben stood stunned, looking down at their fallen attacker, at her deceased father. A rustling from the underbrush pulled their attention to the empty space where Tom had been standing only seconds earlier. A single boot stepped onto the moonlit path, and then another. Richie McGregor looked down at his brother, and let the bloody tree limb fall from his grasp.

"You get all that, Sheriff?" he asked.

"Um, excuse me?" Ben muttered, hands still raised in a posture of surrender from Tom's hold-up.

"That's not what we agreed to, Richie," Blake said as he walked slowly around the corner with a flashlight beaming at their feet. "But yes, I heard it. All of it. It went pretty much exactly as you said."

"That was for Karl," Richie said, "and Lonnie, too. Figured I was headed for hard time as it was; might as well make it worthwhile and get his stain off my soul." He looked up at his niece. "I'm real sorry, Ellie. I'll do all I can to make it right."

Blake pursed his lips and nodded, then reached for the cuffs on his belt. Richie put his hands behind his back without being asked.

Chapter 70

HUMAN nature has a way of enabling people to see most anything they like under certain circumstances, sort of like encouraging their assumptions on a matter. But all of Barry's assumptions were confirmed and accounted for: the Giant, Tom McGregor, some notion about treasure. There were loose ends that could be sorted out in the following days, but the facts were bound in logic and hard matter, much like the wet steel teeth buried in the Giant's bone and muscle. The world was neatly bound. Until it all changed, forever.

Barry stood and turned in one motion, shaking with the sudden recharge of whatever adrenaline was left in his body's war chest. As a former basketball player, his eye naturally measured distances familiar to the court. A free throw line was fifteen feet away from a point directly beneath the backboard; the rim of the basket was ten feet off the ground. Those dimensions, then, were the first synapses to fire in his mind, the latter being the most important. Given the amount of interference raining down on him, it was a small miracle that his brain immediately processed the scene before him in terms of calculable data. He was standing fully erect, but he felt his body drifting backwards, as though a slow and invisible force were pushing against him. Barry realized the source of this effect came from the fact that his eye line kept rising in order to take in the full height of whatever was standing before him.

The shape and display were both generally human in regards to limbs and head, but the proportions were unlike anything his eyes or nightmares had ever encountered. The torso was nearly as long as the legs, and the arms were longer than either. The entire body was covered in a kind of wet, matted, hair. Overall it was thin, but in the form of an endurance athlete: toned, powerful, coursing with potential. The creature's head sat confidently on shoulders that were cocked like trigger fingers, bent forward and daring him to make the slightest move. The eyes were deep set, but noticeably circular and unflinching.

The creature stood completely still, like a coiled spring ready to explode. Its lithe, muscular arms hung loosely alongside the powerful torso; hands slightly opened, fingers unfurled (all of them, he noticed), each one narrowing to a point like ancient gothic steeples.

And suddenly, Barry understood. His past, present, and immediate future locked into place for the first time; he felt a calm release in his mind like a deadbolt resting in a doorframe.

The Giant was a yarn, a ruse, some kind of opportunistic distraction. For a fleeting second Barry checked for any sympathy following this new revelation; still none to be found. Whatever stood before him now undoubtedly killed his mother, very near the place they were standing. The image of her broken body burst into his mind like radio static, and he felt the power of rage and revenge ripple through his rejuvenated muscles.

Barry knew two things at once. First, that he'd been longing for this moment for many years, like a deep, unknown ache of the soul. Second, that he was prepared to die this night; he felt a strange sense of welcome at the thought.

Maybe death itself stood before him now. But whether it be the message or the means, or even the end of his own sanity, he would release every moment of pain and anger that had long since calcified in his spirit. This would serve as his last action upon this earth, and in so doing he would finally rest.

Barry crunched his fingers into tight fists, twisted the toe of his back leg into a groove in the ground below, and launched himself toward the monster, uttering a cry that any foe would have admired as both a bitter greeting and a long farewell.

The creature met his advance with little resistance, and Barry's fists met firm flesh before his world went white hot, the parameters of which collapsed upon him like a warhead. His last memories were comprised of instant pain, a sense of weightlessness, flying through the night, and the mournful sound of a long, low, howl.

***

FALLING. Air rushing past, his stomach rising into his throat at the swift descent. Crashing. Branches breaking across his back, palmetto leaves slicing his skin. Barry's body slammed into the mud, his brain overwhelmed by the amount of information it was trying to process. The creature was standing over him in an instant, kneeling closer now. In his pain and panic, he could sense a distant kind of care, as though the creature was capable of far more than it was serving up. Barry was dying; he was certain of that. His body could sustain no further impact, and the creature seemed to understand. It spoke in a tongue he did not know, and reached toward his throat and head with enormous hands.

PART VI

Healing

Chapter 71

WET, thin flakes against his cheeks; rain. Something else warm and thick dripping off the ridge of his brow. Blood. His own? Even semi-consciousness brought pain all over. Barry was sitting vertically, somewhat at least. He was lying back in the embrace of a large cypress tree; he could vaguely make out its distinct scent. He made no attempt to move anything, but the soft sound of flesh squishing into mud willed his eyelids to flutter open. A man's bare foot stood next to him, and a rough but careful hand pressed against his neck. Then they were gone, and he slipped once again into the merciful unconscious.

***

BEEPING. Compression around his head, monitors near his ears. Nothing on below the waist. Barry let his body discover and experience the sensation of the budget mattress and cheap blanket. After several minutes, he let out a low groan as his brain began informing him of the damage report. Suddenly, a smooth, familiar hand was holding his own, and a kiss lighted upon his bandaged head.

Ellie.

She said nothing but he could feel her presence, her life. Barry rolled his head toward hers.

"Shhh," she whispered. "All in time."

"Ah, c'mon," said a rough voice in a low wheeze, "get yer ass up."

Barry blinked with effort, as if his eyelids were iron shutters, and saw the blurry image of a man lying next to him in his own bed, wearing an assortment of monitors and a Stetson hat.

***

DREAMING isn't the right word to describe what Barry was experiencing. His mind had suddenly decided on action while the rest of his body begged for relief. Anxiety, more like it. He was familiar with the symptoms. He'd kept a legal pad by his bedside during law school and the early years in New York for just such occasions. This way, he could roll over and jot down necessary information to appease his agitated brain cells.

Later, Barry would remember nothing about his orientation to time and space, only that dots were being connected without provocation, and somewhat without permission. He struggled to rest, but pieces of memories were being torn from their linear thread to create a mosaic that his mind insisted demanded immediate attention.

The library.

Historical archives.

The mysterious delivery, and the words, "Forgive me."

The diner.

Chapter 72

MEDICAL doctors deliver all kinds of news, and their days tend to reflect their message. Bad news makes for a hard day; good news makes the job worthwhile. Telling a patient that more tests are required, which is neither immediately good or bad, usually leads to shifts that are tense or anxious. This pretty much covers the range of possibilities. But there are always stories of doctors who have no reasonable explanation for what they see before them, and those days create all kinds of subversive chaos and introspection. The doctor's world, after all, is largely black and white, or at least cause and effect. This ailment, be it disease or injury, either responds to this treatment, or it doesn't. Practices or virtues like prayer and faith may be present in rooms and wards, but they are vastly outnumbered by the monitors and dosage labels. When such a case presents itself in which the patient is either suffering – or most especially, recovering – for no apparent reason, then the campaign for transcendent deity takes yet another PR blow.

The attending physician standing in front of bed number one in room 327 was on her break. She should be at lunch, and her patient should be dead. She'd never seen injuries like these, and everyone around the "accident" was acting odd. The man's hands were the real mystery. Not much in the way of cutting like they would show if concrete or stone were involved, and far more swelling than a single action or incident should cause. No, they hadn't been run over by a machine or crushed under the impact of a fall. The only relatable case she could connect him to was a street fighter she'd treated a few years ago. Even then, it was hard to imagine any man beating something with the amount of fury and perseverance to cause damage to this extent.

Then there was the hair. Her patient's was full of bark and mud, particularly the back of the head at the obvious point of impact. A blow from behind was a viable explanation, but the deep bruising to his chest suggested instead that the source of momentum had come from the front, and thus the tree or branch he hit was the stopping point, not the beginning.

More curious than his own hair, though, was the tray full of dark strands she'd carefully extracted from his fists during the surgery.

Her brow relaxed as a smile crossed her face. She imagined Mr. Barry Grayson beating a horse's ass without mercy, until it finally had enough and kicked him clear into next week, and nearly into the next life.

Chapter 73

BARRY woke with a sudden awareness, as though the mental fog were clearing for the first time in recent memory. Once again, his brain began sourcing through the pain points, but his spirit won out with a demand to answer the call of whatever presence had entered the room.

The room was dark and the blinds were drawn. He could hear Joe snoring nearby; Ellie wasn't there, he realized. Barry shifted his weight painfully in bed and rolled over to see Raymond Muskee standing just inside the door. His senses immediately burst into overdrive and his ears began to ring, as though a whole cascade of internal alarms were sounding off.

Barry made an attempt to welcome him, but his visitor held up a hand in protest.

"No, friend. Rest." Raymond moved slowly, carefully, as though the floor was a thin sheet of ice. He sat in the chair next to Barry's bed, lowering himself with effort.

The two men sat in silence, listening to the omniscient chirp of various medical monitors. Finally, Barry cleared his throat and mumbled, "I know."

"Yes," Raymond answered after a time. "But not all." He reached into his breast pocket and pulled out a folded piece of paper, placing it carefully inside the resting Gideon Bible on the nightstand. "There is much more to tell, and I will return." He stood over Barry, eyes full of what felt like eons of depth and understanding. "Deities make no apologies," he said, looking at the broken man beneath him full in the face, "but I make my own to you now."

Barry shook his head slightly. "Don't," he whispered.

"Not for me," Raymond added. "My sorrow is for you."

Barry wrinkled his brow in confusion.

"A soul with that much anger is like a twisted root ball; the tree may only be saved if it is excavated and broken to the core. But your fury is spent now, friend, and well so. Nothing in this life is wasted on us. It all belongs. Let your wounds heal, inside and out; let your heart be at peace."

Barry closed his eyes and felt Raymond's words wash over him, loosening the scales of pain that had choked out his joy like post-surgery scar tissue. He felt a strange sensation of release, despite the network of bandages and tubes that bound his body. Emotion spilled out of his heart, and a single hot tear stung his eye and escaped out of the corner and down his cheek. He opened them both to blink through the moisture, and Raymond was gone.

**

ELLIE opened the door, sleepless nights in a hospital chair showing under her eyes. "Barry, oh my God," she hurried to this side. "Are – are you ok?"

"Depends," he said slowly. "Is Carter still president?"

She smiled. "You haven't been gone that long, ranch hand."

"Dammit."

"How do you feel?"

"Like I've been run over by a...never mind."

Her smile faded. "You've been out for more than a week."

"Baby steps, El."

"I'm sorry."

"What's the damage?" he asked, straining to find a more comfortable position.

She sighed. "The doctor says you're a lucky man. In fact, she keeps giving you weird looks and shaking her head. She expects you to recover, though," she chirped.

"You've got several broken ribs, and obviously your hands are..." her voice trailed off. "Barry," she said, "what happened to you?"

"That's a long story," he said. "You first."

She started to speak, then dropped her eyes and forcibly withheld the tears welling in them. Ellie then slowly recounted the events that she and Ben shared, the funeral for her father, and the mysterious checks in the mail from churches all over the state, mourning the loss of "Reverend McGregor."

"What about Lonnie?" Barry asked.

"He's been released, or exonerated, or something."

"Exonerated."

"Richie's testimony cleared him of all charges, and, of course, he's now in prison."

Barry nodded his approval. The legal system in Riverview was admirably swift.

"He told us everything. About the Giant, and about…"

"My mother," he finished.

"Yes," she whispered. Ellie pulled a worn tissue from her pocket. "He said the Giant was only supposed to scare your folks into selling the property, so that they could get after some kind of stupid treasure on the refuge across the river."

"Well, he's probably dead now," Barry said, staring straight ahead.

"Who? The Giant?"

Barry looked at her for a long moment. "Yeah, why?"

"They never found him," she said.

"He was caught in a damn bear trap!"

"They found blood, but it was empty," she paused. "He must've pulled it open."

"That's…impossible," Barry whispered.

Ellie allowed the silence to sit with them before speaking again.

"The police dredged the river."

"Nothing?"

"Well, no," she said, "not nothing. They did find a dead gator."

"Ok," he said slowly. "So?"

"Its mouth had been ripped open."

"For God's sake," Barry sighed, "How far can a one-legged freakshow get?"

Ellie nodded in sympathy. "Sheriff's got a manhunt going all the way to Ocala, Kissimmee, and Fort Myers. He's hell-bent on finding him."

The two sat together like fallen leaves trodden under a deluge, Ellie holding one of his heavily wrapped hands and carefully soothing his forearm. "Barry?" she asked, her voice quivering, "I heard you screaming that night." She checked his eyes for permission to continue. "It didn't sound like pain, more like…like a man who was prepared to die."

"Funny thing is," Barry started, "I think part of me did die that night, or at least more of me has been set free than anything else."

"What happened?"

Barry sat patiently, shifting his weight in the bed. "Do me a favor and open that Bible over there."

Ellie walked around and returned to her seat before opening it. She let the pages fall open and then picked out the folded slip of paper. A smaller piece, inserted into the first, fluttered onto Barry's blanket. She picked it up, and drew her breath.

"What is it?" he asked.

"You mean *who?*" she said, turning the old photo around to his view. Barry could see a young girl, barely a toddler, being held by a familiar face.

"Raymond?" he asked.

"I think so," she said.

"And that's you, isn't it?"

"How'd you know?"

"I'd rather him tell you."

"Who?" Ellie asked. "Where'd you get this?"

"Let's just call him the driver of that truck that ran me over."

Chapter 74

BARRY spent a few more days in the hospital under the curious watch of his doctor, who finally agreed to release him when it was clear that he wasn't going to divulge any further information. Ellie gave her solemn promise to take good care of him and make sure he made it back for his check-ups. Joe had already broken free, citing the need to oversee barn reconstruction and livestock management.

Ellie drove slowly out of the parking lot of Tampa General, careful to take wide turns.

"Hey, I'm not an invalid over here," Barry poked.

"Ok, I know, but…"

"But what? Let's get outta here."

"But I almost lost you, that's all." She turned south onto 301. Barry looked over at her.

"I'd hold your hand," he said, "but I'm nearly all bandages these days."

She laughed.

"Where are we going, anyway?" he asked.

"I figured after all that hospital food that you could use a stack of pancakes."

"Oh, now you're talking." He was quiet for a few moments. "That and a tall glass of answers will be perfect."

"How's that?"

"Just you wait, Miss Ellie McGregor. All this talk about treasure might get real interesting."

***

THE two pulled into Hester's Diner. Ellie went to get the wheelchair and Barry called her off. "I don't need that thing." He closed the passenger door and winced. "Ok, but I will take your shoulder." Ellie happily helped her wounded warrior into the nearest booth. It wasn't long before Barry was saddled up to a feast of buttery pancakes and mountains of eggs, grits, bacon, and sausage.

He was hardly a mouthful in when the parade of familiar faces started to spill out of hiding from the other seats.

Ben snuck up behind him and kissed him on the cheek. Barry made a move to punch him, but thought better of his hands. "And I can tell you now that from here on out the answer is '*No.*'"

"No what?" Barry asked.

"To whatever far-fetched adventure you come calling with. I'm out. Forever."

Blake Martin gave his shoulder a firm squeeze, visibly moved at his progress and genuinely thankful for his help. He assured Barry that his department was expanding their search across the state, and that he was confident in their eventual success.

Lonnie McGregor walked timidly up to the booth. "Mr. Barry. I wanna thank you. Thank you for what you done for me. For my family." Barry's world went still for a moment. Lonnie looked like a different person, no longer the tense, caged scrapper with bags under his eyes and bruises on his face. "I – I been helping Joe. Your daddy, Joe." Lonnie wrung the ball cap in his hands. "The shop's all closed up now. Plus Joe says I might as well work for him so long as I'm out there huntin' all the time anyway."

"Lonnie," Barry said, "thank *you*. For more than you'll ever know. It was my honor to help, and I'll see you around the ranch."

Finally, Maryl rolled herself up even with the table. "Listen, you shouldn't knock the life of ease in one of these here chairs." Barry laughed, and groaned at his ribs.

"Barry," she said, "I can't thank you enough. You risked everything for my boy, for us. Not many folks would do that, and that means a helluva lot to me."

"You're most welcome, Ms. McGregor. Despite my current condition, I assure you I'm grateful to be right here rather than where I was a few months ago."

"You ever need me to show you how to do a proper wheelie, you let me know."

Everyone laughed, and their corner of the diner settled into a peaceful chatter of thanksgiving and general small talk. Finally, Sheriff Martin dismissed himself to the office, Ben made an excuse to head over to Dan's Three Corners Bar, and Lonnie cited work to be done at the ranch. Ms. Hester turned the "Open" sign to "Closed" after the last customers shuffled out.

Barry and Ellie sat together quietly, when the sound of blinds snapping closed broke the silence.

"I guess Ms. Hester doesn't mess around," Ellie said.

"It's not her," Barry replied.

Ellie worked her way around slowly and saw Raymond Muskee systematically shuttering the diner. Suddenly, the same sound echoed from the opposite side. Barry and Ellie turned to see Maryl rolling along from window to window, closing blinds as she moved toward them. Raymond and Maryl intersected at their booth, the diner effectively on lockdown.

Barry leaned back and relaxed his shoulders, as though he were settling into a seat at the theater. Ellie did the exact opposite.

"What's going on?" she asked, beginning to rise from her chair.

Barry placed a bandaged hand on her leg. "It's all right," he said, "I think it's story time."

"Story time?"

"Take out that picture," he said. "But I think you better hold on tight."

Maryl glided to her original position at the head of the table, and Raymond quietly sat down across from Barry. Maryl's countenance looked a mile long, the joy in her eyes only moments ago now replaced by a weight that bordered on shame or reproach.

"Ellie," she said softly, "it's time we spoke."

Chapter 75

EVERY few minutes a vehicle rumbled overhead, and the headlights trailed off like a bloated shooting star. Barry's body hurt all over, and he wasn't certain how he'd make it back up the hill. None of that mattered now, though, with Ellie lying quietly in his broken embrace under the Alafia Bridge. The two of them lay there and listened to the whippoorwills and owls trade melodies against a backdrop of contented crickets, their songs combining to create a sort of quiet understanding.

Barry knew Ellie's world was nearly upside down, and he was happy to give her a comforting space to process. His suspicions had been right about most of what Raymond and Maryl had divulged, but even he could hardly believe hearing it aloud. In what now felt like a past life, he thought about the kind of technical writing that would normally be involved in signing away knowledge of this kind, or at least of this magnitude. But then again, the extraordinary comes with its own kind of special seal, something like sanity or plausibility.

Ellie stirred and sat up, staring out into a moonlit tangle of barnacle-covered bridge beams. "How'd you know?" she asked.

"I didn't, exactly. Not all of it, anyway. I found a few documents in the archives of the University Library. That, coupled with what you and I stumbled across here in town, I basically backed into just about the only possible explanation."

"How's that?"

"Well, I figured it was unlikely that Gaspar's *Floriblanca* had any treasure onboard whatsoever during its final engagement. Not in the way that most read it, at least. He was on the verge of retirement, so to speak. Anyway, there's no way a simple life boat would be enough to dispatch the booty of a career pirate such as Gaspar. The treasure had to be something else. It made sense that it was more likely *someone* else."

"But me?" she asked. "Or...my *ancestor* I guess?"

Barry sat up gingerly to join her. "I almost can't believe I'm saying this," he began.

"Tell me about it," she said.

"Gaspar spared Juan Gomez's life. Panther John, remember? He gave him a new life, in fact. That must have been enough to warrant the spirit of Juan's people, the Tall Song, to then protect those whom Jose Gaspar treasured. He didn't send Panther John out from that final battle with his gems or jewels; he sent him away with what he treasured most: his wife and unborn child."

"She was pregnant?"

"Had to have been."

"How's that?"

"Otherwise you wouldn't share his lineage."

"Right. Pirate lineage," she shook her head in disbelief.

"But when the captain never returned up river…"

"The other men in the party wanted to turn on her," she finished.

"Yeah I suppose. Pirates, after all."

"And that's where this *Tall Song* comes in," she emphasized.

Barry scratched his face with one of his bandaged hands. "Yeah. According to the parameters of this crazy narrative, anyway."

"So the Tall Song possesses Juan to protect Gaspar's wife," Ellie pondered.

"And evidently your distant relative. The spirit of the Tall Song has been protecting that lineage ever since, and it seems Raymond was the next in line for the job."

The two returned to silence. A raccoon ambled down to the river's edge and started digging for scallops in the soft, exposed beach. He took an interest in the two people sitting quietly nearby, and increased his efforts with a level of suspicion, as though these strange creatures might be after his dinner.

"Karl," her voice trailed off. Barry said nothing. "I suppose Lonnie was protected as an extension of me?" she asked, in a tone that suggested the question was directed to the river or the cool night air.

"I suppose," Barry offered. But his thoughts were on the contents of his father's freezer.

"So how'd you figure Tom was involved?"

"Well, I told you how we met down in Gibsonton."

"Yeah," she said.

"I made a call after that to the University Library and asked for the names of those who had recently viewed the same historical documents. The librarian read through a list of names, and one of them was Al Templeton."

"Al who?"

"Templeton."

"What's that got to do with anything?"

"Al's the original Gibsonton Giant, the one whose boot is on that monument right off U.S. 41. He's been dead for nearly twenty years. Given the pieces I had already, I figured your dad was the only one who would use that as a fake identity."

"God almighty," she sighed.

A mullet leapt and slapped the surface of the river. Overhead, a large semi-tractor trailer rumbled north on

301, passing through Riverview without any knowledge of the story that was unfolding on the banks below.

"My parents," she whispered, "my real parents."

"You wanna track 'em down?" Barry asked.

"No."

"That was quick."

"Maryl's been more than any mother ever could be to me," Ellie replied. "She's my mother. The fact that she knew this the whole time, though…" her voice trailed off. "We've definitely got some catching up to do, especially now with Tom out of our lives. But she's so much of who I've become."

"I'm glad to hear that."

The raccoon smacked his jaws liberally, enjoying every last morsel of the shellfish.

"Plus," she started, "even if I wanted to, it's not like I'd have any idea where to begin. From the way Raymond describes his involvement, they could be anyone, right? And maybe it's better that way."

"How do you mean?"

"This is who I am. Oddly enough, I suppose everything I've just learned doesn't change that. At least not for any worse. I'm proud of that."

"Me too," Barry said.

"Still…" Ellie rubbed her eyes with her palms, "I guess it's too late for me to feel any kind of empathy for Tom, but I suppose I can't help it."

"It's never too late for that, El."

"Seems most men of his day want a second chance at life through their own sons. Sons like you, maybe. Getting stuck with Lonnie, and then me…maybe I can see how the darkness got into him in the first place."

"First of all, you and I both know that Joe would have words with your assumption of my carrying on his legacy." She smiled. "Second, none of us can escape the responsibility of our lives, or at least what we tell ourselves about the role we play in the narrative. Shit happens, and it happens to everyone, some time or another. The only thing any of us can control is what we do with it, how we respond to it."

Ellie looked at him for a long moment. "That's deep talk, ranch hand."

He shrugged. "God knows I couldn't have said that a few months ago."

"Well, I'm glad to hear you say it now," she said, wrapping her arm under his.

Barry sighed. Her touch was more powerful to heal than any prescription medication he'd been given.

"So what about you?" she asked.

"What about?"

"Can you ever look Raymond square in the face again?"

Barry chuckled and laid his head back on the embankment. "I guess sometimes you finally confront what you've been so angry about, and then it kicks your ass." Ellie's laughter bounced around the underbelly of the bridge, and disappeared down the river, on its way to Tampa Bay.

"C'mon," she said, "let's get this old man to bed." She helped him up with significant effort, and kissed him gently, with purpose and adoration. "But you know what all this means, right?" she asked.

"Do tell."

"Your girlfriend's got the blood of a Spanish pirate coursing through her veins."

"Yeah, I've considered that. Not sure which scares me more: that or Raymond's alter ego."

Chapter 76

ELLIE drove carefully down the dirt road to the Grayson ranch, her headlights scattering cottontail rabbits in their wake. She pulled up near the porch, and they could see Joe's silhouette in one of the rocking chairs. "Damn," she said, "guess we're not making out tonight."

Barry didn't respond; he was staring through the windshield. "You wanna help me go shopping?" he asked.

"What for?"

"A truck."

"*You* want a truck?"

"I figure it's far more pragmatic around here than that," he motioned toward the Jensen Interceptor sitting in front of them. "Although it does have four-wheel-"

"Yeah, yeah, we all know," she interrupted. Her smile held the power of resurrection. "Well, this is an interesting turn of events."

"How so?" Barry asked.

"To be honest, I was trying to wrap my head around how I was gonna fit into some big city."

"What, and leave all this excitement? Hell no." They both laughed. "No," Barry said, "I'm onto something here, El. I can't believe I'm saying this, and maybe it's the meds talking, but I think you were right: I needed Riverview as much as anyone here needed me. Probably more," he added. "Seems there was a lot here that I took for granted – or overlooked." He gently wove a lock of her hair around the back of her ear. Ellie's gaze momentarily broke from his. "What is it?" he asked.

She stared hard at the lifeless dashboard before answering. "Something you said, when we were crossing the river; it's been gnawing at me."

Barry sat for a moment and gave an honest attempt at trying to recall even the last twenty-four hours, much less the timeline she was referring to. In the end, he could only ask, "What?"

A brown, nondescript moth lighted onto the warm hood of the pickup, quartering away from the passengers, as if pretending not to be eavesdropping. Ellie studied it for a spell, then followed the insect's line of sight out across the pasture.

"That we're all a lot more alone in this world than we want to admit," she said, returning to his eyes. "Is that really what you believe?"

Their guest took its leave, as Barry felt anyone – or anything – would, should it stumble upon this part of the conversation. He himself had no such escape route. But then again, a thought struck him that felt refreshingly honest, one that he could get behind. "Belief is a tricky word for me at the moment," he started, "and I'm not trying to sound like a lawyer here."

"I'm listening," Ellie said.

"I'm not at all certain what I believe about a lot of things right now." The stars were in full form now, distinct and warm. "But if you'll let me," he continued, "I'd like to start working it out, with you."

Ellie nodded slowly, and the corners of her mouth rose just enough to indicate a smile. But for Barry, the gesture felt like hope incarnate.

"Somehow," he continued, as much to himself as to Ellie, "I've got to believe that all of this belongs."

They sat together, resonating with his last words.

"Well then, you bet," Ellie said, "I'll help Barry-the-big-city-lawyer find his first truck."

He kissed her goodnight and limped toward the front of the porch steps. Joe met him with his own effort and offered his hand. The two eased themselves down into the rocking chairs.

"You want a beer?" Joe asked.

"God, I'd love one."

Joe returned and carefully handed his son an opened can.

"Barry," Joe began, "thank you."

Barry looked at his can, confused. "Seems I should be thanking you."

"I mean that I have you to thank for the fact that I'm even sitting here."

"Oh, that." Barry took a long pull from his can. "I figure I'm the only one who should be allowed to beat on my old man."

Joe smiled. "I mean it, though. Thank you. You've done more to get me moving forward than just that."

"I gotta thank you, too, Dad. I was a real jerk for a long time. I'm sorry."

Joe nodded. "I suppose the last several weeks have done a number on us both."

"Here's to the better, and to moving on."

"I'll drink to that," Joe said.

They rocked quietly on the old porch for a long time.

"I almost had him, though," Joe said.

Barry crushed his can. "Definitely," he smiled. He rose and opened the screen door.

"What're your plans?" Joe asked.

"Plans? For starters, I'm gonna sleep till New Years." Joe laughed. "From there, I think I'll get a truck. Seems

I'm gonna need one, and you're gonna need help around here, at least for a while."

"Don't go thinking about parking some import over there next to mine."

"I'll take that as another, 'thank you.'"

"Goodnight, son."

"See you in the morning."

Joe rocked gently. No fires blazed before him, either from torches or arson. Only blackness, pierced by starlight. He pulled a frozen, tightly wrapped package from under his flannel. He ran his fingers along the worn tape and folded creases. He took another sip of his beer, and turned the package over to reflect the moonlight. He grunted, and decided right then and there that he'd lay one of the two items in his hands to rest this night.

And he sure as hell wasn't giving up the beer.

Chapter 77

THE Hillsborough County manhunt turned up empty. Nearly fifteen other departments across the state couldn't find a bloodied, one-legged giant. Strangely, the local search turned up the remains of two other men, neither of which could be identified. Authorities figured they were illegal immigrants, making a wage picking fruit, but likely caught up in trouble.

Long after Blake had called off the search, a curious call about something a family pet had brought home tentatively restored his hopes. The bone was enormous, and one the medical examiner suggested would match the femur from a person of the Giant's size. Canine units were summoned, but the dogs refused to enter the refuge and nearly pissed themselves when presented with the bone. Blake stormed off into the jungle, furious at the barriers that kept thwarting his progress, and desperate to present some sense of closure to the Graysons, himself, and the entire state to some degree.

After an hour of aimless walking, a disturbance in the canopy overhead caught his attention. He stepped back several paces to take it all in. Birds typically only roost at night, but this was a huge gathering of various species of vultures and crows, like angels of death demanding a sacrifice. They barked and fought and pulled at something draped across several branches. Blake could see that the dirt on the path directly beneath it was darker and glazed with moisture. Blood.

A deputy who had given chase bumped into the sheriff. "Sorry sir," he panted. "Took us a while to calm the dogs."

Blake was looking up.

"Sir?"

The deputy followed his gaze and drew a breath at the spectacle above them.

"What's got them all worked up?"

"Same thing as us," Blake said.

"What do you mean?"

Blake pushed the tip of his Stetson up onto his forehead. "I believe we've found our beanstalk."

THE END.

Author's Note

I distinctly remember the first time I got my hands onto copies of *Tom Sawyer* and *Huckleberry Finn*. I had finally found my people, my accomplices, my inspiration.

My own boyhood and teenage years were spent making memories along the banks of the Alafia River, directly across from the wild, unsettled jungle of the refuge. Our neighborhood posse spent countless hours catching bass and pan fish on homemade cane poles. We explored the crystal springs of Buckhorn Creek, its sapphire spilling into the black pearl water of the Alafia. (Type the coordinates 27.885061, -82.307328 into Google maps; I grew up on Monette Road. The island you'll see in the middle of the river is the one I reference in the pirate portion of the plot.) One summer we shaped and painted our own skim boards to surf along the low tides. Overall it was a magical experience, and no doubt one that allowed the story of *Balm Riverview* to slowly permeate the fabric of my soul.

I've heard that all fiction carries with it a degree of autobiography. In the case of *Balm Riverview,* mine is only thinly veiled. I wrote this novel in a season of significant disruption in my life, specifically during the arduous task of attempting a full-blown career transition. After months of zero progress, I finally committed to a summer of embarking on a journey I'd long avoided: writing. I drove to a university library, hunkered into a nook on the top floor, opened a new document, and started the first page. I was Barry: angry, depressed, rudderless, and succumbing to the throes of something akin to a loss of adult innocence. Writing this story, then, was a means of working out my life thus far, of trying to square most of what I once believed, and more importantly, how I was going to heal and move forward.

As for the geography and landmarks featured in this book, the vast majority of them are real, though not all of them exist to this day. I used to hit golf balls in the cow pasture down the street, and I described my exact impression of Dan's Three Corners Bar as a boy through Barry's memory. Riverview itself is far more suburban now than when our gang rode bikes through the streets, but the charm of the little library and the sandwich shop harken back to its relatively rural days. (Mr. King and his wife are still dishing out haircuts long after their valiant attempt at my middle school flattop). Goodson Farms has the best strawberry short cake in the continental United States. I eat so much of the stuff on family visits that it's a small miracle I don't have diabetes…yet. Gibsonton is a gem, and its offbeat carny history has been featured on numerous television productions.

In regard to the supernatural and folklore elements, many of those were pieced together from a lifetime of interest in the subjects. Much of Gaspar's tale – what little of it exists – is presented as I found it in these pages, including the theories about Sanibel and Captiva Islands (both of which we vacationed on as kids). The *Tall Song* is a figment of my own imagination, though the Skunk Ape is proudly credited to my home state. I never saw Al's giant boot in person, but my pals and I were chased out of an abandoned house in Gibsonton in the middle of the night, having caught wind that it was allegedly haunted and thus sparking our own ghost-hunter production.

There are many lines throughout this manuscript that I'm particularly proud of, some of which I saw coming a long way off. In all honesty, though, it's possible that I wrote nearly the entire piece just to get to this single line: *I guess sometimes you finally confront what you've been so angry about, and then it kicks your ass.* I believe there are towns like Riverview and Gibsonton all over the country that by nature offer a kind of salve to the prodigals who go searching for the true treasures of life – happiness and hope. The pace is slower, the pretention a little less overt, and the residents marginally more comfortable in their own skin.

So here's to my hometown, and the countless other places of refuge housing folks like myself, those trying to navigate the tension between the cards they were dealt and the life they so desire, and slowly realizing that neither is entirely accurate or out of reach.

About the Author

Wes Gow lives in Virginia Beach, VA with his wife and two young daughters; he's outnumbered and would have it no other way. He writes and performs music locally, surfs badly, and works as a life-story coach in his company Cardinal Coaching Solutions, LLC.

If you're so inclined, connect with Wes on Instagram at @wesgow, and learn more about his work and other projects at www.balmriverview.com and www.wesgow.com.

He'd love to hear from you!

Made in the USA
San Bernardino, CA
05 August 2020

76322252R00263